WHY MERMAIDS SING

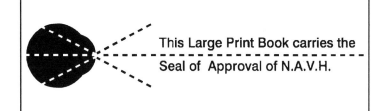

This Large Print Book carries the
Seal of Approval of N.A.V.H.

A SEBASTIAN ST. CYR MYSTERY

WHY MERMAIDS SING

C. S. HARRIS

THORNDIKE PRESS
A part of Gale, Cengage Learning

GALE
CENGAGE Learning

Detroit • New York • San Francisco • New Haven, Conn • Waterville, Maine • London

Thorndike Press® Large Print Historical Fiction.
The text of this Large Print edition is unabridged.
Other aspects of the book may vary from the original edition.
Set in 16 pt. Plantin.
Printed on permanent paper.

LIBRARY OF CONGRESS CATALOGING-IN-PUBLICATION DATA

Harris, C. S.
    Why mermaids sing : a Sebastian St. Cyr mystery / by C. S. Harris.
        p. cm.
    ISBN-13: 978-1-4104-0467-1 (hardcover : alk. paper)
    ISBN-10: 1-4104-0467-6 (hardcover : alk. paper)
    1. Great Britain — History — George III, 1760–1820 — Fiction. 2. Nobility — Crimes against — Fiction. 3. London (England) — Fiction. 4. Large type books. I. Title.
    PS3566.R5877W48 2008
    813'.6—dc22   2007044781

Published in 2008 by arrangement with NAL Signet, a member of Penguin Group (USA) Inc.

Printed in the United States of America
1 2 3 4 5 6 7 12 11 10 09 08

For the people of New Orleans and the Gulf Coast, who suffered so much, and are still suffering, from Hurricanes Katrina and Rita

ACKNOWLEDGMENTS

Why Mermaids Sing will always be, for me, my "Katrina book." I began the first chapter just days before the storm slammed into my New Orleans–area home. In the dark months that followed, as we shifted from one place of refuge to the next and started on the long, hard road to reconstruction, there were many times when I seriously doubted the manuscript would ever see publication. I wrote this book in a Baton Rouge apartment, in a cabin by a lake in central Louisiana, in the back room of my mother's house, and in the gutted office of my own half-built home. That I managed to pull it off is due to the many wonderful people who stood by me.

I am especially grateful to my editor, Ellen Edwards, and all the great people at NAL who were so supportive and understanding; my agent, Helen Breitwieser, who said cheerfully, "You can do it!" every time

I started losing faith; all the many friends who were there for us, including Jon, Ben, Bruce and Emily, Laura, Elora, and Charles; and my incredible, resilient, unbeatable family — my mother, Penny, Samantha, Danielle, and Steve.

Thank you all.

CHAPTER 1

Saturday, 14 September 1811, On the Road Between Merton Abbey and London

Fear twisted Dominic Stanton's stomach, compressed his chest until his breath came shallow and quick.

He told himself he was being a fool. A fool and a coward. He was a Stanton, for Christ's sake. In less then two months, he would be nineteen years old. Men his age — younger, much younger — went off to war. Yet here he was just a few miles outside London and he was acting like some silly girl from the village, about to pee his pants with fear every time the thunder rumbled or the rising wind rustled the oak leaves overhead.

A copse of mingled oak and chestnut closed around him. Dominic kneed his mare into a canter. Dusk was only just beginning to fall, but the heavy cloud cover and the thickness of the grove created their own eerie air of twilight. Over the keening of the wind, he could hear the faint clip-clop of a horse's hooves coming from somewhere behind him. He wasn't imagining it again, was he? He glanced over his shoulder at the empty road curving away out of sight. *"Jesus,"* he whispered.

It was his mother's fault, he decided. She was the one who'd insisted he make it home in time for her stupid dinner party. If it weren't for her, he'd still be back at the pub with Charlie and Burlington and the rest, calling for another round and talking over each blow and rally of the prizefight they'd all ridden down to Merton Abbey to watch. Instead, here he was riding back to London alone at dusk with a storm about to break.

Telling himself he was hurrying because he was going to be late, Dominic urged his mare on faster . . . and felt his saddle begin to slip.

Shit. Stupid ostler, forgetting to tighten the girth. Dominic reined in, his face slick with cold sweat. Casting another quick glance around, he hopped down from the saddle. His fingers were shaky, clumsy. Throwing the stirrup leather out of the way, he fumbled for the buckle and heard the rattle of harness, the clatter of wheels coming up behind.

He whirled around, his mare tossing her

head and sidestepping nervously away from him. A horse and carriage loomed out of the darkness. "Oh my God," whispered Dominic as the driver drew up.

CHAPTER 2

Sunday, 6:45 a.m., 15 September 1811, Westminster

Sir Henry Lovejoy, chief magistrate at Queen Square, Westminster, stood at the edge of the Old Palace Yard. Thrusting his hands into the pockets of his greatcoat, he forced himself to look at the mutilated body sprawled before him.

Dominic Stanton lay on his back, his arms flung wide, his eyes open to the misty sky above. Beads of moisture had collected on the boy's light, softly curling hair, while the dampness left from last night's rain had seeped into the fine cloth of his blue coat to darken it until it looked almost black. From the hips up, the body appeared unmarked except for the traces of blood on his cravat and the strange object shoved in his mouth.

What had been done to his legs was unspeakable.

"For God's sake, cover him up again," said

Lovejoy, his stomach heaving.

The constable reached to flip the sheet of canvas back over the body. "Yes, sir."

The early-morning fog rolling in from the nearby river felt cold and damp against Lovejoy's face. Lifting his gaze, he stared up at the ancient soot-stained walls of the House of Lords beside them.

"Think it's the same killer, sir?"

It had been just three months since they'd found another young man, a banker's son named Barclay Carmichael, in St. James's Park. His body had been mutilated in virtually the same horrid way. Lovejoy glanced over at his stocky, ruddy-faced constable. "You can't seriously be suggesting London has two such killers at work, now, can you?"

Constable Higgins shifted uncomfortably. "No, sir. Of course not."

Henry Lovejoy let his gaze wander around the Yard. They'd roped off the area to keep back the crowds of curious onlookers already beginning to gather. Some half a dozen constables were walking the Yard in a slowly advancing line, their heads bowed as they searched the ground. Lovejoy didn't expect them to find anything. They hadn't found anything before, with Carmichael's son.

"You're certain the lad is Dominic Stanton?" said Lovejoy.

"Appears so, sir. There's an engraved watch in his pocket, and the caretaker who found the body recognized him. Says he used to come here all the time as a little one with his da."

Lovejoy pressed his lips together. Alfred, Lord Stanton was an active member of the House of Lords and an intimate of the Prince Regent. As bad as things had been after the murder of young Barclay Carmichael last June, this time would be worse.

The disembodied sound of a foghorn drifted in with the mist from the river. Lovejoy shivered. It might be only September, but already the morning held a chill that told of the coming of winter.

"Lord Devlin is here, sir."

Lovejoy swung around. A tall, aristocratic-looking gentleman crossed the Yard toward them. His breeches were of the finest doeskin, his coat inimitably tailored, his waistcoat of white silk. But a day's growth of beard shadowed a handsome face set in hard lines, and Lovejoy knew a moment of misgiving. From the looks of things, Devlin had yet to make it to his own bed. And Lovejoy was not at all certain how the young Viscount would react to what the magistrate was about to propose.

"Thank you for coming, my lord," said Lovejoy as Devlin came up to them. "I apologize for the unseemliness of the hour."

Heir and only surviving son to the Earl of Hendon, Sebastian St. Cyr, Viscount Devlin, glanced down at the canvas-covered figure at their feet, then up again. "Why precisely am I here?" he asked, his eyes narrowing as he followed the line of slowly advancing constables.

The man had strange amber-colored eyes that still had the ability to make Lovejoy uncomfortable even after some eight months of acquaintance. Lovejoy cleared his throat. "We've had another young gentleman killed, my lord. And partially butchered. Just like Barclay Carmichael."

The Viscount's brows twitched together. "Let me see."

"I'm afraid it's a rather distressing sight, my lord."

Ignoring him, Devlin hunkered down beside the body and flipped back the canvas.

A faint quiver of distaste passed over his lordship's features, but that was all. Watching him, Lovejoy supposed the Viscount must have seen many such sights — and worse — during his years at war.

Devlin's gaze traveled over the dew-dampened coat to the point where the boy's breeches had been cut away. What was left of the Stanton boy's legs looked like something one might see hanging up for sale in a meat market, the flesh hacked and raw, the exposed bones gleaming white.

"Carmichael's body was butchered like this?"

Lovejoy brought up a handkerchief to wipe his face. "Yes. Only, in Carmichael's case it was the arms. Not the legs."

Devlin studied the boy's smooth-skinned face, framed in soft blond curls. "Who is this one?"

"A young man by the name of Dominic Stanton. Eldest son of Alfred, Lord Stanton. Just eighteen years old."

Devlin nodded. "I still don't understand why I'm here."

Lovejoy hunched his shoulders against the damp cold. He hadn't expected this to be easy. "I was hoping perhaps you might be able to help us understand what is happening."

Devlin held his gaze steadily. "Why me?"

"These young men are of your world, my lord."

"And you think their killer might also be of my world? Is that what you're saying?"

"We don't know, my lord. The boy was obviously killed someplace else and then brought here."

"And the missing flesh?"

"Has not been found, my lord."

Devlin stared across the Yard, to where the apse of Westminster Abbey loomed out of the mist. Beyond that, one could just make out the ancient bulk of Westminster Hall. "Why leave the body here, do you suppose?"

"It's a public spot," suggested Lovejoy. "The killer obviously wanted the body to be seen. And quickly found."

"Perhaps. Or perhaps he was trying to send some sort of message."

Lovejoy fought back a shiver. "A message? To whom?"

From the fog-shrouded river a hundred yards or so away came the sound of another horn, followed by a burst of laughter from unseen men on a passing barge. Devlin pushed to his feet. "Where does Lord Stanton say his son was last night?"

"We've yet to speak to his lordship."

Devlin nodded, his forehead creasing with a frown as he studied the distorted face of the desecrated body before them. "What's that in the boy's mouth?"

Lovejoy had to turn away again and swallow a few times before he could answer.

"We're not certain yet, but it appears to be the severed hoof of a goat."

CHAPTER 3

Leaving the Yard, Sebastian cut behind the massive stone walls of the House of Lords to where a set of stairs led down to the banks of the Thames. The fog was beginning to lift with the strengthening of the sun; in the clear morning light, the water showed flat and silver.

He didn't want this again, he thought, pausing at the top of the steps to stare off across the river to where a wherryman worked his oars in slow, rhythmic strokes. Didn't want to find himself once again sucked into the midst of the kind of tortured emotions that destroyed people's lives. Murder always seemed to lead to more killing, and Sebastian was tired of killing. Tired of death.

He'd spent last night in the arms of the woman he would make his wife, if only she'd let him. But she wouldn't let him, and so he had left her bed before the sun rose.

He'd just reached his own house on Brook Street when Lovejoy's constable found him. He rasped his hand across his unshaven face and wished he'd stayed in Kat's bed.

He heard the magistrate, Sir Henry, come up behind him. "Tell me about the other one, about Barclay Carmichael," said Sebastian, keeping his gaze on the river.

"His body was also found early in the morning," said Sir Henry, "hanging upside down from a tree in St. James's Park. But it was obvious he hadn't been killed there."

"You say he had been mutilated, as well?"

"Yes. The arms." Sir Henry paused at the water's edge a slight distance away. "He'd been with friends the night before. Left them at White's and said he was walking home. According to his friends, he was slightly foxed, but not excessively so."

Sebastian glanced at the magistrate. "That was nearly three months ago. What have you discovered?"

"Very little. No one remembers seeing him after he left White's." Sir Henry lifted the collar of his coat against the breeze blowing off the river. "When we found him, Mr. Carmichael's throat had been slit and his body drained of all blood. The flesh was missing from the arms."

"Who did the examination of the body?"

"A Dr. Martin, from St. Thomas. I'm afraid he was able to tell us little beyond the obvious."

"You'll be ordering a postmortem on Stanton?"

"Of course."

"You'd do well to send him to Paul Gibson on Tower Hill." If Dominic Stanton's body had any secrets to tell, Paul Gibson would find them.

Sir Henry nodded.

Sebastian stared down at the waters of the Thames lapping the algae-covered stones of the steps at their feet. The smells of the river were strong here, the stench of dead fish mingling with the odor of the tanneries on the river's banks. "You say Stanton was eighteen. How old was Mr. Carmichael? Twenty-six?"

"Twenty-seven."

"Nine years' difference. I doubt you'll find the two had much in common."

"Not have much in common, my lord? But . . . both were wealthy young aristocratic men from the West End."

"You think that's why they were killed?"

"I fear it's what people will say."

Sebastian lifted his gaze to the far side of the river, where the bulky outlines of the Barge Houses were just beginning to emerge from the mist. The fortunes of both families were indeed immense, but there were subtle differences. For while the Stantons were one of England's oldest families, Sir Humphrey Carmichael had been born the simple son of a weaver.

Sir Henry cleared his throat, his voice coming out sounding tight, worried. "May I count on your assistance, my lord?"

Sebastian glanced over at the magistrate. He was a funny little man with a shiny bald head, pinched, unsmiling features, and an almost comically high voice. Painstakingly moral, upright, and fastidious, he was also one of the most sincere and dedicated men Sebastian had ever met.

The urge to say no was strong. But the memory of the dew beading on the dead boy's fair curls haunted him. And the kind of debt Sebastian owed this earnest little magistrate could never really be repaid.

"I'll think about it," said Sebastian.

Sir Henry nodded and turned toward the Yard.

Sebastian's voice stopped him. "When you found Barclay Carmichael, was there anything in his mouth?"

The magistrate swung back around, his Adam's apple visibly bobbing as he swallowed. "As a matter of fact, yes. Although we could never determine its significance."

"What was it?"

The breeze from the river fluttered the hem of the magistrate's coat. "A blank page torn from a ship's log. Dated 25 March."

CHAPTER 4

Sebastian arrived at his house in Brook Street to find his father, Alistair St. Cyr, the Fifth Earl of Hendon, just turning away from the door. Hendon's own town house was in Grosvenor Square. He seldom visited his son's residence, and never without a reason.

The Earl was a big man, taller than Sebastian and more solidly built, with a barrellike chest and a massive, bull-like head. His hair was white now, but once it had been dark, nearly as dark as Sebastian's own. "Well," said Hendon, his gaze traveling from Sebastian's unshaven face to his less-than-impeccable cravat, "I thought to catch you before you went out. I see that instead I've come too early, before you arrived home."

Sebastian felt his lips twitch up into a reluctant smile. "Join me for breakfast?" he asked, leading the way into the dining room.

"Thank you, but I breakfasted hours ago. I'll take some ale, though."

Sebastian caught the eye of his major-domo, Morey, who bowed discreetly.

"Your sister tells me you've instituted a search for your mother," said Hendon, pulling out a chair beside the table.

Sebastian paused in the act of spooning eggs from the sideboard dish onto his plate. "Dear Amanda. However did she come to hear of that?"

"So it's true, is it?"

Sebastian brought his plate to the table. "It's true."

Hendon waited until Morey set the ale before him and withdrew. Then he leaned forward, his arms on the table, his vivid blue gaze hard on Sebastian's face. "Why, Sebastian? Why are you doing this?"

"Why? Because she's my mother. When I first found out the truth about what happened in Brighton that summer, I was angry. With you. With her. Maybe even with myself for believing all the lies I was told. I'm still angry, but I've also realized there are things I'd like to ask her."

"But she's on the Continent."

"That's where I'm looking."

Hendon's bushy white eyebrows drew together in a frown. "There's still a war on, you know."

"It's a complication, I admit, but not an insurmountable obstacle."

Hendon grunted and reached for his ale. The relationship between father and son had never been an easy one, even before Kat, even before the revelations of last June. The marriage of the Earl of Hendon and his gay, beautiful countess, Sophia, had produced four children: the eldest child, a girl named Amanda, and three sons, Richard, Cecil, and Sebastian. Of them all, it was Sebastian, the youngest, who had been the least like his father. Yet for most of Sebastian's childhood, the Earl had been content to let his youngest son go his own way, secure in the knowledge that the strange boy with the feral eyes and a fascination for poetry and music would never be called upon to inherit the estates and the exalted position that went with them.

Then death had taken first Richard St. Cyr, then Cecil, and Sebastian had found himself the new Viscount Devlin. There had been times, particularly during the long, hot summer of Cecil's death and Lady Hendon's mysterious disappearance, that it had seemed Hendon hated his youngest son. Hated him for living when both his brothers had died.

"Your aunt Henrietta tells me you've refused her invitation to this ball she's giving tomorrow night," said Hendon, his heavy jaw jutting forward in that way it did when he knew he was about to start a fight.

"I have a previous engagement."

Hendon gave a scornful laugh. "Where? At Covent Garden Theater?"

Sebastian took a deep breath and let his father's barb slide past. "If Aunt Henrietta is particularly desirous that I attend her ball, it's because some acquaintance of hers has a marriageable daughter she's determined to fling in my path." The remark might have sounded arrogant, but it wasn't. Sebastian knew well that if he were still the youngest of three sons, no ambitious mother in London would let him anywhere near her daughter.

"You need someone casting marriageable young females in your path," said Hendon tartly. "You'll be nine-and-twenty in a month."

"The last eligible female my dear aunt inflicted upon me did nothing but prate endlessly about Alcibiades and the Sicilian Expedition."

"That's because when she introduced you to the Duke of Bisley's daughter, you described the girl as a pretty widgeon with more hair than sense." Hendon cleared his throat. "I hear the young woman Henrietta has in mind this time is quite out of the common."

Sebastian laid down his fork. "I already have a woman in my life, as well you know."

"A man can have both a mistress and a wife, for God's sake."

Sebastian met his father's fierce gaze and held it. "Not this man."

Hendon growled a crude oath and pushed up from his chair. He was nearly at the door when Sebastian stopped him by saying, "Rather than wasting your time trying to find me a wife, I wish you'd bend your purpose instead to finding me a new valet."

Hendon swung around. "What? I thought you just hired a new man last summer."

"I did. He quit."

"Quit? Why?"

Sebastian hesitated. In actual fact, the valet had quit because he'd spied Sebastian's tiger teaching the second footman how to pick pockets, but Sebastian wasn't about to tell Hendon that. Instead he said, "*Do* you know of anyone?"

"I'll have my man look into it."

After his father left, Sebastian tried again to apply himself to his breakfast, but soon gave it up. He thought about going over the stack of valets' credentials in his library, or perhaps applying himself to some overdue correspondence. But he knew he wasn't going to do either of those things.

He was going to the City to hear what Dr. Paul Gibson could tell him about the death of young Mr. Dominic Stanton.

CHAPTER 5

"It's the wound across his throat that killed him," said Paul Gibson, tying what looked like a stained butcher's apron around his waist.

They were old friends, Sebastian and this one-legged Irish surgeon with a scholar's mind, a healer's touch, and a secret burning hunger for the sweet relief to be found in poppies. They had met on the battlefields of Europe. Theirs was the friendship of men who'd faced death together, who knew each other's greatest strengths and private demons. No one in all of England could analyze the dead like Paul Gibson. Sebastian knew it, and he also knew why. The human body was Gibson's bible; he ministered to its ills and injuries, he studied and taught it, and on dark nights when men with muffled lanterns prowled the churchyards of London, Paul Gibson was known to offer a ready market for what they had to sell.

They were in the small stone building behind Gibson's surgery near the Tower, where Gibson performed his autopsies and dissections. The mist had long since burned away, revealing a clear, blue-sky morning. Through the open door Sebastian could see the bright golden sunshine of a warm September day, hear the sweet song of a lark and the faint buzzing of bees around the overgrown roses in the yard that stretched between the outbuilding and the surgery itself. But in here the air was close and dank and scented by death.

Sebastian stared down at the naked, ravaged body of Dominic Stanton lying on the thick granite slab before them. Gibson hadn't yet progressed beyond the preliminaries in his postmortem. But even to Sebastian's untrained eye, the slice across the boy's throat looked neat and precise — in sharp contrast to what had been done to his legs.

"I hope for his sake that was the first cut."

"It would appear so." Moving awkwardly on his one good leg, Paul Gibson limped around to the other side of the table. He'd lost the lower part of his left leg on a battlefield on the Continent. "The slash was made from left to right. Probably from behind."

Sebastian looked up at his friend's lean, dark face. "But there was hardly any blood on the cravat."

"I suspect it was removed along with the coat, waistcoat, and shirt before his throat was slit. The body was then drained of its blood and dressed again."

"Jesus. Just like Barclay Carmichael."

Gibson frowned. "You mean the man who was killed last June?"

"I'm afraid so." Sebastian studied the body lying stiff and rigid before them. His experiences in the war had taught Sebastian more than he cared to know about the changes the passing hours bring to the remains of the dead. "At about what time would you say Stanton was killed? Around midnight?" The youth appeared to be in the full grip of rigor mortis.

"Probably. Give or take a few hours either way."

"Any signs of a struggle?"

"A struggle? No. But this is interesting." Gibson picked up one of the body's arms. "There are abrasions on his wrists. See? And signs of irritation at the corners of his mouth."

"He was bound and gagged," said Sebastian.

"So it would appear."

Sebastian studied the boy's well-developed shoulders and tall frame. Dominic Stanton might have been young, but he was still a big, strong lad. It wouldn't have been easy for one man to overpower him. "Any sign of a head wound?"

"No."

Sebastian had to force himself to look at what was left of the boy's legs. "Doesn't strike me as a particularly professional job," he said after a moment.

"No. It's quite clumsy in fact. Done with some sort of cleaver, I'd say. Postmortem, thankfully."

"Do you know a Dr. Martin, at St. Thomas? According to Lovejoy, he did the autopsy on Barclay Carmichael last June."

The Irishman's mouth thinned into a humorless smile. "The man's a bloody pompous ass, but I'll try talking to him. See if he noticed anything that didn't make it into his report."

The stench in the room was starting to get to Sebastian. He went to stand in the open doorway and draw the clean, fresh air of the day into his lungs.

From behind him, Gibson said, "Sir Henry Lovejoy told me he's asked for your help. And why. He said you hadn't agreed."

"I haven't." Sebastian narrowed his eyes

against a sun so bright it hurt. "The boy was obviously brought to the Old Palace Yard after being killed and cut up someplace else. Any idea where?"

Gibson turned away to reach for a scalpel. "Ask me tomorrow."

CHAPTER 6

Sebastian was crossing Whitehall, headed toward St. James's Park and the site where the first victim's body had been found, when he heard an imperious voice call, *"Dev-lin."*

He turned to find Alfred, Lord Stanton striding toward him. A haughty-looking man in his late forties, Stanton had the broad shoulders and substantial height of his son. But when Sebastian looked into the Baron's brown eyes and bony, sun-darkened features, he found himself thinking that the boy, Dominic, must have taken his fair coloring and full cheeks from his mother.

"I understand you're responsible for my son ending up in the hands of some common Irish surgeon."

Sebastian stood and let the Baron walk up to him. "It's within the magistrate's power to refer a murder victim's body for a post-mortem."

"Bloody hell. This is my son we're talking about. My son. Not some back-alley whore to be handed over to a bog Irish nobody."

Sebastian stared off beyond the Guards toward the park and tried to make allowances for the anguish of a father who'd just lost a son in one of the worst ways imaginable. Although from the sounds of things, it wasn't the postmortem Stanton was objecting to as much as the social status of the surgeon conducting it.

"Paul Gibson is the best student of anatomy and death in London. If anyone can help discover who killed your son, it's he."

Stanton's jaw jutted out. "And what business is it of yours, who killed my son?"

There were those, Sebastian knew, who still believed him guilty of the terrible rapes and murders that had frightened London the previous winter. It was always possible that Lord Stanton was one of that number, although Sebastian doubted it.

"Do you know if your son had any enemies?" he asked, as much to see the man's reaction as anything. "Someone who might wish him harm?"

Stanton's face darkened with anger. Sebastian could see a father's grief in the man's slackened facial muscles and bruised eyes. But there was something else there, too. Something that looked very much like fear.

Stanton poked the air between them with one meaty finger. "You stay out of this, you hear? It's no affair of yours. None!"

Sebastian watched the big man stride away toward the Privy Gardens, the September sun golden on his broad shoulders.

"Well, that was interesting," said Sebastian.

He followed the canal in St. James's Park to a slight rise with a single black mulberry tree, where on a warm summer's morning three months before the rising sun had shed its rays on another butchered young man.

Barclay Carmichael had been found with his ankles lashed together by a stout rope thrown over an arching branch of the mulberry. Hoisted high, his mangled arms dangling toward the grass, he'd been found at first light. Just like Dominic Stanton.

Two wealthy young men, thought Sebastian, one eighteen, the other seven-and-twenty. One the son of a powerful banker, the other the scion of one of England's oldest families. Both bodies butchered and left as if on display in very public spaces.

Standing on the rise, Sebastian turned in a slow circle. From here he could see the

Palace of St. James's and the Houses of Parliament, the Old Admiralty Building and the Horse Guards Parade.

Why here? he wondered. And then he thought, *Where next?*

He found Sir Henry Lovejoy descending the steps of the Public Office on Queen Square. At the sight of Sebastian, the magistrate paused and made to swing around. "My lord. Please, come in."

"No. I won't keep you," said Sebastian. "I just had a few questions I wanted to ask. I take it you've had the opportunity to speak with Lord Stanton?"

An indefinable quiver passed over Sir Henry's normally bland features. "Yes. Unfortunately, his lordship was rather upset by the choice of surgeon for his son's post-mortem."

"As well as by my possible involvement in the investigation into the circumstances of his death, I gather?"

Sir Henry blinked. "As a matter of fact, yes. How did you know?"

Sebastian simply shook his head. "Where does his lordship say his son spent last night?"

"It seems the boy made one of a party of friends who rode down to Merton Abbey for yesterday's prizefight."

Bare-knuckle boxing was illegal and could, technically, be stopped by the magistrates, which is why the matches were typically held several hours' ride from London. But the match between the Champion and his Scottish challenger, McGregor, had been the subject of such intense speculation there couldn't be a magistrate in the area who hadn't been aware of it.

"They set out from London for Merton Abbey as a group, just before eleven yesterday morning," Sir Henry was saying.

"So what happened?"

"Mr. Stanton was expected home for a dinner party his mother was giving. He never arrived." Sir Henry paused. "Lady Stanton is said to be hysterical."

The bells of Westminster Abbey began to chime the hour, the rich notes floating out over the city. "Do you have the names of these friends?"

"Yes. Young Lord Burlington, Sir Miles Jefferies's son Davis, and a Charlie McDermott. At the moment they're gathered at a pub in Fleet Street. I was just on my way there to interview them."

Sebastian squinted against the bright September sun. "Let me approach them first."

39

He was aware of Sir Henry studying him. "I didn't think you were interested in the case, my lord."

Sebastian gave a grim smile and turned away. "I've changed my mind."

CHAPTER 7

The Boar's Head on Fleet Street was one of those comfortable old pubs with dark paneled walls and low ceilings that reminded their patrons of winter evenings spent tucked away in the cozy Jacobin inns of Leicester and Derby, Northampton and Worcestershire. Sebastian supposed it was that warm familiarity that had made it an attractive refuge for three young men with bruised spirits and aching memories.

Ordering a pint of ale, Sebastian paused beside the low, ancient bar. The three friends huddled around a table in the corner, unaware of his presence. A somber group, they sat with shoulders hunched, hands cupped around pewter tankards, chins sunk in ambitiously tied cravats. Occasionally one would make a comment and the others would nod. No one laughed.

The eldest of the three, Davis Jefferies, was but twenty, a slight, incredibly gaunt young man who looked more like sixteen. To his left sat Charlie McDermott, another slim youth with the pale skin and flaming red hair of the far north. Only Lord Burlington, a baron's son from Nottingham who'd come into his title as a child, approached Dominic Stanton in size and bulk.

Sebastian watched the men for a time, then walked over to their table, pulled out a chair, and sat down. Three startled pairs of eyes turned toward him. "I'd like a few words with you gentlemen," he said quietly, "if you don't mind?"

The three exchanged hurried glances. "No. Of course not," said Jefferies, stammering slightly. "How may we help you, my lord?"

"I understand you attended yesterday's mill down at Merton Abbey."

Jefferies hesitated a moment, then said, "Yes."

"With Mr. Dominic Stanton?"

The redheaded Scotsman, McDermott, spoke up, saying in a rush, "I beg your pardon, my lord, but what is this about?"

Sebastian leaned back in his chair. "I'm wondering if you know of anyone Stanton might have angered lately. A gentleman annoyed by Mr. Stanton's attentions to his lady, perhaps? Or perhaps someone he bested in a game of chance or a wager?"

The three were silent for a moment, thinking. Then Jefferies shook his head and said, "Dominic wasn't much in the petticoat line. And he never could pick a winner — or run a bluff."

"Was he in any way acquainted with Mr. Barclay Carmichael?"

"Are you roasting me? A bang-up Corinthian like Carmichael? No. We all admired him, but . . . that was it."

Burlington spoke up suddenly. "You're trying to figure out who did it, aren't you?" The boy's face was pale and puffy. When Sebastian looked into his soft gray eyes, Burlington glanced quickly away.

"Do you have any ideas about what happened to him?"

All three boys shook their heads, their eyes wide.

"Where did you gentlemen go after yesterday's fight?"

"To the White Monk," said McDermott. "Outside Merton Abbey."

"Until when?"

"Just before midnight. But Dominic left long before that. His mother wanted him home for some dinner party she was giving."

"So he left alone?"

Again, the three exchanged glances. It was Burlington who swallowed and licked his lips before answering. "He asked me to go with him. Said he didn't want to ride back to London by himself. But I just laughed at him. Made fun of him. Told him he was acting like a shrieking little housemaid." The boy's voice cracked and he looked away again, blinking rapidly.

"What time did he leave?"

"About half past five, I'd say?" McDermott looked around the table for confirmation. The other two nodded their heads. "Yes. Half past five."

"Driving himself in his curricle?"

"No. We all rode. Dominic has — had," he corrected himself quickly, "a sweet-going little mare named Roxanne. Last I heard, she was missing, too."

"What does she look like?"

"A dapple gray. With four white socks and a white blaze."

Sebastian pushed back his chair, then hesitated. "You said Mr. Stanton was nervous. Was he often so?"

"Dominic? No. At least, not until lately."

"When you say lately, what exactly do you mean?"

Again there was that brief consensus taking. "The last month?" said Jefferies.

"Maybe more."

"Do you know what was making him nervous?"

The question was met with a heavy silence. After a moment Burlington cleared his throat and said, "He thought someone was following him. Watching him."

"Did he ever see anyone?"

"No. No one. It was just a feeling he had. He was spooked. It's why we all laughed at him. God help us. We laughed at him."

CHAPTER 8

Riding his neat little black Arab, Sebastian took the road south from London toward Merton Abbey, following in reverse the route Dominic Stanton would have taken the night before.

The afternoon was hot, the sun a golden blaze of late-summer glory. By now the traces of last night's rain had been reduced to an occasional patch of mud drying quickly in the heat. Insects whined; the ripe, uncut fields of wheat and rye stood motionless, unstirred by any breeze. When a stand of oaks and chestnuts near the base of a hill closed around him, Sebastian welcomed the shade.

The road had proved to be little traveled. Sebastian suspected that even with yesterday's mill, by the time Dominic Stanton left the White Monk on the outskirts of Merton Abbey, the surge of spectators returning to London would have already passed. Sebastian might welcome the coolness of this shady wood, but for a young man riding at dusk, alone and frightened by an unseen menace, the shadowy copse must have seemed anything but pleasant.

Sebastian slowed his horse to a walk.

The ground here fell away to the east, deep into a rocky gully where the trees grew close and tangled with vines. As Sebastian scanned the sides of the track, he noticed his mare's ears flick forward and back. Tossing her head, she whinnied softly. Sebastian reined in and listened. From the depths of the gully came a soft answering nicker.

He found the gray deep in the gully, her trailing reins caught fast in a thicket. Dismounting, he approached her with softly crooned words. "Easy there, girl. Easy."

She quivered a moment, her eyes wide, then hung her head. He stroked her neck and let her nuzzle his chest. Slowly, looking for traces of blood, he ran his hand over the saddle leather. His hand came away clean.

"What happened, girl? Hmmm? Do you know?"

He checked her hocks and hooves, but she seemed sound. Then, skimming his fingers along the girth, he found the place where a sharp knife had sliced through the strap.

Not enough to cut it completely, but enough that it would eventually work itself loose and a rider would feel his saddle begin to slip.

Leading the gray, Sebastian followed the faint trail of broken branches and bruised leaves back up to the road above. Last night's rain coupled with the day's traffic had obscured any trace that might have been left on the roadway itself. But at the edge beneath the trees, he found a place where the gray had trampled the earth with nervous sidling feet and, beyond that, tracks left by a two-wheeled carriage or cart that had pulled over to the soft verge. Whether the tracks had been laid down last night or at some other time, he had no way of knowing.

He spent the next fifteen minutes walking the area, looking for any other indications of what might have happened there last night. He was about to give up when a flash of white caught his eye. Reaching down into a tangle of long grass, he found himself holding a small porcelain vial decorated with a blue-and-white flower pattern.

He'd seen such vials before. They were imported by the thousands from China and the Far East. Raising the vial to his nostrils, he sniffed.

And caught the familiar pungent scent of opium.

CHAPTER 9

Leading Dominic Stanton's gray mare, Sebastian arrived at the White Monk in Merton Abbey to discover that Sir Henry Lovejoy's constables had already done a commendable job of setting up the backs of every one of the White Monk's ostlers and serving maids.

Located on the outskirts of town, the White Monk was a rambling, half-timbered country inn with an old-fashioned cobbled yard and busy stables. "We musta 'ad a 'undred or more carriages and gigs through 'ere yesterday after the fight," said the head ostler, fixing Sebastian with a malevolent glare. "Which one you askin' about?"

Sebastian bounced a half crown in his palm. "The one whose driver was behaving in some way out of the ordinary."

The ostler eyed the coin with undisguised longing. He was a thin, wiry man in his late fifties with gray stubble shadowing his cheeks and a prominent Adam's apple that bobbed when he swallowed. "Didn't see that one."

Sebastian tossed the coin into the air and caught it. "Do you recall which ostler took care of this gray?"

"Aye. That were me."

"Really? Did you notice anything amiss with the saddle?"

"Course not. Why you ask?"

"Look at it now."

The ostler cast Sebastian a quizzing glance, then went to run an expert's hand over the rig. At the sight of the cinch, he froze. He fingered the neatly sliced edge, his back held rigid, then swung slowly to face Sebastian.

"You think I did this?"

"No. I think you want this half crown. Who really took care of the mare?"

The ostler hesitated, his chest rising with his labored breathing. At last he said, "It were me. But I swear to you, there weren't nothin' wrong with the cinch when I brung this horse to the young gentleman."

"At the time Mr. Stanton called for his mare, was there a crowd in the yard?"

"Aye. More than a few. Why?"

"Do you think one of them could have sliced the cinch?"

The ostler squinted off across the cobbled yard to where a pair of geese was coming in to land on the holding pond, the rich light of the evening sun turning their outstretched white wings to gold. "I suppose it's possible. But I didn't see nothin'."

"Did you notice exactly who was in the yard at the time?"

"No." He shook his head with what looked like genuine regret. "Not that I recall."

The geese filled the air with their plaintive calls. "You've been most helpful," said Sebastian, pressing the coin into the ostler's palm. "Thank you."

Sebastian spent the next hour drinking a couple of pints of dark ale in the White Monk's public room. Tonight, the patrons were all locals. But yesterday's fight had brought a crowd of young men such as Dominic Stanton and his friends. Sebastian talked to a farmer with ruddy cheeks and a bulbous nose who remembered the young gentlemen clearly.

"I've a son about their age myself," said the farmer, wiping the foam from his upper lip with the back of one hand. "Those lads were in high spirits, to be sure. But no harm in that. A man's only young once, I always say."

"They didn't quarrel with anyone?" Sebastian asked.

"Not that I saw."

Sebastian spent the next hour buying drinks and talking to the inn's various patrons. But they all told him the same tale.

Calling for his horse, he checked the cinch, then rode back to London, Dominic Stanton's pretty little gray trotting contentedly behind him.

Sebastian employed numerous servants, both at his house in London and at the small estate near Winchester left him by a maiden great-aunt. Many were family retainers; almost all were solid, respectable employees. Only one — a twelve-year-old former street urchin named Tom whom Sebastian had taken on as his tiger — was neither.

Returning to the mews behind his Brook Street town house, Sebastian handed his black Arab into the care of one of his grooms. But he entrusted Dominic Stanton's mare to Tom.

"I suppose by now you know all about the body found in Old Palace Yard this morning," said Sebastian.

"Aye." Tom ran an expert's hand down the gray's near flank and bent to study a gash Sebastian hadn't even noticed. "Butchered like a side o' beef, from what I 'ear. They're callin' the cove what did it the 'Butcher o' the West End.' "

"Huh. Sir Henry won't like that."

Tom's nearly lashless gray eyes sparkled with expectation. " 'E's asked fer yer help, ain't 'e?"

"Hasn't he," corrected Sebastian absently. "How did you know that?"

"I knows."

Sebastian eyed the brown-haired, sharp-faced lad beside him. "Any speculation on the streets as to who might be behind all of this?"

"Oh, there's plenty o' spec-u-la-tion," said Tom, pronouncing the word carefully. "People are sayin' it's everything from French devil worshippers to witches. But nobody really knows nothin'." He patted the gray's neck. "This 'is 'orse?"

Sebastian nodded. "I found her just off the road to Merton Abbey."

Tom fingered the cut cinch and pushed a low whistle through the gap in his front teeth. "Look at that."

"Look at that, indeed." Sebastian turned toward the house. "I want you to take the mare to Sir Henry in Queen Square. Tell him I have a few possibilities I intend to pursue."

"So we're gonna be lookin' into these murders, are we?" said Tom with obvious delight.

Sebastian swung back around. *"We?"*

But Tom only laughed.

Chapter 10

An hour later, Sebastian took the stairs of the theater's Covent Garden entrance two at a time. The theater's principal front, with its columned portico and classical bas-reliefs, faced onto Bow Street. But that entrance was still chained closed, for the theater did not officially open for the fall season until Monday night. Tonight's performance was a dress rehearsal only.

Handing a coin to the attendant, Sebastian hurried across the ornate box lobby. Even before he slipped into the row of empty boxes, he could hear a hard-pressed Petruchio exclaiming from the stage, " 'You lie, in faith; for you are call'd plain Kate, and bonny Kate, and sometimes Kate the curst. But Kate, the prettiest Kate in Christendom . . .' "

Easing into a seat, Sebastian watched the woman on the stage below prop her hands on her hips and throw back her head.

" 'Asses are made to bear,' " she told her theatrical suitor with a scornful curling of her lip, " 'and so are you.' " Then, for the briefest instant, her eyes lifted to the boxes and she smiled. She knew Sebastian was there.

Her name was Kat Boleyn, and at twenty-three, she was the most acclaimed actress on the London stage, famous as much for her dark good looks and vivid blue eyes as for her considerable talent on the boards. Once, long ago, Sebastian had asked her to marry him. Much had happened since then, although her love for him remained undiminished. That, Sebastian knew. It was, after all, the selfless strength of her love for him that made Kat determined never to become his wife. She had this idea in her head that by marrying him she would destroy him, and nothing Sebastian could say or do would change her mind.

As the dress rehearsal ended, Sebastian headed backstage. He found Kat seated at her dressing table, busy with the task of wiping greasepaint from her face. She looked up, her gaze meeting his in the mirror. She smiled. "I thought perhaps you meant to renege on your offer to escort me to supper tonight."

He pressed a kiss against the nape of her

neck, where it arched delicately below the upswept tumble of her rich, auburn-lit hair. "I've been to Merton Abbey," he said, resting one hip on the edge of her dressing table.

"Merton Abbey?" She frowned. "Whatever for?"

"It's the last place anyone saw a young man named Dominic Stanton alive. Someone dumped his mutilated body in Old Palace Yard last night, and Sir Henry has asked for my assistance."

"You agreed?" He heard the concern in her voice, saw it in the way she searched his face. Of all the people in Sebastian's world, only Kat — and perhaps the surgeon Paul Gibson — understood what his involvement in this murder would cost him. "Why?"

Sebastian gave her a wry smile. "I'd like to think I agreed simply because Sir Henry asked it of me. But I suspect it's also because the boy's father warned me that it was none of my affair."

Kat frowned. "Why would he do that?"

"Most likely because he — or his son — has something to hide."

Later, as they supped on lobster bisque and a cold joint at Steven's in Bond Street, he told her of the day's events. She listened to him in silence, her intelligent gaze thoughtful. When he finished, she said, "So what are you suggesting? That someone tampered with Dominic Stanton's cinch while he was drinking with his friends in the White Monk, then followed behind him in a carriage until his saddle began to slip?"

Sebastian reached for his wineglass. "There's no way of knowing for certain that the wheel tracks I found on the verge of the London road were made last night. But if I were planning to move a body, I would certainly bring along a carriage."

"Was he killed there, by the side of the road?"

"I doubt it. The marks Gibson found on his wrists suggest the boy was tied up and taken elsewhere. He certainly wasn't butchered there."

She pushed aside her plate. Sebastian smiled apologetically. "Sorry. This isn't exactly supper table conversation."

Reaching out, she cupped her hand over his where it rested on the tabletop. "What do you think is the connection between Stanton and Carmichael? Apart from the fact that both were young men from wealthy families, I wouldn't have said they had much in common."

"Neither would I. Dominic Stanton was a

raw young man newly on the Town, while Barclay Carmichael was a Corinthian, a regular out-and-outer. According to Stanton's friends, he admired Carmichael, but that was all."

"How horrifying to think someone simply chose them at random." She paused. "Although I must admit, I couldn't say why that seems more frightening than the idea that the killer knew them."

"Perhaps because the randomness of it would make us all somehow vulnerable."

A hint of amusement lit up her deep blue eyes. "Perhaps that's it." The amusement faded quickly. "You say Lord Stanton seemed to fear your involvement. Do you think his lordship is doing something he doesn't want anyone to find out about?"

Sebastian reached for the wine bottle to refill her glass. "Or he knows his son was involved in something — something that would disgrace the family were it to become known." Sebastian emptied the last of the wine into his own glass, then sat in silence for a moment, watching the candlelight gleam on the deep burgundy liquid. "I suppose it's possible Dominic Stanton inadvertently attracted the attention of his killer at the White Monk. Although from what his friends said, I think it's more likely the killer was watching Stanton for some time. Following him and waiting for the chance to catch him alone. Last night he got that chance."

He was aware of Kat's gaze upon him. She knew him like no other, knew the dark dreams that haunted his nights, the dark deeds that haunted his past. "You think this won't be the end of it, don't you?" she said.

Sebastian drained his glass in one long pull and set it aside. "No. It won't be the end of it."

CHAPTER 11

Monday, 16 September 1811

Kat Boleyn awoke in the grip of a fear that crushed her chest and left her gasping for breath. It was a dream, she told herself; this time it was only a dream.

A thin thread of light showed around the heavy drapes at the windows, hinting at the dawn to come. Turning her head, she found Sebastian asleep beside her. A smile touched her lips. He had stayed. He didn't often stay.

Her smile faded as the vague feeling of unease left by the dream resurged. In her dream she had been walking down a darkened alley. She couldn't see anyone, but she knew a man was there behind her. She could hear his footsteps, see his shadow. She'd had the same dream every night for a week, and she knew why.

Someone was following her.

She had never seen him, but she sensed him often. At the theater. On Bond Street.

In the stillness of the evening when she went to close the curtains at the windows, he was there. Watching. Waiting. Why?

It was always possible he was simply an admirer. An admirer who lurked in shadows and watched in silence would frighten any actress. But a woman who had spent years spying for the French and passing secrets to Napoleon's agents knew fears that went beyond those of an ordinary actress.

She called herself Kat Boleyn, but she'd been born with a different name, to a woman who'd once been the toast of London, a woman who had taken wealthy, titled men into her bed, then left it all to return to her native Ireland. It was in Ireland that Kat's memories began, in a whitewashed house on the edge of a green in Dublin — a snug little house filled with laughter and so much love. And it was in Ireland that those halcyon memories had ended in a night of terror, when a troop of English soldiers pulled Kat and her mother screaming from their beds.

They'd made Kat and her stepfather watch what they did to Kat's mother. Kat had tried to shut her eyes, but they'd told her if she didn't watch, they'd do it to her, too. And so Kat had opened her eyes. When they were done using her mother like a dog, they'd hanged Kat's mother and stepfather both, and left their bodies twisting slowly in the smoke-filled dawn at the edge of the green.

Everything Kat had done for France she'd done in their memory, to hurt the English so that Ireland might one day be free. She would never regret what she had done, although she had cut her ties to the French months ago, when Devlin came back into her life. Her dedication to Ireland remained, but she could not in all conscience accept Devlin's love while working to aid those against whom he had fought.

Yet Kat knew well that her activities in the past had left her vulnerable. She was vulnerable both to those to whom she had once provided information, and to their enemies — her enemies, the English.

The man who now slept beside her knew nothing of the deeds she had committed in the past. He himself had spent years in the Army, fighting the very country she'd sought to aid. There had been times this past week when she'd been tempted to tell him of the man who watched her from the shadows. But she understood the concept of unforeseen consequences, and she feared Devlin learning the truth about her past even more than she feared the shadowy man who followed her.

She realized that at some point Sebastian had awakened. He lay watching her, his eyes gleaming faintly in the growing light. He had the strangest eyes, the amber color of a wolf's eyes, with a wolf's ability to see in the dark. His other senses were acute, as well — so acute that he sometimes disconcerted her.

"Did I wake you?" she said. "I'm sorry."

A smile quirked up one corner of his mouth. "I'm not."

He reached for her, his fingers tangling in the heavy fall of hair at the nape of her neck as he drew her to him. She brushed her lips against his, felt his hands drift down her bare back. There was peace in his touch, joy in his kiss. She gave herself to him, and let the peace and the joy of his love wash over her and through her.

But the fear remained, a cold and heavy presence like the man who watched unseen in the night.

CHAPTER 12

At just past seven o'clock that morning, Sebastian turned his black Arab mare through the gate into Hyde Park. The morning was clear and cool, the park largely deserted at this hour except for a single rider hacking his gray up and down the Row.

It was the Earl of Hendon's habit each morning he was in London to begin the day with a ride in Hyde Park. As Sebastian watched, the gelding missed its stride, and a gentle breeze brought him the sound of his father's words of admonishment mingling with the familiar drumming of hoofbeats.

It had been Hendon himself who taught Sebastian and his brothers to ride. Even in those days, Hendon was always busy with affairs of state. But the task of teaching his sons to ride was one he would delegate to no mere groom. The Earl had been a relentless taskmaster, his expectations high, his comments at times brutal. But his pride in his sons' accomplishments had been there, too, in the gleam of satisfaction in his eyes, in the rare words of praise for a movement well executed.

Remembering those days now with a smile, Sebastian brought the Arab in beside his father's gray. They posted side by side for a moment in silence. Then the Earl threw Sebastian a quick glance from beneath lowered brows. "You're obviously here for a reason, and it must be damnably important to drag you out of bed at this hour. What is it? Lost your aunt's fortune on the 'Change, have you?"

Sebastian laughed. It was a never-ending source of chagrin to Hendon that his son and heir had inherited a small country estate and comfortable independence from a great-aunt. An heir with an independent income was difficult to control, and control was important to the Earl of Hendon. "Actually, I wanted to ask your opinion of Sir Humphrey Carmichael."

"Carmichael?" Hendon let his breath out between his teeth in a sound of disgust. "Damned upstart. His father was a weaver. Did you know that? A bloody weaver."

"So I'd heard. Owns a number of mills someplace up north, does he not?"

"Yorkshire. That's where he got his start.

Now the man has interests in everything from coal mines to shipping and banking."

Sebastian studied his father's dark face. Hendon possessed all the arrogance and prejudices of his class, but his harshest condemnations were saved for those in political opposition to the ruling Tories. Sebastian smiled. "Carmichael's a Whig, is he?"

"Ostensibly, no. He claims to support the Tories. But in practice the man is a bloody radical. He builds houses for his workers. Imagine that! Hires surgeons to tend their ills. Even feeds them a midday meal. And he won't let a child under twelve work more than ten hours a day in his mills or his mines."

"What is the nation coming to?" Hendon cast him a dark look, but Sebastian kept his gaze fixed ahead. "Does Carmichael have any association with Alfred, Lord Stanton?"

"Stanton's a banker. He has associations with every man of wealth or standing in the City." There was a pause; then Hendon said, "It's because of what they're saying happened to Stanton's son, isn't it? That's why you're asking. Because Barclay Carmichael died the same way."

"Yes."

Hendon frowned, but said nothing.

"What of Stanton's politics?" Sebastian asked. "Is he a Tory?"

"Good God. Of course. The Stantons go back to the Conqueror."

Sebastian laughed. "The implication being, I suppose, that such a proud lineage naturally confers upon its descendants protection against all radical philosophies?"

"Don't be ridiculous."

Again they rode in silence, Hendon working his jaw back and forth in that way he had when he was annoyed or thoughtful. After a time, he said, "It's a ghastly thing, what was done to those two young men. What sort of vile beast would perpetrate such a barbarity upon men of wealth and breeding?"

Sebastian stared off across the park to where the calm waters of the Serpentine reflected the clearing blue sky. Their wealth was the most obvious link between the two murdered men, a link that suggested their killer might harbor a vicious resentment of men of wealth and privilege. Except that Sebastian wasn't so sure it was that simple. Barclay Carmichael had been wealthy, but his family's origins were humble. "What do you know of Carmichael's son, Barclay?"

Hendon shrugged. "I've encountered him in the clubs. He seems to have been well regarded."

"Despite the lingering odor of the shop?"

"Sir Humphrey Carmichael married the Marquis of Lethaby's daughter, Caroline."

"Ah. And paid handsomely for her, I've no doubt."

Hendon grunted. "Pulled Lethaby out of the River Tick."

It was an old story: once proud noble families brought to the edge of ruin by bad luck, dissipation, or bad management, forced to marry off their daughters to rich cits in order to maintain their precarious hold on respectability. Mere wealth could never buy its possessor true acceptance into the innermost circles of Society. But it could buy a lord's daughter and, through her, social acceptance for one's sons.

A sudden thought occurred to Sebastian. "Is there a connection between the Stantons and the Marquis of Lethaby?"

"You'd need to ask your aunt Henrietta about that. The woman's a walking Burke's Peerage. You could ask her about it tonight — if you went to her ball."

Sebastian laughed out loud and turned his horse's head to leave.

"Sebastian —"

Sebastian hesitated, the black Arab tossing her head.

70

Hendon worked his jaw furiously back and forth. "This killer . . . Whoever he is, the man is dangerous. Dangerous and disturbed. You will take care." It was an order, not a request.

Sebastian let his gaze drift over the blunt-featured, white-haired man astride the big gray and felt the annoyance raised by his father's earlier remarks begin to drain out of him. In Sebastian's memories, his father was a commanding, intimidating figure, his vivid blue eyes flashing, his body large and hale. Once Hendon had been unforgiving, merciless, and fearless. He was still unforgiving and merciless, but when had he begun to grow old? Sebastian wondered. Old and afraid.

"I'll be careful."

CHAPTER 13

At twenty-seven, Barclay Carmichael had been just a year younger than Sebastian, a slimly built man with light brown hair and pleasant, even features. Sebastian had known him only slightly, for while Sebastian had been sent to Eton and Oxford, Carmichael had been educated at Harrow and Cambridge. Yet he'd been a familiar face in the clubs of St. James's, at Ascot and Menton's, Crib's Parlor and Angelo's. Sebastian knew nothing to the man's discredit, and a morning's discreet inquiries produced nothing to disrupt that image.

The picture that emerged was of an easygoing, affable man known for both his prowess on the hunting field and his willingness to help a friend. The worst anyone said of him was that he always paid his tailors' bills on time.

Increasingly puzzled, Sebastian turned his steps toward the imposing stone bulk of the

Bank of England.

The Bank was a private institution controlled by some of the wealthiest men in England. Their relationship with the government was both sympathetic and self-serving, and Sebastian doubted there was a man among the Bank's twenty-four directors who was not a staunch Tory. The never-ending war with France had been very good for business — or at least, good for these men's business. Sebastian had heard it said that in 1790 the Bank had employed only two hundred clerks; they now numbered over eleven hundred.

He found Sir Humphrey Carmichael walking briskly across the rotunda toward one of the funds' offices. "Sir Humphrey," called Sebastian. "If I might have a word with you?"

Sir Humphrey turned, an expression of annoyance shadowed by something else crossing his face. He looked to be in his late fifties or early sixties, a jowly man with pale, hooded eyes and an unusually long upper lip. He sucked on his lip for a moment, those secretive lids lowered as if to hide his thoughts. Then he tightened his jaw, said curtly, "For a moment," and led the way to an office of rich green velvet and polished mahogany that overlooked Threadneedle Street.

"I understand you're the man to see if one is interested in making investments," said Sebastian, declining the banker's offer of a seat.

"Yes. But I don't think you're here to discuss investments, are you, my lord?"

Sebastian met the older man's hard stare. His eyes were light gray and utterly inscrutable. Here was a man to be reckoned with, thought Sebastian. In the space of something like thirty years, Carmichael had risen from being a weaver's son to become one of the wealthiest men in London, with a marquis's daughter as his wife. It was a journey no one made without being brilliant and cunning and utterly ruthless. Hendon's talk of factory housing and noonday meals had sketched a portrait of a philanthropist, but that portrait seemed difficult to reconcile with the man now before Sebastian.

Sebastian smiled. "Very well. Let's cut to the chase, shall we? Sir Henry Lovejoy has asked for my help in discovering what happened to Dominic Stanton, and I was wondering if you knew of any possible connection between young Mr. Stanton and your son, Barclay."

Sir Humphrey Carmichael went to stand on the far side of his broad, gleaming desk, his hands clasped behind his back, the features of his face utterly composed. They might have been discussing the price of cotton or the latest American challenge to Britain's naval supremacy, rather than the brutal murder and mutilation of his first-born son just three months before. Only the gleam of pain in the banker's eyes, quickly hidden by those heavy lids, betrayed the raw agony of a father's loss.

"Apart from the manner of their deaths," said Carmichael slowly, "no. I know of no connection between them."

Sebastian let his gaze wander the office. It was an elegant chamber, the walls hung with dark oils depicting sleek horses and racing hounds, the paintings sandwiched between massive bookcases crammed with books and curious objets d'art that could come only from a lifetime of travel. "Is there a connection between you and Lord Stanton?"

"I have dealings with most of the wealthy and influential men in this city, Lord Stanton being no exception."

Which didn't exactly answer the question, Sebastian noticed.

"I understand you're a follower of Robert Owen and the reformers."

Carmichael grunted. "Not me. My wife."

Sebastian knew a flicker of surprise. So it was the marquis's daughter rather than the weaver's son who had interested herself in the needs of the working poor, who had built houses and hired surgeons and served soup. It said something unexpected about the relationship between the banker and his lady wife, that he had allowed her to indulge her concern for his workers even if he didn't share it.

"Yet you encourage her," said Sebastian.

"Her projects have proved to be surprisingly good for business. I encourage anything that's good for business."

"And Barclay? Did he interest himself in his mother's projects?"

"At twenty-seven? Hardly."

Sebastian's gaze fell on a dark wooden statue prominently displayed on a table near the window. Some fourteen inches high, it depicted what he thought might be a woman, although the figure was wrapped in an Eastern cloak, making it difficult to be certain. Seated on a lion, she waved something like eight or ten arms in the air. "An interesting piece," said Sebastian, moving to examine it more closely.

"It's from Ceylon." Carmichael's tongue flicked out to moisten his lips in a quick gesture. And Sebastian thought, *He's nervous. Why is he nervous?*

"I have interests in a firm that imports tea," Carmichael was saying. He moved to take the statue into his large hands. The hands were scrubbed so clean they were pink, the nails carefully manicured. But these were no gentleman's hands; the fingers and palms still bore the calluses left by the labors of his youth. "It's a statue of the Hindu goddess Shakti."

"Have you been to India?"

"Several times."

Sebastian thought about the page from a ship's log shoved in Barclay Carmichael's mouth by his killer. "What about your son? Did he ever travel with you?"

"I travel on business. My son was a gentleman," snapped Carmichael. It was, after all, the reason Sir Humphrey Carmichael had paid through the nose for the privilege of marrying the daughter of a marquis, so that his son might call himself a gentleman. A gentleman's wealth came from land, or investments, or inheritance; he never actually took a direct hand in the vulgar business of earning money.

"Your son was a remarkably well-liked man," said Sebastian. "Do you know of anyone who might have wished him harm?"

77

"No." Carmichael's eyes narrowed. "But if I did, do you really think I would tell you?" It was said without any apparent heat, only a glimmer of something that was visible for an instant in those hooded eyes, then gone.

Sebastian stared at the man's sad, fleshy face. "It might help to make sense out of what is happening in this city."

"And what concern might that be of mine at this point?"

"To ensure that such a thing doesn't happen again?" Sebastian suggested.

"My son is dead. You think I care if it happens to some other man's son?" He swiped one large, work-worn hand through the air in a quick, dismissive gesture. "Well, I don't."

Sebastian's fingers twitched on the brim of his hat. "If you change your mind, you know where to find me. Good day, sir," he said, and strode from the room.

Behind him, Sir Humphrey Carmichael's hand tightened around the head of the Shakti. With a sudden oath, he whirled, his arm jerking to send the statue hurtling across the room.

CHAPTER 14

"A curious conversation," said Paul Gibson, when Sebastian met with the surgeon later that day.

They were drinking ale and dining on a joint of cold ham at a battered old table overlooking the surgery's neglected back garden. "It reminded me of my meeting with Lord Stanton yesterday morning," said Sebastian. "There's more than arrogance going on here, more than suspicion or resentment of my involvement. Their re-action is simply not . . . natural."

"Grief can drive men in strange ways."

Sebastian swallowed the last of his ale and set aside his tankard. "Perhaps."

Gibson pushed awkwardly to his feet. "Come see what I've found . . . although I'm afraid it's not much."

Sebastian followed the surgeon through the weed-grown garden to the small stone building behind the surgery. The scent of blood and decaying flesh hit them halfway across the yard. Sebastian breathed through his mouth.

What was left of Dominic Stanton lay on the room's altarlike table, covered with a sheet. Sebastian stared at that long, silent form and said, "I suppose in all honesty it's impossible for anyone to truly grasp what it would be like, knowing this had been done to his son."

"Probably." Gibson flipped back the sheet. "Unfortunately, I can't tell you much more about his death. I still believe it's the wound across his throat that killed him . . . which I suppose would be a relatively merciful way to die, considering the horrors of what came after."

"It's the way you'd slaughter a lamb," said Sebastian, his gaze on the boy's face. Dominic Stanton's features were relaxed in death; he might have been sleeping.

"Except this was no lamb but a big, hale young man. I would think it must have taken more than one assailant to subdue him." Gibson rolled up the sheet and shoved it aside in a rough gesture. "Although it's difficult enough to imagine one man committing such an act of barbarity, let alone two."

Slipping a hand into his pocket, Sebastian

drew forth the small blue-and-white Chinese vial he'd picked up from the grassy verge on the road to Merton Abbey. "I found this where I think the boy was set upon."

Taking the vial, Gibson raised it to his nostrils and sniffed. He looked up, one eyebrow raised. "Opium?"

Sebastian watched Gibson's hand clench around the vial, then relax. Gibson's own dark love affair with opium dated back three years or more, to the blood-soaked surgeon's tent in Portugal where he'd lost the mangled remnant of a leg left him by a French cannonball.

"Is there any way to tell if Stanton ingested the drug before he died?" Sebastian asked.

Gibson sighed and held the vial out to him. "Unfortunately, no. You think Stanton was a habitual user?"

"I suppose it's possible, although I've found nothing that would suggest it. I'm thinking perhaps the drug was used to make him more manageable."

"It would do that. Particularly if the lad were unused to its effects. But to force it down his throat wouldn't have been easy if he resisted."

"No. But if someone held a gun on him and gave him a choice between the opium and instant death, he would drink it."

As bad as the room had smelled yesterday, today it was indescribably worse. Sebastian went to stand in the open doorway and breathe. "According to Mr. Stanton's friends, the boy was nervous the past few weeks, convinced someone was following him. Whoever killed him must have been watching him. Waiting for the chance to catch him alone. His friends thought he was imagining it. They even laughed at him for being afraid."

"Aye, he was afraid, poor lad. He wet himself at some point before he died."

"Not at the moment of his death?"

"No. It was when he was still wearing his shirt."

Sebastian turned to gaze at the fair curls and full cheeks of the silent face on Paul Gibson's granite slab. Dominic Stanton had probably thought himself a downy one, awake on every suit. Whereas in fact, he'd been little more than a child. A scared child. *"Jesus."*

His gaze rose to the enameled basin on a nearby table, where something bloody and vaguely familiar lay. "The object he had stuffed in his mouth, what was it?"

Gibson followed his stare. "The hoof of a goat. It probably came from a butcher's stall. Whoever dismembered that goat was far more familiar with a cleaver than the man who hacked up Stanton's legs. Any idea what it signifies?"

Sebastian shook his head. "No. According to Lovejoy, Barclay Carmichael had a page from a ship's log stuffed in his mouth."

Gibson nodded. "I spoke to Martin, the surgeon who did the postmortem on young Carmichael." His lip quivered in disdain. "The man's a bloody idiot. I asked him if the body showed signs of having been bound and gagged before death, and he said he'd never thought to notice. But you were right: Carmichael's throat was slit and the body drained of all blood. The flesh was hacked from his arms."

"Not the legs?"

"No. Just the arms."

Sebastian walked around the slab. He had to force himself to look, really look, at the mangled boy. "Barclay Carmichael's body was found at dawn in St. James's Park," he said, "hanging upside down from a mulberry tree. Dominic Stanton was found in Old Palace Yard, again at dawn. Both very public places. Both young men were last seen the night before their deaths by friends whom they then left. Sometime between when they were last seen and when their bodies were discovered at dawn, both young men were set upon by at least one assailant, perhaps more. They were taken God only knows where, stripped of their shirts, their throats slit, and the blood drained from their bodies. Then the killer — or killers — hacked the flesh from Carmichael's arms and from Stanton's legs and dumped the bodies where they'd be quickly found the next morning." He glanced up to find Gibson watching him. "Does that sound right?"

"I'd say so, yes."

Sebastian blew out a long, slow breath. "Was there nothing to indicate where Stanton might have been killed?"

"Just these." Gibson walked over to pluck what looked like pieces of straw from the table and hold them out. "I found one in his hair, the others caught in his shirt and coat."

Sebastian took the fragile stems between his fingers and sniffed. "It's hay."

"I asked Martin if Barclay Carmichael had hay in his hair and clothes. He said yes — although he couldn't imagine why it might be significant." Reaching for the sheet, Gibson shook it out over the body, his motions unexpectedly gentle as he smoothed the covering over the boy's mutilated feet.

He stood for a moment, his gaze on the silent, shrouded form before him. When he spoke, his voice was hushed. "What kind of person would do something like this? Butcher a human body like a slab of meat?"

"You do it."

Gibson looked up, his lips pressed together so tightly that two white lines bracketed his mouth. "I dissect cadavers for knowledge, to help save lives, and I respect and honor every body that comes to me. Whoever killed those two young men was acting out some twisted hatred, not pursuing any scientific inquiry. He desecrated their bodies in a way that violates every standard of decency, every tenet of civilization as we know it."

"Yet we've both seen men do such things — and worse. Well-bred young men of birth and fortune."

There was a silence as both men's thoughts drifted back to another time and another place, and a fellow officer who had once delighted in the pain and dismemberment of his enemies.

"That was war," said Gibson. "This isn't war. And besides, he's not here."

"No, this isn't war. But he is here in London."

"Quail?" said Gibson.

Sebastian nodded. "Captain Peter himself."

Captain Peter Quail was not the kind of fellow officer one easily forgot. A tall, lanky barrister's son from Devon with cornflower blue eyes, a shank of straight blond hair, and a ready laugh that came loud and often, he had served with Gibson and Sebastian in Portugal. He was every regiment's dream with a cricket bat and poetry in motion on horseback. And he had taken a fiendishly sadistic delight in butchering informers — or men he suspected of being informers. He used to dump his victims' mutilated bodies on their families' doorsteps. As time passed, he developed what he considered his calling card — various parts of his victims' anatomy sliced off and stuffed into their mouths.

"I'd heard he lost an arm at Ciudad Rodrigo."

"He did. But he was able to use an inheritance from his wife's people to buy a transfer to the Horse Guards." Commissions in the Horse Guards were the most expensive in the Army.

Gibson stared at the silent figure before them. "What possible reason could he have to do this?"

"I don't know," said Sebastian. "Maybe he simply developed a taste for it."

■ ■ ■ ■

"I want you to find someone for me," Sebastian told his tiger, Tom, as he drew Sebastian's curricle up before the surgery.

Tom handed over the chestnuts' reins and scrambled back onto his perch. "Who?"

"A captain in the Horse Guards named Quail. Peter Quail."

Chapter 15

Kat set the *casquet* at a rakish angle on her head, then turned this way and that, studying her reflection in the shop's looking glass. Once she'd dressed in rags, a frightened child alone on the streets of London who'd learned to beg and steal just to stay alive. Now she owned a wardrobe full of clothes, but it wasn't enough. It would never be enough to make her forget.

After the death of her mother and stepfather, Kat had found a brief refuge with her mother's sister, an ostentatiously religious woman named Emma Stone. Determined to prevent Kat from following her mother's path to sin and damnation, Aunt Emma had wielded her whip with brutal purpose. But it was the lecherous advances of Mr. Stone that had finally driven Kat to escape into the night. The experience had left her with a bitter contempt for sanctimonious piety and a child's delight in the joys of soft sheets and fine clothing.

This particular hat's brim was of cherry velvet, with a bunch of silk flowers tucked beneath a darker ribbon at the crown, and the entire effect was —

"Charming," said a deep male voice behind her.

Kat spun around to find a tall, dark-haired man regarding her through a quizzing glass. Nattily dressed in buff-colored breeches, an olive coat, and gleaming Hessians, he leaned casually against the frame of the shop's open doorway. Behind him, she could see the bright sunshine of a fine September afternoon, the street crowded with dowagers and matrons in elegant carriages and town bucks on horseback. Yet she felt — and understood herself to be — utterly alone.

She knew him, of course. His name was Colonel Bryce Epson-Smith. Once an officer in the Hussars, he had for some three or four years served as the personal agent of Charles, Lord Jarvis, cousin to the King and the acknowledged power behind the Regent.

"Why, thank you." Lifting the cheery confection from her head, Kat reached for a chip hat with a forest green velvet band and a matching wisp of a veil. "Or do you prefer this one?"

"Why not take both?"

Kat smiled. "Why not, indeed?" She turned to the woman behind the counter, a thin slip of a thing who had suddenly gone very quiet. "Wrap them up for me."

Dropping his quizzing glass, Epson-Smith pushed away from the doorframe and took a step toward her. "Miss Boleyn will be sending someone to pick them up." He spoke to the girl behind the counter, but he kept his gaze on Kat.

Kat met his inflexible stare. "I'd rather take them with me now."

"Unfortunately, that won't be possible. Lord Jarvis would like a word with you. He doesn't appreciate being kept waiting."

In spite of herself, Kat knew a flutter of fear. People had been known to simply disappear when Jarvis expressed an interest in seeing them. Others were later found dead, dumped in outlying fields after frightening things had been done to their tormented bodies. "And if I refuse?"

Epson-Smith's eyes were gray and hard. It took all of Kat's courage and determination to continue to hold his stare. "I don't think you're that stupid."

CHAPTER 16

That afternoon, following a tip from Tom, Sebastian tracked Captain Peter Quail to the horse auction yard of Tattersall's.

Even in that crowd, Captain Quail was easy enough to spot: a tall, blond-haired man with the left sleeve of his regimentals hanging conspicuously empty. He was inspecting a carriage horse, a glossy bay with a gracefully arching neck and regally held tail, when Sebastian came up behind him.

"Showy," said Sebastian. "But a bit short in the back, wouldn't you say?"

Quail turned, the expression on his face closed and watchful. "I wouldn't have said so, no. But then, you always did have the best horses in the regiment."

"I heard you'd purchased a transfer to the Horse Guards. How comforting for your wife to have you once again by her side."

Quail's eyes narrowed. When they'd served

together in the Peninsula, Quail had never been without a Portuguese mistress, sometimes keeping two whores at a time. "What's this about, Devlin? I don't flatter myself that you've sought me out simply for the sake of auld lang syne."

Sebastian ran one hand down the bay's neck. She really was a splendid animal. "I suppose I'm curious. You didn't by any chance know a young gentleman named Dominic Stanton?"

"You mean the lord's son who just got himself butchered?" Quail gave an abrupt huff of laughter. "Not hardly."

"Yet you've heard what happened to him."

"Who in London has not?"

The bay nosed Sebastian's pockets, looking for a carrot. "What about Barclay Carmichael? Did you know him?"

A muscle twitched along the man's handsome jawline, his nostrils flaring on a quickly indrawn breath. "I know where you're going with this."

"I should rather think you would," said Sebastian, his attention seemingly all for the horse. "That's what happens when you acquire a reputation for torture and mutilation. Young men start showing up butchered, and suspicion naturally turns toward you."

Quail's chest swelled, the brass on his regimentals gleaming in the late-afternoon light. "I did what I did in Portugal for King and country."

"And loved every minute of it, didn't you?" Sebastian turned to study the man beside him. "So what happened? Did you acquire a taste for it, and then find you missed it when you had nothing to do besides parade up and down the Mall and provide an ornamental backdrop for the Prince?"

Quail stared back at him, breathing hard but saying nothing.

The afternoon sun struck the dust in the air, turning it to gold. The smell of expensive horseflesh and manure drifted on the afternoon breeze. "Where were you Saturday night, anyway?" Sebastian asked.

"At home. In bed with my wife." Quail leaned in close, his blue eyes like ice. "Why? Whose bed were you in? *My lord.*"

Sebastian smiled. "Not my wife's." He started to turn away.

Quail stopped him, his voice rising. "You're wrong about this. You hear me, Devlin? You're wrong. I had nothing to do with either Carmichael or Stanton."

"Really?" Sebastian gathered the bay's lead and slapped it against the captain's

93

chest. "Then why are you lying?"

Sebastian stood in the shadows of the auction yard's Palladian facade and watched as Quail glanced quickly around, then disappeared into one of the subscription rooms.

"Follow him," Sebastian told Tom. "I want to know where he goes, whom he sees."

Tom pulled his hat low enough to shade his eyes and grinned. "Aye, gov'nor."

CHAPTER 17

Charles, Lord Jarvis lifted a pinch of snuff to his nostrils and sniffed. He was a big man, tall and fleshy, with large appetites and a power unmatched by any in England.

Although he could claim a distant kinship to the King, Jarvis owed his position of power not so much to his birth as to the nearly incomparable brilliance of his intellect, his shrewd ability to manipulate men, and a fierce dedication to King and country that no one could question. If it weren't for Jarvis, the Hanovers would have lost their fragile hold on the throne of England long ago, and both the Regent and the old King knew it. Or at least, the King knew it when he was in his right mind, which was seldom these days.

Jarvis kept offices in both St. James's Palace and Carlton House, although it was at Carlton House that he spent most of his time since the proclamation of the Regency some seven months before. His own house, in Berkeley Square, he visited as seldom as possible. The place was overrun with females, a species for which Jarvis had little patience and even less tenderness. His mother was a foul-tempered, grasping harpy, his wife an idiot, while his daughter, Hero . . . Jarvis felt his chest burn and rose to pour himself a brandy. At the age of twenty-five, Hero was headstrong and stubborn, forever engaged in a nauseating string of good works and unlikely ever to wed.

Once Jarvis had had a son, a weak-willed namby-pamby named David. But David was dead, which left only Hero. If she'd been born a son, Jarvis would have been fiercely proud of her — except for those radical notions of hers, of course. As it was, she was a sore trial to him.

He took a sip of his brandy. The woman he'd ordered brought to him today was of a sort he understood well. A whore, she used her beauty and the ecstasy to be found between her legs to entice and ensnare men. It mattered not whether she served the French out of conviction or for greed. She would tell Jarvis what he wanted to know and allow herself to be used, or he would crush her. Her and Devlin both, if need be.

The discreet knock at his door brought

his head around. He watched Kat Boleyn sweep into his chamber with a regal bearing that Princess Caroline and her horsey daughter, Charlotte, would do well to emulate. She held her head high and was pretending not to be afraid, although he knew she was. Only a fool wouldn't be afraid, and this little actress was no fool.

She was a beautiful woman, even if she wasn't his type. Jarvis's taste ran to delicate, flaxen-haired women, while Kat Boleyn was dark and tall. She fixed him with a fierce blue stare and said, "I understand you wanted to see me."

"Admirable," he said, and saw her eyebrows rise in inquiry and surprise. "But unnecessary. We both know why you're here. I trust you won't waste either my time or yours with protestations of innocence."

"It's difficult to protest my innocence when I don't know what I'm being accused of." She had her voice flawlessly under control.

Jarvis took another sip of his brandy. He did not offer her wine; nor did he invite her to sit. "Your association with the French is known. Has been known, actually, for quite some time now."

"Really? If this is a fishing expedition, I'm not biting." She turned toward the door.

"May I go now?"

He went to lounge in a chair beside the empty hearth, his legs crossed in front of him. "No."

She hesitated, then swung slowly to face him again.

"We have a report, compiled by two of our agents last winter. A copy of it is there on the table." He nodded to the black notebook that lay on a nearby ebony side table. "Do take a look at it. I'm convinced you'll find it fascinating reading."

She picked up the book with a hand that did not tremble and flipped through the pages. Once or twice she paused, her lips parting on a quickly indrawn breath. When she finished, she set the book aside and looked up at him, her famous blue eyes huge in a pale face.

"I deny it all."

"It doesn't matter. I didn't bring you here to discuss the contents of that most interesting little book."

"Then why am I here?"

Jarvis folded his hands together and rested them on his broad chest. "As you are no doubt aware, Monsieur Pierrepont's activities on behalf of Paris were known to us. We left him alone because it suited our purposes. But his hasty departure last February has disrupted what was a nice, tidy situation. Our agents tell us Napoleon has a new spymaster in London. We want his name. You're going to give it to us."

She started to say something, but he held up his hand, stopping her. "It's immaterial if you know his name now or not. But if you do not know it, I suggest you learn it. Quickly. You have until Friday."

She stared back at him, her head held high, her posture defiant. He knew what she was thinking. He smiled.

"You're thinking I've given you something of a reprieve. That left to your own devices until Friday, you will simply flee the country for France. That would not be wise. You are being watched. If you make any attempt to flee — or to warn the gentleman whose name I seek — you will be seized." He pushed up from the chair and walked toward her. "I have men in my employ who enjoy hurting people, and they are very good at what they do. It wouldn't take them long to extract whatever information you might possess. Only, I'm afraid they wouldn't stop there. Before they finished with you, you would no longer be pretty. Or whole. You would be begging them to kill you, and they would. Eventually."

Reaching out, he touched her cheek.

Before she could stop herself, she flinched.

"And if that still is not enough to convince you of the wisdom of cooperating, then I suggest you give some thought to the consequences for Viscount Devlin, should it become known that his mistress is a French spy. You think you wouldn't implicate him, but believe me, by the time my men were through with you, you would."

She stared at him with a cold, murderous fury that almost gave him pause. He dropped his hand from her cheek, but he was careful not to turn his back on her. "You have until Friday."

CHAPTER 18

Sebastian was in his dressing room, shrugging into a black evening coat with the clumsy help of his footman Andrew when Tom came to deliver his report.

"Discover anything of interest?" Sebastian asked, nodding the footman's dismissal.

"Quail spent most o' the afternoon in St. James's, in 'is club. Then he went 'ome."

"To his wife? That's unusual. Do you think he knew you were following him?"

"I don't think so, no. Want I should trail 'im again tomorrow?"

Sebastian smoothed his lapels. "Yes. I won't need you in the morning. I'm interviewing some gentlemen's gentlemen who look promising."

Tom dug the toe of his shoe into the carpet and tried to look innocent.

Smiling to himself, Sebastian reached for a small flintlock and slipped it into his pocket. Pistols weren't exactly standard evening wear, but the low-heeled pumps that were de rigueur for balls meant he couldn't carry a knife in his boot.

Tom's eyes widened. "Expectin' trouble?"

"When it comes to murder, I always expect trouble."

Henrietta, Dowager Duchess of Claiborne, stood at the top of the imposing stairs of her Park Street town house, her hands clenched into fists at her sides. She had been receiving her guests, but the arrivals had long since begun to thin, and Henrietta was forced to admit that her handsome if wayward young nephew, Viscount Devlin, was not coming. Turning away, she blew out a harsh, ungenteel breath of disgust.

Beside her, her son, the present Duke of Claiborne, leaned toward her to say, "You didn't really expect him to show, now, did you?"

"Of course not. But I'm still annoyed with him."

At the age of seventy, the former Lady Henrietta St. Cyr was one of the grand dames of society. She had never been beautiful, but she had always been fashionable. And very, very astute.

She had erred, she knew, in presenting both Bisley's daughter and the Fenton girl to Devlin; the one was too frivolous, the other too severe. But she had high hopes for this newest possibility, the Dillingham girl. Lady Julia was breathtakingly lovely and satisfyingly intelligent without being a dead bore. As Devlin would discover if he'd simply condescend to meet the poor girl.

Abandoning her post at the top of the stairs, Henrietta moved through her guests with the practiced ease of an accomplished hostess. She was steering a wayward buck toward a shy young girl in ivory figured silk when she became aware of a stir around her, like the fluttering of hens when a wolf threatens the chicken house.

Turning, she saw a solitary figure climbing the marble steps. Devlin.

He wore the standard male evening attire of black silk knee breeches, black dress coat, and black silk waistcoat with a graceful ease that somehow managed to be both negligent and exquisite at the same time. Reaching the top of the steps, he paused, his gaze scanning the crowded rooms. He had his mother's tall, fine-boned good looks, with dark hair and the strangest pair of yellow eyes Henrietta had ever seen. Eyes that lit up with a smile as he came toward her.

"Aunt," he said, bowing low over her hand.

She rapped his knuckles with her fan, hard. "Don't think to turn me up sweet. I'm surprised you bothered to show up at all, as late as it is."

Devlin grinned. "I hadn't intended to, but I had some questions I wanted to ask you."

Far from being annoyed, Henrietta knew a quickening of curiosity. "Questions? About what?"

Taking her arm, he steered her toward a small withdrawing room. "Not here."

"I have guests," she protested.

His smile widened into something devilish. "I can come back tomorrow morning. Early."

Henrietta sighed. It was well known that she never left her room before one o'clock. "You unnatural young man. I don't know what sordid mess you've involved yourself in this time, but I refuse to tell you anything until you promise to at least dance the quadrille with Lady Julia."

"Who?"

"Lady Julia Dillingham."

She thought he might balk, but he only laughed and said, "A fair-enough exchange. The quadrille it is. Now tell me what you know about the Stantons and the Carmichaels."

Henrietta felt her smile slide off her face.

"What have you to do with that ghastly business?"

"A friend has asked for my help." He closed the door behind him and leaned back against it. "I understand Sir Humphrey Carmichael married the daughter of the Marquis of Lethaby. Is Lethaby in any way related to the Stantons?"

"Only very distantly." She went to lower herself into a curving chair of puce velvet, and sighed. "He was such a charming young man, Barclay Carmichael. He had every girl of marriageable age in London on the scramble for him. What a pity."

"Do you know of any connection between Stanton and Carmichael?"

"The fathers or the sons?"

"Either one."

Henrietta tapped one finger thoughtfully against her lips. "I do seem to recall they were both involved in something a few years back, but I couldn't say now exactly what it was."

"A scandal?"

"No. I don't believe so. If I remember correctly, Russell Yates was also involved in some way."

Devlin raised one eyebrow. "Russell Yates? Now that's interesting."

Russell Yates was one of society's more

colorful characters, a born gentleman who'd made his fortune as a privateer. There had always been whispers about Yates, about his murderous past and the connections he still maintained with smugglers and free traders. But lately there had been other rumors, dark hints about certain activities that seemed to belie his virile image and that weren't discussed in mixed company. It was all said in whispers, of course, for in an age in which vice and sin were commonplace, there still remained this one taboo, this one prohibition, the violation of which could lead not to mere ostracism, but a sentence of death.

Henrietta studied her nephew's face, but he was giving nothing away. "Have you heard the rumors about him?"

"I've heard them."

"Do you believe there's anything to them?"

"I don't know. But it does suggest a new angle of inquiry."

"You can't be serious. I don't know about young Stanton, but no one ever questioned Barclay Carmichael's interest in the ladies."

Devlin shrugged.

Henrietta pressed her lips together and made an exasperated sound deep in her throat. "Hendon told me you'd involved yourself in these latest murders. Don't you think it's a bit, well, *common,* Devlin?"

His brows twitched together into a frown that was there, then gone. "Common? Dreadfully so. In fact, if you had the least regard for the reputation of this Lady Julia, you would most definitely advise her not to dance the quadrille with me."

Henrietta pushed to her feet with a grunt. "I fear it would take far more than an unnatural interest in murder to render you anything other than an enviable catch, my dear." She looped her arm through his. "Now take me back to my ball, you troublesome child. I believe the quadrille is next."

CHAPTER 19

Kat stood beside the heavily draped windows of her bedroom, her arms wrapped across her chest. The room behind her was dark. The night watchman had long since called out, *Two o'clock on a fine night and all is well,* but she still wore the *robe en caleçon* of blue satin piped in white that she'd worn home from the evening's performance. She had not been to bed.

She didn't want to look, but she had to. Touching the edge of the curtain, she shifted it so that she could peer down on the street below. The night was unusually bright, the moonlight mingling with the light from the streetlamps to bathe the pavement in a soft glow. She searched the shadows, looking for a shape that shouldn't be there, a hint of movement on a still night.

Sebastian would have seen the figure in an instant; it took Kat several minutes. She had almost given up looking when he raised his hand to his mouth, like a man stifling a yawn.

She let the curtain fall back into place, then simply stood there, her breath coming hard and fast. She had no illusions about the situation she was in. Jarvis was not a man given to idle threats; he had meant everything he said. She had until Friday.

She'd found it curious, at first, that he'd given her several days to deliver up to him the spymaster's name. Then she'd realized he must have had agents watching her for months, ever since Pierrepont's flight last February. It must have been when Jarvis grew frustrated by his inability to ascertain the spymaster's identity by stealth that he had decided to approach Kat directly. Convinced that she did not, indeed, know the new spymaster's name, he had decided it necessary to allot her that brief span of time in which to discover it.

Pressing the fingertips of one hand against her lips, Kat swung away from the window. She had no need to discover the name of Napoleon's new spymaster in London, for she knew it. Aiden O'Connell was an Irishman who cooperated with the French for the same reason Kat once had: for Ireland. He had approached her last summer hoping to reestablish the connection she had once enjoyed with his predecessor, Leo Pierrepont. She had told him at the time she wanted out of the game, but that wouldn't save her now from Jarvis.

Her options were limited and she knew it. She could attempt to escape, but Jarvis was notorious for his network of spies, and her stomach roiled at the thought of the things his henchmen would do to her if they caught her. She could wait until Friday and nobly refuse to give up O'Connell's name, but Jarvis would then simply wrench the information from her by torture. She knew she would tell them anything they wanted to hear — anything, even as she knew it wouldn't be enough to save her. Or . . .

Or she could betray O'Connell freely, and hope it would be enough.

With a groan, Kat sank to the floor, her arms drawing her bent knees against her chest. Jarvis had left her no real choice, and he knew it. On Friday, she would tell him Aiden O'Connell's name. The trick would be to find a way to do it on her own terms. Because she harbored no illusions. Now that Jarvis had his hooks in her, she would never be free, never be safe.

And neither would Devlin.

Leaving his aunt Henrietta's ball, Sebastian

descended the torchlit steps to discover a man in a rough greatcoat and slouch hat lounging against the wall near Sebastian's carriage, his hands in his pockets. As Sebastian approached, the man pushed himself upright and took a step forward.

Sebastian's footmen made to stop him, but Sebastian waved them back.

"Nice evening," said the man, the skin beside his eyes crinkling in a smile. He looked to be about thirty years of age, with broad shoulders and a kind of coiled restlessness that reminded Sebastian of men he'd known in the Army, in the secret service.

Sebastian casually slipped one hand into his own pocket and felt the smooth, well-crafted wooden stock of his pistol. "Then why the coat?"

This time the man's smile showed his teeth. "You know why." His speech was not that of a gentleman, yet not of the streets, either.

Moving deliberately, Sebastian brought the small flintlock from his pocket to hold it loosely at his side. He was careful to keep a calculated distance between them. "What do you want?"

For an instant, the man's eyes left Sebastian's face, his gaze flicking to the flintlock at Sebastian's side. The man's expression never altered. "I've come to offer you some friendly advice."

"Advice?"

"Advice. I was hired to give you a warning. You know the kind. A dead cat on your doorstep. A brick through your window in the middle of the night. But then I thought, Why play games? There's something the gentleman needs to understand, so why not simply explain it to him?"

"Hence the advice."

"That's right." The man in the slouch hat brought up his left hand to scratch the side of his nose. "The thing is, you see, you've been asking too many questions. The gentleman who hired me wants you to stop."

"You mean, asking questions about Barclay Carmichael and Dominic Stanton."

The man smiled again. "That's right. See? I knew you'd understand."

"Who hired you? Lord Stanton or Sir Humphrey Carmichael?"

The man's smile slid away. "Now there you go, asking questions. Not a good idea, remember?"

The man was starting to annoy Sebastian. "Just who are you, anyway?"

"My name isn't important. I'm just the messenger."

"And the adviser."

"So to speak."

"And if I fail to heed your advice?"

The man's smile was completely gone now. "That would be unwise."

Sebastian signaled his footman, who leapt forward to let down the carriage steps. "Give your employer some advice from me, why don't you?" Sebastian said.

The man pivoted to keep his face toward Sebastian as Sebastian moved past him to the carriage. The man's right hand never left his pocket. Sebastian never raised the pistol from his side. "Tell your employer I don't like people who kill cats. I have a real objection to heavy rocks being thrown through my windows. And if he sends anyone after me again, I'll kill him."

Something glittered in the other man's eyes, something that was both a warning and a promise. "Till we meet again, then," he said, and faded into the night.

Sebastian settled into the corner of his carriage, the flintlock resting against his knee. He could hear the distant strains of music from his aunt's ballroom and, from nearer at hand, a woman's laughter.

His questions were obviously making someone uncomfortable. The threat against him had been serious, the man who delivered it a professional. Leaning forward, Sebastian signaled his coachman to drive on. He had no intention of heeding the man's warning, of course. Which meant that he'd be meeting the gentleman in the slouch hat again.

Only next time, Sebastian knew, he wouldn't see the man coming.

CHAPTER 20

Tuesday, 17 September 1811

Early the next morning, Sebastian received an unexpected visit from a furtive little man with sun-darkened skin and an accent that could change from Geordie to Cockney or from French to Spanish to Italian and back again in an instant. His name was Emmanuel Jones, and he had once worked for Sebastian in the Army. Now he was working for Sebastian again in an entirely different capacity. He was searching for Sebastian's mother.

"That ship you was askin' about," said Jones. "The *San Remo?* You were right. It didn't sink seventeen years ago. It made port at the Hague, then worked its way along the coast in slow stages, through the straights of Gibraltar and around the toe of Italy, to Venice."

Sebastian rested his elbows on his library's broad desktop and studied the enigmatic features of the man who stood before him. "And the Englishwoman who was on it?"

"She calls herself Lady Sophia Sedlow now."

Sebastian nodded. Sedlow had been his mother's maiden name. "And?"

"She lived for a time in Venice, with a poet. He died. Nine years ago."

"Where is she now?"

"She left Italy in the company of a Frenchman, sometime around 1803. One of Napoleon's generals."

"Which one?"

"Becnel."

Sebastian stood from behind his desk and went to fiddle with the inlaid Moroccan box he kept on a shelf near the hearth. It was a moment before he trusted himself to speak. "She's in France now?"

"Yes. But I don't know exactly where."

Sebastian swung to look at him. "Then why are you here?"

Something flickered across the man's normally impassive face. "I'm not messing with Becnel."

Crossing to his desk, Sebastian opened a drawer and drew forth an envelope from which he counted a stack of banknotes. "Speak of this to anyone," he said, shoving the notes across the desk, "and I'll kill you.

It's as simple as that."

Jones folded the money out of sight with a sniff. "I know how to keep me mouth shut."

After he had gone, Sebastian went to stand, again, beside the empty hearth, his gaze fixed unseeingly on the cold, empty grate. He would need to find another agent, someone both trustworthy and unafraid to venture into the heart of Napoleon's France.

It wouldn't be easy. But it could be done.

He spent much of what was left of the morning interviewing applicants for the position of valet.

"We come highly recommended," said one of the applicants, a softly rounded man named Flint who affected a thin black mustache and punctuated his words with soft flutterings of his flawlessly manicured white hands. "Highly recommended, indeed."

Sebastian glanced through the valet's glowing credentials and felt a spurt of cautious optimism. In a field of applicants distinguished by nothing so much as mediocrity, the man looked promising. "So I see. You take considerable pride in your work, I understand."

"We consider our work more than a vocation," said Flint, sitting painfully upright in a chair on the opposite side of Sebastian's desk. "For us, taking care of our gentleman is akin to a calling. No measure is too extreme to achieve the best presentation. If a gentleman is a bit thin in the calf, we add padding to the stockings. If a gentleman grows corpulent in his advancing years, we are conversant with the discreet use of the corset. And for that unfortunate tendency displayed by some gentlemen to grow hair on the backs of the fingers, we are well versed in the art of hot waxing."

Something of Sebastian's reaction to this speech must have shown on his face, for the valet hastened to add, "Not that your lordship requires any of these extreme measures."

"Thank God for that."

The valet tilted his head, subjecting Sebastian to an intense scrutiny that made him feel like a nag being offered for sale at Tattersall's. "We would, of course, press for a bit more precision in the presentation. Sporting gentlemen can sometimes be a tad too careless in their dressing, if you know what we mean? A few extra hours spent at the toilette each morning can make such a difference."

"A few extra hours?"

Flint nodded. "No more than two or three."

Sebastian leaned back in his chair and pressed his fingertips together. "I'm something of an eccentric creature, I fear. There are times when I find it expedient to dress in the type of garments one customarily sees for sale in places such as Rosemary Lane. I trust you would have no difficulty with that?"

Flint gave a nervous titter. "Your lordship is . . . most droll."

"On the contrary, I am entirely serious."

The valet's pained smile fell, just as Tom came catapulting into the room, bringing with him the scent of sunbaked streets, hot boy, and the pervasive, earthy odor of the stables.

"I've a message from Sir 'Enry," said the tiger, breathing hard. " 'E's discovered another murder 'e thinks might be linked to the two young gentlemen what snuffed it here in London. Seems they found a body in a churchyard down in Kent, way last April. Gutted like a bleedin' fish, 'e was —"

"Merciful heavens," said the valet, pressing a snowy handkerchief to his lips.

"— and Sir 'Enry," continued Tom, casting the valet a curious glance, " 'e wants to know if'n you'd be interested in drivin'

119

down there with 'im this mornin'."

Sebastian pushed back his chair and turned to the valet. "If you'll excuse me, Mr. Flint —"

But the little man with the neat black mustache and soft white hands was already gone.

"The boy's name was Thornton," said Sir Henry Lovejoy, one hand held up to anchor his round hat more firmly to his bald head, the other hand gripping the edge of the seat beside him. "Mr. Nicholas Thornton."

Lovejoy was beginning to regret his decision to make the journey down to the Kentish town of Avery in Viscount Devlin's curricle, with that irreclaimable pickpocket Tom ensconced on the tiger's perch in the back. Lovejoy did not have a fondness for horseflesh; nor did he share his lordship's obvious delight in speed. Lord Devlin feathered a turn, his horses' flashing hooves eating up the miles. Lovejoy closed his eyes.

"How old was he?" asked the Viscount.

Lovejoy forced himself to open his eyes. There was no denying that the Viscount seemed to have his horses under perfect control. Lovejoy loosened his hold on the seat and drew in a deep breath. "Just nineteen. He was a divinity student up at Cambridge. Studying to enter the church, like his father."

"The church?" said Devlin in surprise.

Lovejoy nodded. "The boy's father is the rector at St. Andrews. The Reverend William Thornton."

"What makes you think there's a connection between his death and the London murders?"

Lovejoy himself found the similarities in the deaths difficult to comprehend. A rector, while considerably more distinguished than a vicar or a mere curate, was of a social rank far different from that enjoyed by either Stanton or Carmichael. "As I understand it, the boy's body was hacked open and his organs removed. I know little beyond that. I'm afraid young Mr. Thornton's killing attracted considerably less attention than the recent murders in London. Avery is, after all, some distance from Town."

"And the boy's father was only a clergyman," said the Viscount.

Lovejoy kept his face wooden. "Just so."

The white gate of a toll appeared up ahead. The urchin Tom blew a blast on his yard of tin as Devlin drew up and waited for the keeper to amble out of his cottage.

"You say the boy was killed last April?" said Devlin, after the toll was cleared.

"When he came down for the Easter holiday. Took a pole and went out fishing sometime in the late afternoon."

"By himself?"

"So it would appear. They later found his pole beside a stream that runs behind the vicarage."

"And the body?"

"Wasn't discovered until the next morning at dawn. The killer left the boy in the rector's own churchyard, lying atop one of the tombs."

CHAPTER 21

Avery proved to be a sleepy Kentish market town with a wide High Street curving down a gentle hill toward the banks of the Medway below. It was dominated by its old Norman church, St. Andrews, which stood in the midst of an ancient but well-tended churchyard of scythed grass dotted with worn gray tombstones. To the south of the church lay the rectory, a pleasantly proportioned house of mellow red brick built late in the last century, with twin, two-story bay windows protruding gracefully on either side of a small white porch.

The Reverend William Thornton received them in a study overlooking the rambling untidy gardens that stretched away from the rear of the vicarage. The study was a scholar's refuge, filled with piles of manuscript pages and ancient leather-bound volumes that overflowed the room's many bookcases to spill onto tables and across the floor.

They found him seated in a green leather chair beside the empty hearth, a frail-looking man with wispy gray hair and a prominent nose made more conspicuous by the gauntness of his cheeks. A rug covered his legs. He did not stand at their entrance.

"You must forgive me for not rising to greet you," he said when the stout middle-aged housekeeper in a mobcap ushered them in to see him. "I fear my legs no longer support me. But please do not allow my infirmity to lead you to deduce that you are unwelcome. It's not often I receive visitors from London. Please, sit down. Mrs. Ross, some tea."

"Please accept our apologies for intruding upon you," said Lovejoy, taking a seat on a nearby comfortably worn sofa. "But we must ask you some questions about your son."

Declining a seat, Sebastian went to stand with one hip resting on the low sill of a window overlooking the garden. He watched as Thornton's pale cheeks sagged, his lips trembling for a moment before he pressed them tightly together.

"It's because of these killings in London, isn't it? You think there's some connection?"

"There may be," said Lovejoy.

One of the Reverend's bony, heavily

veined hands tightened on the edge of the rug in his lap. "Mrs. Ross told me about this last one, the Stanton boy. It's terrible, just terrible."

"What can you tell us about the day your son disappeared, Mr. Thornton?"

The rector sat in silence for a moment. When he spoke, his voice was hushed and oddly flat, as if he could speak only by sealing off his every emotion from the tale he was telling. "Nicholas was up at Cambridge, but he'd come down for the Easter holidays. He used to spend every minute he could when he was home in the wood behind the house, and that was where he went that morning. It was a Wednesday. He was due to return to Cambridge in just a few days."

"He went fishing?"

"He took a pole with him, but I think it was something in the nature of a prop, so he'd look productive." Amusement gleamed, then was gone in an instant. "He said he'd be back in an hour or two, in time for nuncheon."

"But he didn't come back?"

"No. I didn't worry at first. You know what boys are like. But as the afternoon wore on, I became concerned. Nicholas was not usually so careless. When the shadows began to lengthen toward evening, I finally decided to go looking for him. I found his pole and his shoes beside the stream, near his favorite fishing hole. But nothing else. It was as if he had vanished."

"Was there any sign of a struggle?"

"No. Some men from the town volunteered to help me search the wood and beyond." Thornton restlessly shifted his legs. "I wasn't so infirm then, you see. We fanned out over the entire area, but we found nothing. Not until the following morning."

"When his body was discovered in the churchyard."

The Reverend's lower lip quivered. "Yes."

Sir Henry hesitated, as if reluctant to press on. He glanced at Sebastian, who said, "Was your son by any chance acquainted with either Dominic Stanton or Barclay Carmichael?"

Thornton's eyes widened. "No. Not to my knowledge. Nicholas was up at Cambridge, studying divinity. I can't imagine he would have met either one."

"Tell us about your son, Reverend," said Sir Henry, his voice unusually gentle. "What was he like?"

A sad smile touched the rector's lips and brought a brief spark of life to the tired old eyes. "He was one of the most curious

126

children I've ever known, always asking questions, wanting to see how things worked."

"And as a young man?"

"He was little changed. He was still a child in so many ways. Not in his mind," the clergyman added quickly. "He was always very bright. But in his ways and interests."

"Have you other children?"

"No."

Sebastian let his gaze drift over the neglected garden to the small glebe and, beyond that, the stretch of wood where the boy had disappeared.

"Can you think of anyone who might have had a grudge against your son," Sir Henry asked, "either real or imagined?"

The Reverend drew a deep breath that lifted his thin chest, then let it out in a sigh. "Not that I know of. Nicholas was a very quiet boy. Quiet and serious. My wife used to worry about him. She used to say he was more at ease with books than with people." Again that wistful smile touched his lips only to vanish, leaving him looking more stricken than before. "I thank God every day she didn't live to see what happened to him."

"Your wife is dead?"

The Reverend nodded sadly. "She died

this past January, right after Christmas."

Sebastian was careful not to look at Lovejoy. He'd heard it said that once the magistrate had had a wife. A wife and a child both, now long dead.

"You have our deepest sympathies," murmured the magistrate.

Sebastian found his gaze drawn again to the scene outside the window. To the north of the garden with its brick paths and overflowing clumps of marigold and santolina, lavender and roses, lay the church of St. Andrews. Through a gap in the high yew hedge he could see the church's squat medieval buttresses and an ancient square tower that thrust up broodingly against the blue September sky. The churchyard was an expanse of carefully tended green, far tidier than the rectory's own garden and crowded with a scattering of ancient gray headstones and tombs. He wondered if the Reverend had been the one to find his son's body, although it wasn't a question Sebastian felt inclined to ask.

"Do you mind if we ask who examined your son's body?" said Sebastian.

The Reverend appeared surprised by the question, although he answered it readily enough. "No, of course not. It was Dr. Newman. Dr. Aaron Newman. He lives here in

Avery, just across the green. Perhaps he can help you in a way I have been unable to do." The Reverend paused. "I keep reminding myself, 'Vengeance is mine, saith the Lord.' But it doesn't help. The man who did that to my son —" His voice broke. He paused to swallow hard, then said more quietly, "Whoever did that to my son was evil. To visit such an end on a poor innocent lad of nineteen . . ." His voice failed him again, and this time he made no attempt to continue.

Lovejoy rose awkwardly. "Please forgive us for intruding on you, Reverend. We won't trouble you any longer."

The Reverend passed a trembling hand across his eyes. "But you must stay for tea."

The magistrate gave one of his peculiar little bobbing bows. "Thank you, but no."

Sebastian pushed away from the window, conscious of a sense of frustration. What could possibly be the connection between this clergyman's serious, studious son and a spoiled nobleman's son like Dominic Stanton, or a sophisticated town buck like Barclay Carmichael? He remembered what Kat had said about the seeming randomness of the killings making everyone feel vulnerable. He wondered if that was why he was so anxious to find some link among the three murdered men: because the lack of a link in these savage murders made the act somehow that much more horrifying.

"Are you from around here, Mr. Thornton?" he asked suddenly.

The Reverend shook his head. "I come from Nayland, in East Suffolk. Near Ipswich. This living was presented to me by my wife's uncle. When I was a young man, it was always my intention to devote my life to missionary work, carrying the good news of our Lord to the unfortunate heathens dwelling in sin and darkness in the benighted regions of the world. I never thought to have a parish of my own, let alone a benefice of this size."

Sebastian knew a flicker of interest. "Did you ever go on a mission?"

Mr. Thornton pushed himself up straighter in his chair. "As a matter of fact, yes. I spent six years in the Horn of Africa before I married. And then Mrs. Thornton and I had occasion to go on another mission nine years ago, when I was able to leave my parish in the care of a curate."

Nine years ago, Sebastian thought, Nicholas Thornton would have been ten years old. "And Nicholas?" Sebastian asked. "Did he go with you?"

"Oh, no. Nicholas was at Harrow by then.

He never did come out, even for a visit. Mrs. Thornton was very jealous of the child's health, and she feared he'd take ill in such an insalubrious climate. He spent his school holidays with her brother."

"Where precisely did you and Mrs. Thornton go?" asked Sir Henry, although Sebastian knew the answer even before Thornton gave it.

"India."

"A coincidence, surely?" said Sir Henry, when Sebastian told him of the conversation with Sir Humphrey Carmichael. They were crossing the village green, headed toward the doctor's rambling white frame house. As they walked, a gaggle of white geese scattered, complaining, before them, the sun bright on the birds' gleaming feathers. "I daresay thousands of Englishmen have visited the Indian subcontinent at some point in their lives. Have you?"

"Yes."

"There. You see? Besides, we don't know that Lord Stanton has ever been to India."

"No, we don't." Sebastian stared off across a cluster of stone cottages half hidden beneath a riot of climbing roses putting on a final display of fall blooms. "All the same, if I had a son, I think I'd be worried."

CHAPTER 22

Dr. Aaron Newman was a slim man in his mid- to late forties, with the prematurely silvered hair and kindly yet strained face of a man whose job required him to witness the private joys and agonies of too many lives.

He received them in a parlor furnished simply with good, old furniture, and listened while Sir Henry explained the purpose of their visit. He offered them brandy, which Sebastian accepted and Sir Henry, predictably, declined.

"It's been over five months now, and I still haven't managed to come to terms with what happened to Nicholas," said the doctor, pouring himself a drink. "Such a tragedy. Reverend Thornton and his wife were childless for so many years, and then they had the boy. He seemed a special gift from God, a child conceived so late in his parents' lives." Newman removed his spectacles and rubbed a hand across his eyes, his face slack with emotion. "But God took him back, didn't he?"

Sir Henry cleared his throat uncomfortably. "How long have you known the Reverend?"

"Since he took up the living here in the village, more than twenty years ago now. I assisted with Nicholas's delivery, you know." Dr. Newman replaced his spectacles and came to settle in one of the deeply upholstered chairs encircling the tea table. "Tended him through all his childhood illnesses."

Sir Henry nodded sympathetically. "I understand the Reverend found the boy?"

The doctor's lips tightened into a grimace. "I'm afraid so. Lifted Nicholas into his arms and tried to carry him here. He collapsed halfway across the green."

"He suffered a seizure?" asked Lovejoy.

The doctor nodded. "It affected his left side. He has gradually regained the use of his arm, but I'm afraid he still doesn't walk well."

"We understand the boy was left in the churchyard."

A spasm of distaste crossed the doctor's features. "Yes. Reverend Thornton saw him when he went to open the church that morning. It was horrible, quite horrible. The killer had left the body atop one of the old tombs near the south transept door. It's the door the Reverend always uses."

"Interesting," said Sebastian. "Whoever killed the boy must be familiar with the Reverend's habits."

The doctor's eyes widened. "I suppose so. I hadn't thought of that."

"What can you tell us of your examination of the body?" asked Sir Henry.

Dr. Newman pushed up from his seat and went to a writing table covered with a scattering of books and notes, one hand restlessly riffling the pages of a worn volume lying near the edge of the table. It was a moment before he spoke. "Nicholas's throat had been slit."

"From behind?" asked Sebastian.

The doctor hesitated. "I couldn't say, actually." He drew a deep breath and let it out slowly. "I console myself with the thought it was a relatively merciful death, considering what came after."

"There were other wounds?"

The doctor nodded. "The torso had been slit open and the heart, lungs, and liver removed. Rather inexpertly, I might add."

"Hacked in anger?" Sebastian asked.

Newman looked thoughtful, then shook

his head. "I wouldn't have said so, no. There were no extraneous wounds to the body. Just the slice across the throat, the opening of the body cavity, and the removal of the organs."

Lovejoy pressed a cleanly folded handkerchief against his tightly held lips.

"Had the blood been drained from the body?" Sebastian asked.

"As a matter of fact, yes. How did you know?"

"From the condition of the two most recent victims found in London."

"You think there's a connection?"

"There would seem to be, wouldn't you say?"

"Yes, I suppose so. But . . . Do you have any idea who's doing this? Any idea at all?"

"We're working on it," said Lovejoy, tucking his handkerchief away. "Had the Thornton boy been bound and gagged before he was killed?"

"I'm a physician, Sir Henry, not a surgeon. I'm afraid I have never made such things a study." It was said with gentle pride, for in the hierarchy of medicine, physicians were gentlemen. Educated at Oxford and Cambridge, they could discourse at length in Latin on the medical texts of the ancients. They used their learning — and their observations of their patients' pulse and urine — to prescribe drugs, or physics. They did not involve themselves in such vulgar practices as physical examinations; nor did they deal with broken bones. They certainly did not perform surgeries or carve up cadavers in an attempt to learn the secrets of life. Because of the rarified nature of their husbands' activities, the wives of physicians, like the wives of barristers, could be presented at court; the wives of solicitors and surgeons such as Paul Gibson could not.

The doctor drew a pocket watch from his waistcoat and smiled apologetically. "I'm afraid you gentlemen must excuse me, but I've an elderly patient I promised to see before two o'clock. I'll ask my housekeeper to bring you some tea, shall I?"

"Thank you, but no." Lovejoy pushed to his feet. "If you think of anything else that might be considered relevant, you will contact Queen Square?"

"Yes, of course." Rather than ringing for the housekeeper, Dr. Newman walked with them to the front door himself. As they passed the stairs, an old beagle stretched to its feet and padded over to the physician's side.

"By the way," said Sebastian as he prepared to follow Lovejoy into the bright sunshine, "did Nicholas Thornton have anything in his mouth when he was found?"

"Actually, yes." Newman bent to pull absently at the dog's ears, his face troubled. "I can't imagine how I could have forgotten to mention it. It . . . it looked like a star. A silver papier-mâché star."

CHAPTER 23

There was a peace to be found in grave-yards. Sebastian had always felt it as a gentle acceptance of the passage of time and the cycles of life. A peace tinged with sorrow, perhaps, but rarely with violence.

Standing beneath an ancient elm tree near the south transept of the ancient Norman bulk of St. Andrews, Sebastian looked out over a churchyard of neatly scythed grass dotted with moss-covered headstones and crumbling gray tombs. Bees buzzed a nearby scarlet rosebush that was scattering spent petals across the grass. Yet there was no peace to be found here, Sebastian thought; the very air seemed charged with expectation and unassuaged anger.

Sir Henry cleared his throat. "This one, wouldn't you say?"

Sebastian turned to find the magistrate peering at a low tomb that lay just off the worn path leading from the rectory to the ancient iron-banded door of the south transept. Sebastian walked over to stare down at the simple stone monument formed of gray stone sides some eighteen inches high surmounted by a cracked flat slab. Its inscription was so weathered and encrusted with lichen as to be virtually unreadable.

"Probably." He glanced up. From here he could see the High Street and the village green, and beyond that, the stone bridge that arched over the stream. "A rather public spot for a killing, wouldn't you say?"

Sir Henry nodded. "According to the Reverend, the boy disappeared in the afternoon while fishing. They searched the woods and fields behind the rectory to no avail. It wasn't until early the next morning that his body was discovered here. Which would suggest the boy was killed, then taken to an out-of-the-way spot to be butchered before being brought back here to be found by the Reverend at first light."

Sebastian shook his head. "Nicholas Thornton's throat was slit. If the boy had been killed beside the stream, the men who searched for him that evening would have seen blood. They didn't. Whoever killed the boy might have overpowered him in the wood, but I suspect he was killed wherever he was butchered."

"Yes, of course." Sir Henry stared off across the churchyard, lost deep in thought. "I wonder how many others there have been," he said after a moment, half to himself. "There could be a dozen or more such killings scattered across the length of England and beyond. How would we know? I learned of this one only by chance."

"I suspect this was the first," said Sebastian.

Sir Henry swung to look at him. "How could you possibly assume that?"

Sebastian squinted against the bright sunlight. "Are you familiar with the poetry of John Donne?"

"Somewhat. Why? Whatever has Donne to do with any of this?"

"The objects left in the victims' mouths," said Sebastian.

Sir Henry shook his head. "I still don't understand."

"They're from a poem." Sebastian hunkered down to search the grass beside the weathered tomb. " 'Go and Catch a Falling Star.' Do you know it?"

"I don't believe so, no."

"I don't remember all of it. Only the beginning. But listen . . .

" 'Go and Catch a Falling Star

Get with child a mandrake root,
Tell me where all past years are,
Or who cleft the devil's foot,
Teach me to hear mermaids singing,
Or to keep off envy's stinging,
And find
What wind
Serves to advance an honest mind.' "

"Merciful heavens," said Sir Henry. "The killer is following the poem. First the star, then the page from the ship's log, and now the goat's hoof. Only the mandrake root is missing." His lips tightened into a grim line. "There must have been another murder. A murder that took place at some point between April and June that we have yet to discover."

Reaching out, Sebastian traced the faded, incised cross on the tomb with his fingertips. "Perhaps. Or perhaps the killer simply skipped that line for some reason."

"Skipped it? What possible reason could he have for doing such a thing?"

"I suspect he has a reason for everything he's doing." Brushing off his fingertips, Sebastian pushed to his feet. "The objects left in each man's mouth. The different ways in which each was mutilated. The manner in which each body was displayed after death.

141

It's all been very deliberate. This killer has a reason for it all. And if we're to have any hope of stopping him, we need to find out what that reason is."

CHAPTER 24

The drawing rooms and ballrooms of Mayfair would forever be barred to women such as Kat Boleyn — women who displayed their charms on the stage, who had known a succession of men in their beds. But Kat was a frequent and welcome guest in those salons of Bloomsbury and Richmond, where the entrée depended not on birth or wealth but on possession of a keen wit and a sharp intellect, where conversation turned not so much to fashion, horses, and hunting as to art and philosophy, literature and science.

On the afternoon following her fateful meeting with Jarvis, Kat put in an appearance at the select salon of a general's daughter named Annabelle Hershey. Miss Hershey was a small woman with pale skin and dark hair, green eyes, and a mind that might have made her an Oxford don had she been born a man.

She greeted Kat with a peal of merry

laughter. "Miss Boleyn, you have been sent by the very gods! You find us in desperate need of a Shakespearean expert to solve our dispute. Do tell us, please: in *The Merchant of Venice,* is Jessica's father Shylock or Tubal?"

Kat cast a quick glance around the crowded salon. The assembled company ranged from scientists such as Humphrey Davy to the renowned literary hostess Miss Agnes Berry and a moody, brilliant, but little-known poet named Lord Byron. The man Kat sought was not here. "Shylock," Kat said. "Tubal is his friend."

Annabelle Hershey threw up her hands in mock surrender. "You were right, Miss Berry! It's back to the schoolroom for me."

From there the conversation slipped easily into a discussion of the rebuilding of the Drury Lane Theater. Kat stayed chatting for some fifteen minutes, and was about to take her leave when Aiden O'Connell strolled into the room. Kat flashed him a wide smile, then immediately looked away.

He approached her a few minutes later. A lean man in his late twenties, he had beguiling green eyes and a dimpled smile that made him a favorite with the ladies despite his unfortunate position as a younger son. "Any other man in the room would be in

144

transports to have received such a welcoming smile from the most beautiful woman in London. So why am I filled with trepidation?"

"Because you're not the fool you would have others think you, perhaps?"

He opened his eyes wide. "Do I play the fool?"

"Very well." She leaned into him under cover of flirtatious laughter. "I must speak with you. Urgently and alone."

His gaze met hers, and whatever he saw in her eyes drove the amusement from his. "When and where?"

"I am being watched. Come to my dressing room at the theater. Tomorrow night after the performance."

He was silent for a moment, considering this. "Very well. Until then." He moved away from her, to where Sir Thomas Lawrence was entertaining a small group with a tale of the antics of his latest subject's ferocious pet parrot.

Kat watched the Irishman out of the corner of her eye. It had occurred to her that by warning Aiden O'Connell, she was running a serious risk. If he knew she meant to betray him, he could very well decide to have her killed himself. Yet it was a risk she had decided she must take. She could not betray him to Jarvis without first giving the Irishman an opportunity to escape.

How she would deal with Jarvis's fury when he discovered his quarry flown was a quandary she had yet to satisfactorily resolve.

That evening, the wind blew in from the northeast, bringing with it the biting chill of the North Sea. Devlin sat in a wing chair beside the fire in Kat's bedroom, a volume of John Donne's poetry open on his lap. He was flipping through the pages when Kat came to stand behind him and loop her arms over his shoulders.

"What are you looking for?" she asked.

"Listen to this," he said, and began to read.

" 'Go and Catch a Falling Star
Get with child a mandrake root,
Tell me where all past years are,
Or who cleft the devil's foot,
Teach me to hear mermaids singing,
Or to keep off envy's stinging,
And find
What wind
Serves to advance an honest mind.

" 'If thou be'st born to strange sights,

Things invisible to see,
Ride ten thousand days and nights,
Till age snow white hairs on thee.
Thou, when thou return'st, wilt tell me,
All strange wonders that befell thee,
        And swear,
        No where
        Lives a woman true and fair.

" 'If thou find'st one, let me know,
Such a pilgrimage were sweet;
Yet do not, I would not go,
Though at next door we might meet.
Though she were true, when you met her,
And last, till you write your letter,
Yet she
Will be
False, ere I come, to two, or three.' "

"Well," said Kat, "Mr. Donne didn't like women much, did he?"

Devlin smiled. "He was a clergyman. It's something of an occupational hazard."

Kat ran her fingers through the dark curls at the nape of his neck, felt the tension coiled within him. "The young man who was killed down in Kent last April . . ." She left the rest of the question unsaid.

"Was found with a papier-mâché star in his mouth."

"Dear God." She came around to curl up on the rug at his feet, her hands folded together on his knee, her head tilted back so she could see his face. "What does it all mean?"

He closed the book and set it aside. "I wish I knew."

She rested her cheek against his leg. "Tell me about today."

He told her in soft, measured tones. When he finished, she lifted her head and said. " 'Get with child a mandrake root.' It's the second line of the poem. Why would the killer skip one line of a poem he's obviously following so deliberately?"

"Lovejoy thinks there must have been a similar killing someplace in England between April and June, a killing he simply hasn't heard about yet."

"But you don't think so?"

"I don't know what to think."

She sat back, her hands trailing down his leg in a gentle caress. Turning her head, she stared into the fire. For a moment she thought of the clergyman's son in Avery, the lines of Donne's poem running over and over in her head. But it wasn't long before her thoughts slid away to her own problems, to Jarvis's threat and her meeting with O'Connell tomorrow.

Devlin touched her hair, his hand cupping her chin to turn her face to him again. "What is it?" he asked.

She gave a startled laugh and shook her head. "What do you mean?"

"Something's troubling you. Something you're trying to hide from me."

She laid her hand over his and shifted to plant a kiss against his palm. She kept her voice light, her smile in place. "Are you suggesting I'm a poor actress?"

"I'm suggesting I know you."

"Do you?" She took his hand and placed it on the swell of her breast. "What does this tell you?"

His hand tightened over her breast, caressing her through the thin muslin of her gown. She saw the leap of desire in his eyes and let her own eyes slide shut, her head tipping back as she sucked in a quick, delighted breath.

He slipped from the chair, his knees denting the carpet beside hers, his lips warm against the bare flesh of her throat. His hands found the tapes of her high-waisted gown, loosened them. He eased the gown from her shoulders, taking with it the light chemise she wore beneath it.

Her lips closed over his, hungry now. Pressing her naked body against his clothed one, she drove all thoughts but *this* from her mind — this man, this love, this moment — and surrendered herself to it utterly.

Later, as she lay naked and spent in his arms, he traced the features of her face with one softly sliding finger and said, "Marry me, Kat."

A pain swelled in her chest, a pain of want and longing that could never be eased. But she was an actress, and so she was able to summon up a smile, even though her voice shook slightly. "You know why I can't."

He propped himself up on one elbow, his fierce eyes glowing in the dying light of the fire. "My aunt Henrietta has found another suitable bride for me. A Lady Julia Something-or-other." He entwined his hand with hers and kept his tone light, although she knew he was intensely serious. "If you truly loved me, you would rescue me from the matrimonial machinations of my family by marrying me yourself."

"You need a Lady Something-or-other as a wife."

"No. I need you."

"I would destroy you." Her voice was a torn whisper.

He slid his hands beneath her, drawing her up close so that he could bury his face in her hair. "No," he said, all hint of lightness gone from his own voice. "Not having you in my life would destroy me."

CHAPTER 25

Wednesday, 18 September 1811

Early the next morning, Sir Henry Lovejoy was just leaving his bed when one of his constables banged at his door.

"What is it, Bernard?" Henry asked when the constable came stomping in, bringing with him the cold damp of the morning.

"You know that case you was telling us about yesterday? The one you think might be linked to some poem about mermaids and mandrake roots?"

Henry felt a twist of anxiety deep within his being. "Yes."

Bernard ran a hand across his beard-roughened face. "I think there's somethin' down near the docks you need to see."

In the dim light of dawn, the forest of masts out on the river were mere ghostly things without form or function. Sir Henry Lovejoy thrust his hands into the pockets of his greatcoat and suppressed a shiver. The mist coming off the water swirled around him, cold and damp and smelling strongly of hemp and tar and dead fish.

"Oye. You there." The bulky form of a constable appeared out of the gloom. "T'ain't nobody allowed any farther 'ere. Orders of Bow Street."

"Sir Henry Lovejoy, Queen Square," snapped Henry. He brushed past the constable, his footsteps echoing on the wooden planking of the docks.

He could see a knot of men clustered near an old warehouse up ahead. Henry paused, aware of a hollowness yawning deep inside and trying to swallow the thickness that had come to his throat. The sight of violent death was never easy for Henry. He had to steel himself for the sight of yet another human being butchered like a side of beef.

At Henry's approach, one of the men near the warehouse straightened and came toward him. A fleshy man with protruding watery gray eyes and loose wet lips, Sir James Read was one of Bow Street's three serving magistrates, a small-minded man Henry knew to be both ambitious and fiercely jealous of his dignity.

"Sir Henry," said the magistrate with a show of bluff good humor, "no need for you to have braved the cold on such a foul morning. This one had the courtesy to get himself offed well away from Queen Square."

The Thames-side docks in the city fell under the authority of Bow Street, and Sir James's words were carefully chosen to let Henry know his presence here was both unnecessary and unwelcome. Henry looked beyond the magistrate, to the shadows of the warehouse. "I heard the victim has a mandrake root stuffed in his mouth."

Sir James's show of bluff good humor slipped away. "Well, yes. But what has that to say to anything?"

"I believe this gentleman's death may be linked to the recent murders of Mr. Barclay Carmichael and young Dominic Stanton."

"You mean the Butcher of the West End?" Sir James gave a harsh laugh. "Hardly. No one's been carving up this gentleman."

Henry knew a moment's confusion. "The body wasn't mutilated?"

"No. Just a neat knife wound through the side . . . and that bloody mandrake root in his mouth, of course."

Henry let his gaze drift around the docks. In the growing light, he could now make out the dark hulls of the ships lying at anchor out on the river. He had to force himself to bring his gaze back to the sprawled figure beside the warehouse.

The man lay on his back, one leg buckled awkwardly to the side, as if he'd simply been left where he had collapsed. No butchering of the body. No careful display of the remains. The cause of death was different, as well: a knife wound to the side rather than a quick slitting of the throat from behind. Yet the presence of the mandrake root in the man's mouth surely tied this man's death to the murders of Thornton, Carmichael, and Stanton. So why the differences?

Henry's footsteps echoed dully as he approached the body. No one had covered the man up. He lay with his eyes staring vacantly, the features of his face relaxed in death.

He was young, as Henry had known he would be — probably somewhere in his early twenties. A handsome young man, with light brown hair and even features and the sun-darkened skin of a man who lives his life on the sea. He wore the uniform of a lieutenant in His Majesty's Navy, the brass of his buttons and buckles neatly polished.

"He's a naval lieutenant?" said Henry.

"That's right. Lieutenant Adrian Bellamy, from the HMS *Cornwall*. A far cry from the likes of your banker's son and future peer."

It was said with a faint sneer that Henry ignored. "How long has the *Cornwall* been in port?"

"Put in Monday night, I believe. They were meant to sail again at the end of the week."

Lovejoy frowned. It had been less than a week since Mr. Stanton's murder, which meant that after leaving a lapse of two or more months between his other killings, their murderer had struck again within days. Why?

"You've spoken to the captain of the *Cornwall?*" Henry asked.

"Of course. According to the captain, the lad came ashore last night after receiving a message."

"From whom?"

"From his family, it would seem. At least, he told the captain he was going to visit them in Greenwich." Sir James stared down at the body at their feet. For a moment the cloak of bluff insensitivity slipped, and a muscle ticked along the man's fleshy jawline. "He didn't make it far, did he?"

"No," said Henry. "No, he didn't."

CHAPTER 26

Sebastian found Sir Henry seated behind his desk in Queen Square. The magistrate had his head bowed, his forehead furrowed by a frown as he scribbled furiously on a notepad.

"I heard about Lieutenant Bellamy," said Sebastian as soon as the clerk Collins had bowed himself out.

Sir Henry removed the small set of spectacles he wore perched on the end of his nose and rubbed the bridge. "It's puzzling. Most puzzling. There was no mutilation of the body, and the young man was killed by a knife wound to the side. Yet the presence of that mandrake root surely links his murder to the other three."

"I would have said so."

Sir Henry picked up a volume from his desktop and rose from his chair. "When I saw him on the docks, Sir James was dismissive of my conclusions. I then spoke to his colleagues Aaron Graham and Sir William and presented them with my notes on the case. Both agreed the evidence suggests the death of Mr. Nicholas Thornton may well be linked to the murders of Mr. Carmichael and Mr. Stanton. However, they remain skeptical of the relevance of the poem by John Donne. They therefore agree with Sir James that the docks killing is unrelated to the other three."

Sebastian watched the magistrate lock the volume away in a glass-fronted case beside the door. "And they've taken over the investigation."

"Yes. It was inevitable, given the breadth of the case."

Sebastian nodded. Bow Street was the first public office formed in London, back in 1750. The original Bow Street magistrate had been Henry Fielding, followed by his brother John. Together the brothers had been so successful at stemming the rampant spread of crime in the growing metropolitan area that another half dozen public offices were established in 1792, including the one at Queen Square. But of them all, only the magistrates of Bow Street exercised authority over the entire metropolitan area and beyond. Bow Street's famous Runners operated the length of England.

"My jurisdiction is limited," Sir Henry was saying. "Technically I should have contacted Bow Street after our discoveries in Kent."

Sebastian watched Sir Henry resume his seat behind the desk. "So what can you tell me about Adrian Bellamy?"

"Little you won't be able to read in the papers, I'm afraid. The young man was from Greenwich. His father is one Captain Edward Bellamy."

"Also a Navy man?"

"No. Retired merchant captain." Sir Henry hesitated, then said, "The differences in the murders are considerable. Not simply in the manner of killing and the lack of mutilation, but in other ways, as well. Bellamy was left where he fell, in the shadow of one of the warehouses beside the docks. There was no public display of the remains, no flaunting of what had been done."

"Perhaps the killer was pressed for time," Sebastian suggested.

Lovejoy carefully fitted his spectacles back on his face. "You may be right. You were certainly correct about the mandrake root. It's as if the killer deliberately skipped that line of the poem, fully intending to return to it later. But why?"

"Because Bellamy's ship was out of port.

The designated victim was beyond his reach."

Sir Henry looked at Sebastian over the top of the spectacles. "You think he's putting his victims in some sort of order?"

"So it would appear."

" 'Teach me to hear mermaids singing,' " whispered Sir Henry.

"What?"

"It's the next line of the poem. 'Teach me to hear mermaids singing.' If he's putting his victims in order, he must already have the next one selected."

Sebastian blew out his breath in a harsh sigh. "And Bow Street doesn't believe any of it."

CHAPTER 27

Sebastian studied his reflection in the mirror, then leaned forward to add a touch more ash to his hair, blending it in until he gave all the appearance of a man just beginning to go gray.

He wore a decidedly unfashionable coat and sturdy breeches of a cut that would give his aunt Henrietta an apoplexy if she were to see them, for they'd come not from the exclusive shops of Bond Street but from a secondhand clothing dealer in Rosemary Lane. There were times when Sebastian's aristocratic bearing and the trappings of wealth gave him a decided advantage. But there were other times when it served his purpose better to pretend to be someone else.

He was just slipping a slim but deadly knife into a sheath in his right boot when Tom came hurtling into the dressing room, bringing with him the scent of the rain that had been threatening all morning.

"There's somethin' you might want to know about that captain in the 'Orse Guards, that Captain Quail you asked me to trail. I think he mighta run into debt. Seems 'is wife threatened to leave 'im if 'e didn't spend more time with 'er. And seein' as 'er da is the one with all the blunt, that's why 'e's been sticking pretty close to 'ome."

Sebastian kept his attention on the task of tying his dark cravat. "Keep looking into it when you have the chance. There's no doubt the man's hiding something. I'm just not certain it's related."

Tom eyed Sebastian's unfashionable rig. "What's this fer, then?"

Sebastian adjusted his modest shirt points. "Greenwich." He turned away from the mirror. "How would you like to take a ride on a hoy?"

"Gore," said Tom on a breath of pure ecstasy as the hoy slid past the Tower of London and the docks beyond, past merchantmen lying heavy in the water with their cargoes of sugar and tobacco, indigo and coffee, their masts thick against the cloud-filled sky.

Sebastian stood at the rail, the moist wind cool against his face as he watched the tiger

162

dart from one side of the boat to the other, dodging coiled lines and scattered crates and some half a dozen fellow passengers. Sebastian smiled to himself. "Ever been to Greenwich?"

Tom shook his head, his eyes wide as the hoy slipped past the massive bulk of India House and, beyond that, the docks and warehouses of the West India Trading Company on the Isle of Dogs.

"We should have time to take a look at the Queen's House and the Naval Academy, if you're interested."

"And the Observatory?"

Sebastian laughed. "And the Observatory."

Tom squinted up at the rusty red-brown canvas flapping in the wind. The hoy was spritsail rigged, with a topsail over a huge mainsail and a large foresail. Its flat-bottomed design made it perfect for the shallow waters and narrow rivers of the Thames estuary it plied. "This cove ye want me to nose out about — this Captain Edward Bellamy — what you expectin' to find?"

"I'm hoping for something that might link either the captain or his son to Carmichael, Stanton, and Thornton."

Tom screwed up his face. "It don't seem

likely. A clergyman, a ship's captain, a banker, and a lord?"

"You'd be surprised at the threads that can bind one man to the next, across all levels of society. Or one woman to the next."

"You want I should listen to the jabber about Mrs. Bellamy while I'm at it? If there is one?"

A line from Donne's poem kept running through Sebastian's head. *And swear, no where, lives a woman true and fair. . . .* It had occurred to him that he'd given little thought to the *mothers* of these murdered young men: the Reverend's recently dead wife, Mary Thornton; Lady Stanton, who'd insisted her son return early for her dinner party and was now said to be so hysterical her doctors were keeping her sedated; and Barclay Carmichael's mother, the marquis's daughter, the woman who tended to the needs of the working poor and had lobbied her husband to limit the hours labored by children in his factories and mines. He'd been focused on finding a tie among the young men's fathers. Yet couldn't the link as easily lie with the victims' mothers?

Sebastian settled back against the rail. "I think that might be a good idea."

CHAPTER 28

Captain Edward Bellamy lived in a sprawling white-framed house trimmed with dark green shutters and set in expansive gardens overlooking the river.

Slipping into the demeanor of Mr. Simon Taylor of Bow Street, Sebastian climbed the short flight of steps to the front door and worked the knocker. His peal was answered by a slip of a towheaded housemaid who looked to be no more than fourteen or fifteen. She started to deny both her master and mistress, but hesitated when Sebastian removed his hat and said loftily, "Mr. Simon Taylor, from Bow Street. Please announce me."

The little housemaid opened her eyes wide and scuttled off.

Captain Bellamy proved to be a tall man, well over six feet and robust, despite his sixty-plus years. A life at sea had given him a weathered, deeply grooved face and left his flaxen hair liberally streaked with white. His stunned grief at the death of his son could be read in every feature.

He received Sebastian in a spacious sitting room overlooking the gardens and the river beyond. With him sat a small, olive-skinned woman with dark hair and liquid brown eyes, her pretty, unlined face streaked with tears. Looking at her, Sebastian at first assumed her to be the murdered man's sister, but Bellamy introduced her as his own wife.

"My apologies for intruding on you at such a time," said Sebastian, bowing low over her hand.

"Plees, sit down," she said in Portuguese-accented English.

"Brandy?" offered the Captain in a gruff voice, going to lift the stopper from a crystal decanter on a nearby table.

Sebastian took a seat on a graceful settee covered with green-and-cream-striped silk. "Thank you, but no." He let his gaze drift around the room. It was elegantly furnished with heavy mahogany tables and glass-fronted cases filled with everything from Chinese jade carvings and delicate ivory statues to Murano glass from Venice. Captain Bellamy had obviously prospered in his voyages.

"The constable who was here this morning said someone would be calling later," said Bellamy, splashing a hefty measure of brandy into a glass for himself. "But I must admit I hadn't expected to see you so soon."

"Bow Street is most anxious to come to a better understanding of this dreadful series of killings."

Bellamy paused with his glass raised halfway to his lips. "Series of killings? What other killings are you referring to?"

"The recent murders of Barclay Carmichael and Dominic Stanton."

Bellamy took a long, slow swallow of his drink. What little color he'd had seemed to drain from his face. "What makes you think my son's death is in any way related to the deaths of those other young men? My son was stabbed on the docks. What happened to young Carmichael and Stanton was an abomination."

"Whoever killed your son left a mandrake root in his mouth. Mr. Stanton was found with the severed hoof of a goat in his mouth, while Mr. Carmichael was found with a page torn from a ship's log. There's also another young man, a student of divinity at Cambridge named Nicholas Thornton, who was found with a papier-mâché star in his mouth. We believe all four killings are related in some way."

Bellamy downed the rest of his brandy in one swallow and turned to pour another drink with a hand that was not quite steady. "I heard what happened to Carmichael and Stanton, but not Thornton. When was that?"

"Last April."

"And he was butchered? Like the others?"

"Not exactly. Certain of his internal organs were removed."

"Mãe de Deus," whispered Mrs. Bellamy, bringing a black-edged handkerchief to her lips.

Sebastian turned to her. "I beg your pardon, madam. But I must speak of these things."

"I don't understand," she said, her fist tightening around her handkerchief. "What does it all mean?"

"We believe the objects refer to a poem by John Donne. 'Go and Catch a Falling Star.' Do you know it?"

"I know it," said Bellamy. He went to stand at the window overlooking the green sweep of the front garden and the river beyond. "But I don't understand what any of this has to do with my son."

"Are you in any way acquainted with Sir Humphrey Carmichael or Alfred, Lord Stanton?"

"No."

"What about the Reverend William Thornton?"

A muscle jumped along the Captain's tight jaw. "Who is he?"

"A clergyman at Avery, Kent. The father of the first murdered man."

Bellamy shook his head. "No. I don't see how Adrian could have known any of them, either. He was just a lad when he first went to sea. He was a midshipman on the *Victory,* you know." A father's pride shone through the heavy grief. "Saw action with Nelson at Trafalgar."

"I understand his ship docked in London just this week?"

"That's right. Monday."

"Did you see him?"

"Right after he docked. He gave me a tour of the *Cornwall.* They took on some damage when they captured an American merchantman trying to run the blockade last month. It's the reason they put into port."

"Did you send a note last night, asking your son to come to Greenwich?"

The Captain's face went slack. "No. Of course not. Why? Did he receive such a note?"

"So we understand. Although the note itself has not been found."

Sebastian watched Captain Bellamy move to pour himself another drink. He walked with the careful deliberation of a man who holds his liquor well, yet has been drinking heavily for some time.

"You're from Greenwich, Captain Bellamy?"

Bellamy shook his head and replaced the stopper on the carafe. "Gravesend. My father was a sea captain in his time. And his father before him."

"What made you settle in Greenwich?"

"My first wife was from Greenwich."

"She was Adrian's mother?"

"Yes. She died fourteen years ago now."

That must have been shortly before young James joined the Navy, Sebastian thought. He looked at the sultry Portuguese beauty now sitting quietly, her gaze on her husband, and wondered if the Captain's remarriage had precipitated his son's entry into the Navy.

"You have other children?"

"A daughter," said Mrs. Bellamy softly. Sebastian realized that she, too, was watching her husband's brandy consumption. A frown line had appeared between her brows. "Francesca. She is twelve."

"You're from Brazil," he said, giving her a smile.

She returned his smile shyly. "Yes. How did you know?"

"I spent some time there when I was in the Army." He glanced back at Bellamy. "You sailed to South America and the West Indies, I gather."

"Frequently. And to China and the East Indies, Africa and the Mediterranean. There are few places with a port I haven't been."

"Spend much time in India?" Sebastian asked casually.

Bellamy's eyes narrowed, and he took a sip of his drink before answering. "Been there many times. Why do you ask?"

"His last voyage was to India," said his wife.

Sebastian turned toward her. "When was that?"

The woman faltered, aware of her husband's intense gaze upon her. "Five years ago," she said in a small voice.

"This has all been most distressing for my wife." Bellamy came to stand behind her and rest a hand on her shoulder. "Perhaps we could continue the discussion some other time, Mr. Taylor?"

Sebastian met the Captain's steely gaze. "Yes, of course." Sebastian pushed to his feet. "Someone from Bow Street will be contacting you again." *And no doubt asking some very different questions,* thought Sebastian as he turned to leave. "Mrs. Bellamy."

Shown to the front door by the nervous little housemaid, Sebastian was letting himself out the garden gate when he became conscious of being watched. Tilting back his head, he looked up into a pair of big brown eyes framed by dark ringlets. A half-grown girl perched on the stout branch of the spreading oak that grew near the gate, her brown scratched legs dangling from beneath the torn hem of what had once been a neat muslin gown.

"You must be Francesca," he said, tipping his head back farther. "How do you do?"

She regarded him intently for a moment without smiling. "Gilly says you're from Bow Street."

Gilly, Sebastian assumed, must have been the towheaded housemaid who'd opened the door to him. "Yes, I am." He executed a flourishing bow. "Mr. Simon Taylor at your service, Miss Bellamy."

She frowned. "How do you know I'm Miss Bellamy?"

"I'm a detective. It's my job to know these things."

"Where's your baton?"

"I carry my baton only when I'm chasing

172

criminals."

She considered this explanation for a moment and didn't seem to find it wanting. "Something's happened to Adrian, hasn't it?"

Sebastian felt an ache pull across his chest. They hadn't told her yet. How could they not tell her?

"I'm afraid that's a question you'll have to ask your papa," he said.

"I know it's true. His ship's in, but he hasn't come home."

"Does Adrian usually come home when his ship is in port?"

She nodded. "He brings me presents." She fished a silver chain from beneath the ruffled neck of her dress, a chain from which dangled a filigreed representation of a hand. The hand of Fatima. "He brought me this from North Africa once."

"But he didn't bring you anything this time?"

"I don't know. Papa wouldn't let me go with him when he went to see Adrian."

"Did your papa say why Adrian wasn't coming home?"

"He said Adrian had to stay on his ship."

"Did he say why?"

She shook her head, her curls bouncing

173

around her face. "Only that it would be better."

She slid from the tree in a rush to stand before him, all skinny arms and legs and big brown eyes. "I saw Mrs. Clinton making a black wreath. He's dead, isn't he? Adrian is dead."

"You ran out here and hid when you saw the wreath, did you?"

She nodded. "Mama thinks I'm in my room."

"I think you need to go talk to your mama."

Tears welled up in her eyes, one escaping to run down her cheek. Sebastian watched, helpless, as another tear brimmed over to slide down her face, then another.

"Are you really a Bow Street Runner?" she asked in a small, broken voice.

"No."

"But you'll find out who killed Adrian, won't you?"

"How do you know someone killed him?"

"I know," she said, and Sebastian had no doubt that, somehow, she did.

CHAPTER 29

Sebastian noticed the man right away.

He stood with one shoulder propped against the trunk of a chestnut tree near the banks of the river, his head half turned away so that Sebastian could see only his profile. Young and of medium height and build, the man wore a double-breasted olive coat with wide-flaring lapels, full sleeves, and a long-tailed skirt. Once the coat must have come from a Bond Street tailor. But Sebastian suspected the coat, like the man's wide-brimmed hat and shiny leather breeches, had passed through one or two used-clothing dealers before reaching its present owner.

Sebastian had seen the man before, amongst the handful of fellow passengers on the hoy down from London. At the time Sebastian had paid him little heed. Now, without looking at the man again, Sebastian closed Bellamy's gate behind him and turned toward the cluster of elegant eighteenth-century buildings that formed the heart of Greenwich. The olive-coated man lingered for a time looking out over the wide expanse of the river. Then he pushed away from the tree to follow at a distance.

The day was cool and overcast with high white clouds. Sebastian crossed into the park, his gaze scanning the tree-shaded hillside for his tiger. He finally found the boy in a crowd of laughing children gathered before a Punch and Judy show. Tom threw one last look at the puppets, then came on the run, one elbow crooked skyward as he clapped his tiger's hat to his head.

"Walk with me toward the top of the hill," said Sebastian as Tom came up to him. "There's a man following us — no, don't look back," he added hastily when Tom's head jerked to do just that.

"Who is 'e?"

"I don't know. He followed us from London."

At the top of the hill, they paused to look back toward the river. From here, they could see the white jewel known as the Queen's House and, beyond that, the stately bulk of Wren's Naval College on the banks of the river. London was a vast, crowded sprawl to the west, bristling with spires and towers. "See him now?" asked Sebastian, his gaze on the distant city.

"Aye."

"Did you notice him earlier, when you were asking questions around town?"

Tom shook his head. "No."

"Learn anything interesting about Captain and Mrs. Bellamy during the course of your perambulations?"

"Of my what?"

"Perambulations. Travels or inspections by foot."

"Oh. Well, I 'eared this Mrs. Bellamy ain't the dead Lieutenant's mum. She's Captain Bellamy's second wife. The Captain's first wife died of consumption back in ninety-seven. It's 'er 'ouse they're living in now. Belonged to 'er da."

"And the neighbors are suspicious of the new Mrs. Bellamy because she's a foreigner."

Tom looked up in surprise. "How'd ye know?"

"Lucky guess. What else do they say about her?"

"Not much, 'cept that the Captain is 'eld to 'ave married beneath 'im."

"Because she's from Brazil?"

"Because she can't read or write."

"Really? That's interesting."

"They've got a little girl. Name o' Francesca. Seems the Lieutenant fair doted on 'er, even if she is 'alf foreign."

"What do they say of the Lieutenant himself?"

"Sounds to 'ave been a likable sort of lad when 'e were younger. Folks ain't seen 'im much since 'e joined the Navy."

"And the Captain?"

"I'm thinkin' there's somethin' queer about 'im, although no one would come right out and say it. 'E's been retired these last five years or so, ever since 'e lost 'is last ship."

Sebastian brought his full attention back to the tiger. "Really? What happened?"

"Come to grief in a storm. It were an East Indiaman, name o' the *Harmony*." Tom shifted restlessly from one foot to the other, his gaze drifting from the olive-coated man now watching the Punch and Judy show to the twin turrets of Flamsteed House. "What we gonna do about that cove?"

"Let him follow us to the Observatory, if he likes."

Tom's eyes shone with excitement.

They turned together to descend the hill toward the neat seventeenth-century house designed by Wren himself. Sebastian's gaze narrowed as he studied the thunderheads building to the west. "According to Adrian Bellamy's little sister, the Lieutenant always came to see her whenever he was in port. Yet he didn't come this time. Instead Captain Bellamy went to see him as soon as his ship docked. I'm wondering if Captain Bellamy didn't perhaps warn his son not to leave the ship — that his life was at risk."

"But the Lieutenant did leave 'is ship."

"Someone sent him a note saying he was needed at home."

Tom did a little skip. "Maybe the killer's getting tired of 'aving to follow these young gentlemen all over the place."

"Perhaps," said Sebastian. "Or perhaps he feels he's running out of time."

The wind was stiffening when they boarded the hoy for the return journey up the Thames, the clouds hanging low and ominous. The river had turned into a dancing cauldron of choppy waves that filled the air with spray and set the small, eighty-foot-long boat to rocking and pitching against its moorings.

Tom lurched up the gangplank, laughing as the deck rose up to meet him, then fell away sharply. While the boy darted across the deck, talking nonstop to the skipper and his mate and setting the boat's dog to barking with excitement, Sebastian went to stand near the forward hatchway, his face turned toward the wind.

The man in the olive coat was one of the last passengers to board. He went to lounge at the stern, his collar turned up against the mist-filled wind as the mate cast off and the hoy pulled away from the wharf. The wind filled the brown canvas, setting the sails to snapping against the gray sky. Olive Coat braced his legs wide against the steep pitch and fall of the deck, like a man who'd spent his share of time at sea.

It was some ten minutes later that Sebastian noticed Tom had grown increasingly quiet. His mouth hung slack, and his skin had taken on a greenish hue. Sebastian hauled the boy up from behind the crate where he'd sought shelter and half steered, half carried him to the bow.

"You need air. Lots of air. No, don't watch the deck. Keep your eyes on the horizon. Pick a point in the distance and concentrate on it. It's no different from riding in a well-sprung carriage."

"I never wanted to empty my breadbasket in no carriage," said Tom, wiping his sleeve across his mouth.

Sebastian cast a glance back at the stern.

Olive Coat was still there, his attention seemingly focused on the stately East Indiaman just off their port side, making its way downstream.

"How much longer?" said Tom in a small, reedy voice.

Sebastian put a hand on the boy's shoulder and squeezed. "A while. The hoy's leeboards allow for a fairly effective windward performance, but she's sitting low in the water. Her cargo's heavy."

Tom groaned.

The boy lost it a few times over the side, but he stayed at the rail, grim-faced and plucky until the hoy bumped up against its London wharf. The air filled with the whine of lines being uncoiled, the salt-cracked voice of the skipper shouting his orders, the scrape of the gangplank being slid out at midship.

"Can I get off now?" asked Tom.

Sebastian glanced down at the boy's ashen cheeks. "You go ahead. I'll stay behind and keep an eye on our olive-coated friend. Just be careful on the gangplank. The spray will have made it slippery."

Tom nodded, his step unsteady as he lurched to midship.

Sebastian hung back, letting most of the other passengers push past him. He was aware of his olive-coated shadow doing the same, falling behind him as Sebastian moved toward the gangplank. Sebastian had taken one step, two, out onto the gangplank when he felt a rough hand clap on his shoulder.

"He's got a knife!" screamed Tom from the wharf.

Sebastian dropped to one knee and spun around, his hands coming up to close on the man's outstretched arm and jerk him sideways. Caught off balance, the man staggered, his feet sliding on the wet wood, the knife clattering as it fell.

Sebastian let go and ducked back. For one unforgettable moment, their gazes locked. The young man's gray eyes widened with quick comprehension and terror, his arms windmilling as he sought to catch his balance. Sebastian surged up, reaching for him, but it was too late. The man pitched sideways off the gangplank to splash into the narrow triangle of water between the wharf and the hoy's hull.

The air filled with the snap of canvas, the creak of timbers as the wind caught the hoy and swung it toward the wharf. The man's head surged up to break water, his eyes wild, his arms flailing as he sought to kick out of the way. The hoy's black hull loomed over him, smashing him against the wooden embankment with a grinding, sickening *thwump* that shook the wharf and ended the man's scream.

"Bloody hell," whispered Tom.

CHAPTER 30

"Your inquiries are obviously making someone nervous," said Paul Gibson, leaning back in his chair. They were in a coffee shop near the Mall. The morning's fog had returned to settle over the city like a cold, wet blanket that spoke of the coming end to summer's balmy days and soft sunshine.

"Obviously," said Sebastian with a wry smile. "The question is, who?"

The surgeon stared down at the hot steam rising from his coffee. "Are you so certain this latest killing near the river is related to the other three? The docks are a dangerous place."

"What sort of dockside killer takes the time to stuff a mandrake root in his victim's mouth but doesn't bother to relieve him of his purse and watch?"

"You do have a point. But the method of killing is entirely different. And there was no draining of the blood, no butchery of the corpse."

Sebastian leaned forward. "You talked to the surgeon who performed Bellamy's post-mortem?"

A slow smile touched Gibson's eyes. "I thought you might be interested."

"And?"

"The consulting surgeon found nothing beyond the stab wound. And the mandrake root, of course."

Sebastian frowned. "Perhaps the killer was interrupted. The other young men — Thornton, Carmichael, and Stanton — all seem to have been waylaid and taken elsewhere to be killed. If Bellamy tried to resist his attacker, the murderer might have been forced to kill him on the spot. He wouldn't have been able to butcher the body in such a public place, so he simply left the mandrake root and fled."

The tramp of marching feet brought Sebastian's head around. Through the paned glass of the coffee shop's front window, he could see a troop of pressed men marching down the street on their way to the docks and a life of service in His Majesty's Navy. Hemmed in close by their press-gang, the men looked to range in age from fifteen to fifty, their faces haggard with fear, their wrists manacled like criminals.

"Poor bastards," murmured Gibson, following Sebastian's gaze. "I never see the unlucky sods without thinking of that line from 'Rule, Britannia.' You know the one . . . 'Britons never, never, never shall be slaves'?"

Sebastian choked on his coffee, while Gibson leaned forward suddenly, his face intent. "That poem you were telling me about, the one by Donne. It suggests a life spent in travel. Perhaps this Lieutenant Adrian Bellamy is the key to it all."

Sebastian shook his head. "The man was at sea for half his life, since he was a lad. What kind of contact could he have had with the other three? No, I think the answer lies with the murdered men's fathers — or their mothers."

"An unfaithful woman?"

"Or unfaithful women."

Gibson ran a finger thoughtfully up and down the side of his cup. "You say Reverend Thornton, Sir Humphrey Carmichael, and Captain Edward Bellamy have all visited India. What about Lord Stanton?"

"I don't know yet. But they're all obviously hiding something. And at least one of them seems willing to kill me in order to conceal it."

"What kind of man continues to hide a secret that puts his own children at risk?"

"All manner of men, or so it would seem."

Gibson stared out at the street, empty now in the flat light of the dying afternoon. "It must be a terrible secret," he said, draining his cup to the dregs. "A terrible secret indeed."

Sebastian was walking up the Mall, headed for the public office in Queen Square, when he became aware of an elegant town carriage slowing beside him. Glancing sideways, Sebastian recognized the crest of Charles, Lord Jarvis emblazoned on the carriage door. He kept walking.

"My lord." A footman descended to hurry after him. "Lord Devlin! Lord Jarvis would like a word with you."

Sebastian kept walking. "Tell his lordship I'm not interested."

He turned the corner. He was aware of the carriage turning with him, then heard the sound of a window being let down. Lord Jarvis's voice was pitched low, but Sebastian had no difficulty hearing his words over the clip-clop of horses' hooves and the rumble of passing carriage wheels. "I know of your visit to Greenwich. I know Sir Henry Lovejoy asked for your assistance in solving this rather lurid series of murders, and I know that while Sir Henry has been removed from the investigation, you are obviously still determined to catch this killer."

Sebastian swung to face him. "And?"

Jarvis gave a grim smile. "And I know something that can help you."

CHAPTER 31

They faced each other across the elegant expanse of the library in Lord Jarvis's massive Berkeley Square town house.

"Why?" Sebastian demanded. "What is your interest in any of this?"

Jarvis drew a gold enameled snuffbox from his pocket. "Have a seat."

"Thank you. What is your interest in this?" Sebastian demanded again.

Jarvis flicked open the snuffbox with one deft finger. "I've brought you here because I'm concerned for the safety of my daughter, Hero."

"Miss Jarvis?" The answer caught Sebastian by surprise. "What has she to do with any of this?"

Jarvis lifted a pinch of snuff to one nostril and sniffed. "I had a son once, David. David was a year younger than Hero." Jarvis tucked his snuffbox away and dusted his fingers. "He was a strange child. Very . . .

dreamy. At the age of eight he announced he wanted to be a poet, but by the time he was ten, he'd decided he preferred to be an artist."

Sebastian studied the big man's curling lip and narrowed eyes, but said nothing. Sebastian knew only too well what it was like for a son to disappoint his father, to never quite measure up to expectations.

"He spent several years at Oxford," Jarvis was saying, "but found nothing to hold his interest. Six years ago, I sent David to my wife's younger brother, Sidney Spencer. Spencer's regiment was in India, and I thought the experience would do the boy good. Toughen him up a bit."

Sebastian sat forward, his attention now well caught. "And?"

"The climate didn't agree with David. He was always sickly as a child, although it was my opinion that his mother and grandmother coddled him." Jarvis's jaw tightened. "After eight months, Spencer decided to send him home."

Sebastian thought he knew where this was going. "Let me guess. The ship was the *Harmony,* captained by Edward Bellamy."

"That's right. All went well at first. But three days out of Cape Town, the ship was struck by a fierce storm that lasted days.

Her sails were ripped asunder, her masts lost, her timbers strained and leaking badly. It seemed obvious to all aboard that the ship was sinking. Captain Bellamy prepared to abandon ship. But most of the ship's boats had been lost in the storm. Recognizing that there was not enough space for all those left alive, the ship's crew mutinied."

"And took the remaining boat?"

Jarvis nodded. "Along with most of the food and water. The Captain, his officers, and the passengers were left to die."

"So what happened?"

Jarvis went to stand beside the empty hearth, one arm resting along the mantel. "The ship didn't sink. The Captain and his officers managed to rig up a makeshift mast and sails, but it was useless. They were becalmed."

"How long did it take the food and water to run out?"

"Not long. They were a day or two from death when they were rescued by a naval frigate that happened to come upon them. The HMS *Sovereign*."

"And your son?"

Jarvis turned his head away to stare down at the empty hearth. "David was injured in the mutiny. He died within hours of their rescue."

Sebastian studied the big man's half-averted profile. His grief appeared genuine enough. Yet things were rarely as they seemed with this man. "I understand the connection to Adrian Bellamy. But what does any of this have to do with the murders of Dominic Stanton, Barclay Carmichael, and Nicholas Thornton?"

Jarvis's head came up. "I don't know about Thornton, but Lord Stanton and Sir Humphrey Carmichael were both passengers on the *Harmony*."

Sebastian frowned. When he'd asked Captain Bellamy if he'd known either Stanton or Carmichael, the Captain had answered no. "You're certain?"

"Of course I'm certain. Both men testified at the mutineers' trial."

"The crew was caught?"

"Caught and hanged. Four years ago. The trial caused something of a sensation."

Sebastian's eyes narrowed. Four years ago he had been in the Army on the Continent. "What makes you think Miss Jarvis is in danger? You weren't on that ship; her brother was."

"And it's not Captain Bellamy, Sir Humphrey, or Lord Stanton who have died, but their sons. David had no son, but Hero is his sister."

From the street outside came a hawker's cry: "Chairs to mend! Old chairs to mend!"

"How did you know I'd taken an interest in the murders?"

"I know," Jarvis said simply.

Sebastian turned toward the door. "Then I suggest you take some of your spies off the streets and set them to guarding your daughter. Good day, my lord."

He expected Jarvis to stop him. He did not. But then it occurred to Sebastian that the big man had probably said all he'd intended to say: it was up to Sebastian to use the information or not, as he chose.

He was crossing the hall when he encountered Miss Jarvis herself. She was a tall woman with plain brown hair, a direct gray gaze, and her father's aquiline nose. If ever there was a woman who could take care of herself, Sebastian had always thought, it was Jarvis's formidable daughter.

"Good heavens," she said, pausing at the sight of him, "what are you doing here?" She tilted her head, making a show of studying him. "And not a gun or a knife in sight."

The first time he'd encountered her here, in her father's house, he'd held a gun to her head and kidnapped her. He held up his empty hands and gave her a smile that showed his teeth. "Not in sight."

The smile was not returned. The fiercely intelligent eyes narrowed. "What *are* you doing here?"

"I suggest you ask your father."

"I believe I shall." She headed toward the library door, pausing only to say over her shoulder, "Oh. Do kindly refrain from kidnapping any of the maidservants on your way out, if you please?"

CHAPTER 32

For several years now, Sir Henry Lovejoy had made his home in a neat row house on Russell Square. The district was genteel but far from fashionable, which suited Henry just fine. Once Henry had been a moderately successful merchant. But the deaths of his wife and only daughter had wrought changes in his life. Henry had undergone a spiritual revelation that turned him toward the Reformist church, and he had decided to devote the remainder of his life to public service.

He sat now in his favorite chair beside the sitting room fireplace, a rug tucked around his lap to help ward off the cold as he read. The fire was not lit; Henry never allowed a fire to be laid in his house before October first or after March 31, no matter what the weather. But he felt the cold terribly and was about to get up and ring for a nice pot of hot tea when he heard a knock at the door below, followed by the sound of voices in the hall.

Mrs. McCoy, his housekeeper, appeared at the sitting room door. "There's a Lord Devlin to see you, Sir Henry."

"Good heavens." Henry thrust aside the rug. "Show him up immediately, Mrs. McCoy. And bring us some tea, please."

Lord Devlin appeared in the sitting room doorway, his lean frame elegantly clad in the buckskin breeches and exquisitely tailored silk waistcoat and dark blue coat of a gentleman.

"Well," said Henry, "I see you've put off your Bow Street raiment."

Amusement gleamed in the Viscount's strange yellow eyes. "You've heard from Sir James, I take it?"

"And Sir William. Please have a seat, my lord."

"Do they still doubt the relevance of Donne's poem?" Devlin asked, settling himself in a nearby chair.

"At the moment, I think Bow Street would investigate the Archbishop of Canterbury himself if someone were to suggest it might be relevant to these murders. It seems Lord Jarvis has taken an interest in the case. An intense interest."

"Ah. I've just had a rather remarkable

conversation with the man myself."

"Lord Jarvis?"

Sebastian nodded. "It seems his son was a passenger on a ship that sailed from India some five years ago. A merchantman named the *Harmony,* captained by Edward Bellamy. Among the other passengers were Sir Humphrey Carmichael and Lord Stanton."

"Merciful heavens." Henry sat up straighter. "I remember the *Harmony.* It was in all the papers."

His lordship hesitated as Mrs. McCoy appeared in the doorway bearing a serviceable tray piled with a teapot and teacups and a plate of small cake slices. Lord Devlin waited until she had poured the tea and withdrawn; then he gave a terse recitation of his conversation with Jarvis.

"I wasn't in England five years ago," he finished. "But you say you recall the incident?"

"Oh, yes. It was quite the sensation." Henry set aside his tea untasted and arose to pace thoughtfully up and down the small room. A lurid explanation was taking form in his imagination. He kept trying to push the idea from his mind, but the tie between the murders and the *Harmony's* harrowing experience raised a grisly possibility he could not seem to banish. At last he said,

197

"You know what this suggests, don't you?" He turned to the Viscount. "The butchering of the bodies . . . the draining of the blood . . ." His voice trailed away.

Devlin met his gaze and held it. "Englishmen have resorted to cannibalism before when faced with starvation and death."

Henry drew a handkerchief from his pocket and coughed into its snowy folds. "I don't believe there was any suggestion that while they were becalmed the officers and passengers of the *Harmony . . .*"

"That doesn't mean it didn't happen," said Devlin, when Henry left the rest of his sentence unsaid. "It's an unwritten rule of the sea that the prohibition against cannibalism may be suspended in the case of shipwreck survivors or men becalmed. Think of the *Peggy,* or the raft of the *Medusa.* Sometimes the survivors admit to what they've done. At other times there is only a suspicion that lingers over them."

"Usually they eat the bodies of their companions who are the first to die — is that not true?"

"Usually. But lacking that option, lots can be drawn and the loser sacrificed for the good of his companions. Only somehow I can't see Sir Humphrey Carmichael or Lord Stanton putting their names in a hat for the chance to become their companions' dinner."

"No," agreed Henry.

"Which leads to the suspicion that the victim, if there was one, was selected more arbitrarily. We need to know the names of any other passengers aboard the *Harmony* on that voyage, as well as the owners of the ship and its cargo."

"The records of the inquiry should be on file at the Board of Trade," said Henry.

Devlin set aside his cup and rose to his feet. "Good. Let me know what you discover."

"You forget, my lord. Bow Street has taken over the case."

Devlin smiled and turned toward the door, then hesitated. "One more thing. There's a captain in the Horse Guards named Peter Quail. When he was with my regiment on the Continent, he took a fiendish delight in torturing and mutilating prisoners. I know of no link between him and the *Harmony,* but you might set one of your constables to discovering his whereabouts on the nights of the murders. Good evening, Sir Henry."

Henry thought about that morning's terse conversation with the magistrates of Bow Street and sighed.

Later that night, Kat sat before the mirror in her dressing room at the theater. In the flickering candlelight, her reflection looked pale, strained. The scent of oranges, grease-paint, and ale still hung heavy in the air, but the theater stretched out quiet around her. The farce had long since ended.

Aiden O'Connell had not come.

With a hand that was not quite steady, she locked away the rest of her costume and stood. Two more days. She had two more days, and she was, if anything, farther from finding a way out of her dilemma than she had been before.

That night, Sebastian dreamed of broken bodies and torn flesh, recent images of young men with butchered limbs blending with older memories of endless bloody carnage on the killing fields of Europe. Waking, he reached for Kat, not remembering until his hand slid across the cool empty sheet beside him that he slept in his own bed, alone.

He sat up, his heart pounding uncomfortably, the need to hold her in his arms strong. Slipping from his bed, he went to jerk open the drapes.

The waning moon cast grotesque patterns of light and shadow across the street below. It had been his intention to meet Kat at the theater after her performance, but she'd told him no, she wasn't feeling well. She certainly didn't look well, her cheeks pale, her eyes heavy lidded. But he knew from the way she failed to meet his searching gaze that she was lying. Another man might have been suspicious, jealous. Sebastian knew only a deep and powerful sense that something was terribly wrong.

He was failing her; he knew that. She was in trouble, and for some reason he couldn't understand she felt unable to confide in him. Or had she tried to turn to him for help, he wondered, only to find him so pre-occupied with stopping this killer that she came away thinking he had no time for her? He realized he couldn't even be sure.

Which was, he supposed, a damning conclusion.

CHAPTER 33

Thursday, 19 September 1811

Sebastian hesitated in the cool morning shadows of the ancient arcade, his gaze on the gentlewoman ladling porridge at a table set at the far end of the courtyard.

The poor and hungry of the city pressed past him, their gaunt frames clad in filthy rags, their faces drawn and desperate. The smell of unwashed bodies, disease, and coming death mingled with the dank earthy scent of the old stones around them. Once, before Henry VIII cast his covetous eyes upon the wealth of the church, this had been the cloisters of a grand convent. Now it was a half ruin that served as an open-air relief center, part of a vast yet woefully inadequate network of private charities that struggled to alleviate the worst of the sufferings of London's burgeoning population of poor.

A young girl clutching a wailing baby cast

Sebastian a curious look, but he kept his attention fixed on the gentlewoman quietly dispensing porridge: Lady Carmichael. A tall, starkly thin woman in her late forties, she wore a plain black apron tied over a fine walking dress also of unrelieved black, for she was in deepest mourning. Beneath a simple black hat covering dark hair heavily laced with gray, her face looked nearly as gaunt and drawn as those of the men and women who crowded around her, cracked and chipped bowls clutched eagerly in desperate hands.

Sebastian had known other women dedicated to good works. Most were nauseatingly condescending and self-righteously conscious of their ostentatious benevolence. Not Lady Carmichael. She worked with a quiet selflessness that reminded Sebastian of the nuns he'd encountered on the Iberian Peninsula and in Italy. She was as generous with her smiling words of encouragement as with her porridge. Yet she did not strike Sebastian as either gentle or soft. There was a firmness there, along with a calm self-possession that marked her as a strong, formidable woman.

Sebastian continued to hang back, watching her, until the last of the porridge was distributed and the throng began to thin.

Only then did he step forward.

"Lady Carmichael?"

She turned at his words, her gaze assessing him. He had the impression she'd been aware of him, watching her from the shadows. "Yes?"

Sebastian touched his fingers to the brim of his hat. "I'm Lord Devlin. I'd like a word with you, if I may?"

Considering the way Sir Humphrey Carmichael had reacted, Sebastian knew he was taking a chance, identifying himself to her. She continued looking at him steadily for a moment, then said, "You wish to talk to me about my son." It was not a question.

"Yes."

She drew a deep breath that flared her nostrils, then nodded crisply. "Very well."

She motioned to her servant to continue packing up the supplies, then turned to walk with Sebastian beneath the ancient arcade.

"Why have you involved yourself in this, my lord? What prompts a wealthy young nobleman to participate in a murder investigation? Hmm? Morbid curiosity? Arrogance? Or is it simple boredom?"

"Actually, it was at the request of a friend."

She glanced sideways at him, one eyebrow raised in inquiry.

"Sir Henry Lovejoy," he said.

"Ah. I see. Yet it's my understanding Bow Street has taken over the investigation. And still you persist. Is that not arrogance?"

Sebastian found himself faintly smiling. "I suppose in a sense it is. But that's only part of it."

"And what's the other part? Don't tell me it's a desire to see justice done. There is very little justice in this world, and you know it."

"Perhaps. But I can't allow something like this to continue, if I can stop it."

Again that arch of the eyebrow. "You think you can stop it?"

"I can try."

A brief flicker of what might have been amusement softened the grim line of her lips, then faded. "And have you discovered anything, my lord?"

"I think so, yes." Sebastian studied the gentlewoman's delicately boned profile. "Did you by any chance accompany Sir Humphrey on his trip to India five years ago?"

"India?" She swung to face him, the dark skirts of her mourning gown swirling softly around her. "Whatever has India to do with my son's death?"

"Sir Humphrey and Lord Stanton were both return passengers aboard a ship called the *Harmony,* captained by Edward Bellamy."

He watched her lips part on a quickly indrawn breath. "You think that's the connection between the deaths of Dominic Stanton and my son? The *Harmony?*"

"Considering what happened to Adrian Bellamy on Tuesday night, yes."

She brought up one hand to press her fingers to her lips. "You mean the young naval lieutenant killed on the docks? That was Captain Bellamy's son?"

"Yes."

"But his body wasn't . . ." Her voice trailed off.

"No. But there is evidence his death is connected, nevertheless. *Were* you a passenger on that ship?"

She shook her head. "No. I do sometimes travel with my husband, but not on that trip, thankfully." She turned to continue walking, the soft soles of her shoes whispering over the worn stones. "You've heard what happened to them?"

"Yes."

"Sir Humphrey was ill for months after his return. I sometimes think he's never entirely recovered from the ordeal."

"Do you know who else was on that ship besides your husband and Lord Stanton?"

She hesitated, the frown lines between her eyebrows deepening with thought. Then she shook her head. "No. There were some six or seven others, but I don't recall their names."

"Was one of them a clergyman?"

"Actually, yes. A missionary and his wife returning from some years' stay in India. I remember because he annoyed Sir Humphrey excessively." Her gaze flickered over to Sebastian. "Why?"

"There was a young man murdered down in Kent last Easter, in Avery. The son of one Reverend William Thornton."

"And this Reverend Thornton was on the *Harmony,* as well?"

"I don't know for certain yet, but I suspect so, yes. I do know that he and his wife spent some years on a mission in India."

They walked along in silence for a time, their footsteps echoing in the stone-vaulted corridor. At last she said, "It makes no sense. Why would someone be killing the children of the *Harmony's* passengers?"

"Someone who wanted revenge, perhaps."

"Revenge for what?"

Sebastian met her gaze and held it, and the air between them crackled with all that remained unsaid. The desperate, starving men and women of the *Harmony* might have kept their secret for five long years, but there was no escaping the implications suggested by the butchered bodies of their children.

Lady Carmichael's eyes widened. She shook her head fiercely, her throat working hard as if she were forced to swallow a rise of bile. "No. You're wrong. Nothing like that happened on that ship."

"Can you be certain?"

Her voice throbbed with emotion. "My husband is a hard man, Lord Devlin. A hard, brilliant man who can be brutal in business if he must. But only in business. He could never, ever have done what you are suggesting. Never."

Sebastian stared off across the now silent, half-ruined cloister, all that remained of what had once been a thriving community. "Most of us probably think we could never do such a thing," he said. "Yet when faced with the stark choice between that and death, I suspect we'd all be uncomfortably surprised by how few would choose death."

"You're wrong," she said again. But she was no longer looking at him, and Sebastian suspected she spoke the words in a futile effort to convince herself.

CHAPTER 34

Kat was seated at the elegant little writing table in her morning room, attempting to draft a terse note to the Irishman Aiden O'Connell when she heard Devlin's rich voice in the hall below, mingling with the desultory tones of her maid, Elspeth. Quickly shoving the note out of sight, Kat stood and turned just as he entered the room.

He was dressed in doeskin riding breeches and top boots, and brought with him the crisp scent of the September morning. He caught her to him for a quick kiss and said, "Come ride with me in the park."

She held him just an instant too long, then laughed. "I'm not dressed for riding."

"So change." He touched his fingers to her cheek, his expression suddenly, unexpectedly serious. "I've hardly seen you the last few days, and when I do, I find you looking . . . tense."

The urge to confide the truth to him welled up within her, hot and desperate. Yet even more than she feared Jarvis, she found she feared watching the love in Devlin's eyes turn to hate. And so she kept silent, although the need to confide in him remained, filling her with a bittersweet ache.

She brushed her lips across his and somehow managed to summon up a smile. "Give me fifteen minutes."

"Fifteen minutes?" he said with exaggerated incredulity, then threw up his hands to catch her playful punch.

Some half an hour later, as they trotted side by side through the streets of the city, he told her of Captain Bellamy, his beautiful young Brazilian wife, and little Francesca. Kat knew a pang of fear when he told her of the knife-wielding assassin on the Thames. And then he told her of last night's meeting with Charles, Lord Jarvis.

She listened to him in silence. "And you believed him?" she asked when Devlin had finished.

He glanced over at her, a light frown touching his forehead. "Sir Henry is checking into the particulars of the ship. But yes, I believe him. It simply fits too well. I suppose even Jarvis must tell the truth at times."

She made an inelegant sound deep in her

throat. "Without an ulterior motive? Never."

She was uncomfortably aware of him watching her as they turned through the gates of the park and rode in silence for a moment. She could fool all of London from the stage, but she couldn't fool this man.

He said, "Why won't you tell me what's wrong?"

She considered trying to laugh the question away, but knew she would never convince him. Forcing herself to meet his fierce yellow stare, she said in a low, strained voice, "I'm sorry. I can't speak of it."

He continued to hold her gaze, his face drawn with worry. But he said no more.

She looked away, her attention caught by a small man in a round hat and spectacles hurrying toward them across the park. As she watched, he raised one hand in a discreet attempt to catch their attention.

Devlin reined in and swung to his feet.

"My lord," said Sir Henry Lovejoy, coming up to them. Pivoting, he gave Kat an awkward little bow. "Miss Boleyn. My apologies for the interruption. Your young tiger told me I might find you here, and I thought you would be interested to hear that I've been to the Board of Trade."

"And?" said Devlin.

"Their records of the inquiry into the

Harmony's loss appear to be missing. The clerk assures me they've simply been misfiled and he has instituted a thorough search for them, but it's curious. Very curious."

Kat heard Devlin utter a soft oath. "You think someone could have taken the records?" she asked.

"Surely not," said Sir Henry. Reaching into his coat, the magistrate drew forth a slip of paper. "I was, however, able to ascertain the names of the owners of both the ship and the cargo."

"What was she carrying?" asked Devlin, taking the paper.

"Tea. In an effort to stave off the mutiny, Captain Bellamy was forced to allow the crew to throw the entire shipment overboard in an attempt to delay the ship's sinking. The owner of the cargo — a Mr. Wesley Oldfield — was ruined. Utterly ruined. He's in debtors' prison, at the Marshalsea."

"That's interesting." Devlin glanced down at the paper in his hand and gave a wry smile.

"What is it?" said Kat, watching him.

Devlin handed her the paper. "The ship's owner. It's Russell Yates."

Sir Henry cleared his throat. "You know Mr. Yates?"

"Mr. Yates is a well-known figure around

the West End," said Kat. "The man used to be a pirate."

"A pirate?"

She smiled. "Well, a privateer. He was the younger son of an East Anglian nobleman, but ran off to sea as a boy and came home a wealthy man. He still wears a gold hoop in one ear and talks like a pirate. Society professes to be scandalized, but they tolerate him because . . . Well, because he's Yates, and he was brought up a gentleman, and he is both amusing and very, very wealthy."

Sir Henry was looking serious. "You think he could have something to do with these savage murders?"

"Yates?" Kat thought about it. "I suspect he could be savage, if driven to it. But to coldly murder four young men for something their fathers might have done? No. I don't think he could do that."

"What finally happened to the *Harmony?*" Devlin asked. "Do you know?"

Sir Henry nodded. "According to what I've been able to discover, a partial crew from the HMS *Sovereign* tried to patch her up and sail her back to London, but she was too far gone. They finally had to abandon her when she floundered in heavy seas off Lisbon."

"So Mr. Yates suffered a loss, as well."

"So it would seem. Although the ship might well have been insured. I plan to spend the afternoon in the offices of the city newspapers, reading their back issues for more details on the incident."

"I thought you were off the case?" said Devlin with a smile.

A rare gleam of amusement lit the magistrate's serious gray eyes. "I am."

CHAPTER 35

Having exchanged the black Arab for his curricle, Sebastian rattled across the worn stones of London Bridge into Southwark. The sun shone warm and golden on the river, but the lanes around the Marshalsea prison were dark and dank, the air heavy with the foul stench of rubbish and rot and despair.

"Wesley Oldfield," said Devlin, pressing a coin into the shaky hand of an old man he came across within the prison's high gray brick walls. "Where might I find him?"

"Up the stairs. Last door to your right," said the man in a surprisingly cultured voice.

"Thank you."

Holding a handkerchief to his nose, Sebastian climbed the noisome, urine-stained stairs and made his way down a cold passage. The sound of a violin playing a sad, sweetly lilting tune came to him from the far side of the scarred old door at the end of the corridor. The music stopped when Sebastian knocked.

"Who is it?" called a tight, anxious voice.

"Viscount Devlin."

The door jerked open.

An unkempt man stood on the far side. According to what Sebastian had been able to learn, Wesley Oldfield was in his late thirties. But the man before Sebastian looked a good twenty years older than that, his long, matted hair the color of a winter sky, his face sunken and gray with ill health. He stood hunched over, one hand on the edge of the door as if for support, the other arm cradling a battered violin. He peered at Sebastian through watery, washed-out blue eyes, his jaw slack. "Do I know you?"

"Mr. Wesley Oldfield?" said Sebastian.

The man ran one hand across the stubble on his chin in a self-conscious gesture. "That's right."

"May I come in?"

Oldfield hesitated, then took a step back and swept a flourishing bow. "Come in. Do come in. Pray accept my apologies for the less than salubrious nature of my accommodations."

Sebastian stepped into a small, low-ceilinged room with a meager, empty fireplace and a single, barred window. The room was as unkempt as the man, and smelled foully of stale sweat and excrement and the slowly creeping madness that can come from a once-promising life now hopelessly derailed.

Oldfield moved awkwardly to clear the clutter of papers and books from the threadbare seat of a once grand chair. "Please. Sit down. I get so few visitors these days I fear I'm forgetting my manners. May I offer you brandy?" He reached for a bottle that stood open on a rickety table, then said, "Oh, dear," and *tssk*ed softly to himself, staring down at the empty bottle. "I must have finished it last night."

"I have no need of refreshment, thank you." Looking at the broken man before him, Sebastian found it difficult to believe Oldfield could have anything to do with the murders. He wasn't sure the man was even capable of remembering anything of significance about the *Harmony* or its last, fatal voyage.

"You're the Earl of Hendon's son, are you not?" said Oldfield, turning away to lay the violin in its case with an almost reverent air.

"You know my father?"

"I know of him." The man swung back to fix Sebastian with an unexpectedly steady

217

stare. "Why are you here?"

"I wanted to talk to you about the *Harmony.*"

The man's reaction to this bald statement was utterly unexpected. The *Harmony* might have led to his ruin, but at the mention of the ship's name, he came to perch on the edge of his unmade bed, a strange excitement animating his features as he leaned forward. "You've noticed it, too, have you?"

"Noticed what?"

"These killings. First the Reverend Thornton's son —"

"You know about Nicholas Thornton?"

"Oh, yes, I know. First Thornton. Then Carmichael and Stanton. And now Bellamy. Someone is killing their sons."

Sebastian stared into the man's tortured, mad eyes. "Do you know why?"

"Why? Not exactly, no. But when you think about the way those young men were butchered, it gives you some ideas, does it not?" He broke off to cast Sebastian a sideways glance. "Is that why you're here? You think I'm responsible?"

"You're in prison," said Sebastian.

An eerie smile played around the other man's lips. "Yes. But we're sometimes allowed out, you know."

"Only during the day," noted Sebastian.

"Carmichael, Stanton, and Bellamy were all killed at night, when you're locked in."

Oldfield's smile slipped. "True." Then he brightened. "I could have hired someone."

"You're bankrupt."

"There is that." Oldfield sighed. "And I've no motive."

Sebastian glanced around the cold prison cell. "No?"

Oldfield *tssk*ed again and shook his head. "It was the crew who insisted my cargo be thrown overboard. They thought the ship was going to sink."

Sebastian started to remind him that the ship actually had sunk in the end. Then he changed his mind.

"It's the crew who ruined me," Oldfield was saying. His nostrils quivered, his hatred twisting his lips cruelly with each word. "Dirty, ignorant scum. Panicking. Abandoning the ship the way they did. Taking all the food and water. Leaving the others to die. I would gladly butcher every last one of their God-rotted carcasses. But —" He broke off, his voice and features suddenly returning to normal. "They're already dead."

"They're dead?"

"That's right. Most of them were killed by natives when their boat landed on the west coast of Africa. The few who survived were picked up by His Majesty's Navy and brought back to London to hang."

"You attended their trial?"

Oldfield cast him a scornful look. "What do you think? Every minute of it. Their trial and their hangings. One of the crewmen — I think his name was Parker — he made a bad end of it. Struggling and shouting even after they had the rope around his neck. He kept swearing the men who testified at his trial were lying."

Sebastian sat forward. "Lying? About what?"

Oldfield shrugged. "I don't recall now. It had nothing to do with me." He scratched thoughtfully at the skin behind one ear. "But I do remember the man had a brother, a docker. He was there at the trial and at the hanging. Swore he'd see that the buggers paid for his brother's death."

"See that who paid?"

"Why, those who testified at the trial, of course."

"And who was that?"

Oldfield smiled. "Bellamy. Stanton. Carmichael." The smile slipped. "But not Thornton." He looked confused. "At least, I don't think Thornton was there."

"Who else?" asked Sebastian, even as Oldfield turned to glance out the window.

220

The man didn't answer.

Sebastian raised his voice and tried again. "Who else was at the trial?"

Oldfield swung his head to stare directly at Sebastian. The watery blue eyes widened with confusion. "What trial?"

Sebastian found Tom outside the prison, walking the chestnuts up and down the lane.

"Learn anythin'?" Tom asked as Sebastian leapt up to the curricle's seat.

"Perhaps. Perhaps not. I'm afraid Mr. Oldfield's misfortunes have addled his brain." Sebastian took the reins. "I want you to find someone for me. A docker by the name of Parker. He had a brother hanged four years ago for the mutiny on the *Harmony*."

Tom stepped back from the horses' heads, one hand coming up to hold his hat in place. "You think he might be the cove what's been doin' the killin'?"

"He could be. Then again, he could also be a simple figment of Mr. Wesley Oldfield's imagination."

Sebastian gathered his reins. He knew a powerful urge to confront both Lord Stanton and Sir Humphrey Carmichael with what he had learned. Yet it would be a mistake, he knew, to approach either man now, before he'd learned the full story of the *Harmony*'s final voyage.

It was time, Sebastian realized, for another visit to the Reverend Thornton in Kent.

CHAPTER 36

Returning from her ride with Devlin, Kat tore up her half-written note to the Irishman Aiden O'Connell and burned the scraps.

It had occurred to her that sending any written communication — no matter how carefully composed — would be folly. The danger of such a note falling into the hands of Jarvis's agents were simply too high.

She had just over twenty-four hours left. Closing her writing desk with a snap, she went to change into a walking dress of straw-colored lawn decorated with plaiting at the bodice and waist and set out to track down the Irishman herself.

The spymaster continued to be elusive. But as she mingled with a crowd of well-dressed onlookers cheering their favorite teams in the summer's last regatta on the Thames, Kat found herself in the company of Russell

Yates, ex-privateer and former owner of the ill-fated *Harmony.*

For a woman with Kat's talents, it was easy enough to maneuver herself next to Yates and engage him in conversation. He was an imposing figure, tall and large boned, with broad shoulders and a solid physique he kept well honed at Jackson's and Angelo's. He wore the buff-colored breeches, striped silk waistcoat, and dark blue morning coat of a gentleman, but he still looked like a pirate, with his hawkish nose, sun-darkened skin, and dark hair he kept just a shade too long.

"I saw you at Covent Garden last night," he said, the gold hoop in his left ear catching the light as he bowed over her hand. "I must say, you make a charming shrew. But then you also make a regal Cleopatra and an incomparable Juliet."

Kat smiled. "We're considering doing *Othello* next. I thought of you when I read the text. You owned a ship that was lost at sea, did you not? The *Helpmate* or the *Handsome* or some such thing."

He lifted a glass of wine from the tray of a servant who hovered at his elbow and took a slow sip. "The *Harmony.* Singularly inappropriately christened ship, considering its fate."

"You've heard the rumors, I suppose? That these grisly murders are somehow linked to the ship's ordeal?"

"No. I hadn't heard any talk. But I'm not surprised. Devilish business, that. Frankly, I'm glad the ship sank off Portugal. It would have been impossible to crew with that kind of history, and then what would I have done with it?"

A cool breeze from the river flapped Kat's straw hat. She put up one hand to steady it. "The ship was insured, was it?"

Yates laughed. "Oh, yes. I believe in insurance — unlike Wesley Oldfield, poor sod."

"Oldfield?"

"The *Harmony* carried a shipment of his tea. Lost it all. Third cargo in as many months. Turned his brain, I'm afraid — that and the accommodations in the Marshalsea, I suppose."

A shout went up from among the crowd of spectators. Kat swung to look out over the water, to where the lead crew was fighting hard to maintain their advantage, the spray from their oars sparkling in the sunshine. "Was Oldfield a passenger on the *Harmony?*"

"Oldfield? No."

She glanced back at the man beside her. "Were you?"

A slow smile spread across his pirate face. "You know, I'm getting the distinct impression you engaged me in conversation this afternoon for the sole purpose of learning everything you could about the *Harmony*."

"Acute of you," said Kat, returning his smile.

He laughed, then abruptly sobered. "It's because of Devlin, I suppose. I've heard he's looking into these murders. I must admit, I didn't think about the possible connection to the *Harmony* when it was just Carmichael and Stanton. But now that they've found Captain Bellamy's son dead, as well . . ."

Kat studied his handsome, sun-darkened face. "Do you have sons, Mr. Yates?"

"No. Thank God, considering the circumstances." He brought one hand to his chest and gave an exaggerated sigh. "I've never yet found a woman to steal my heart."

She laughed politely, as she was meant to do, then said, "Who else died on that ship besides Lord Jarvis's son, David?"

"Let me see . . ." Yates dropped his hand to his side and stared thoughtfully out over the river. "Two or three of the crew were killed in the storm, I believe; the rest either died under some African's spear or at the end of a rope. But that's it. The ship's log was lost in the wreckage, so there's no real record."

"None of the other passengers died?"

He shook his head. "There were only some half a dozen besides Stanton and Carmichael. And no, I don't recall their names," he added when she opened her mouth to ask exactly that. "You know, if you ever tire of the stage, you ought to consider applying at Bow Street. You're a natural."

"It's my understanding they don't employ females."

"More fool they. I've heard Aiden O'Connell say no one can ferret out information faster or more reliably than a female. I'm beginning to think he's right."

Kat brought her wandering attention back to his face. It seemed a strange thing for him to have said, and she wasn't convinced it was as offhand as it sounded. "You're acquainted with Aiden O'Connell?"

A light gleamed in his eyes, then was gone in an instant. "We've been known to do business together."

Kat kept her voice casual and disinterested. "Has he left town? I haven't seen him for a few days."

"Not that I'm aware of. Do you intend to hound him about the *Harmony* as well? If I see him, I'll warn him you were asking after him."

Kat gave a soft laugh. "What has Aiden O'Connell to do with the *Harmony?*"

"Nothing that I know of."

She stayed talking nonsense with him a few more minutes, then moved on. It was some quarter of an hour later, as she was preparing to leave the terrace, that Yates approached her again.

"It's occurred to me that there was indeed another death on the *Harmony,*" he said, leaning in close so that his words would not be overheard. "Bellamy's cabin boy. A spar fell on him during the storm, injuring him badly. He died several days before the *Sovereign's* appearance."

"The cabin boy? What was his name?" Kat asked, her voice coming out more sharp than she'd intended it to.

"That I can't recall. But if it comes to mind, I'll be sure to let you know."

Kat had almost reached the steps of her house in Harwich Street when she became aware of a tall, well-dressed gentleman walking toward her, his bootheels tapping ominously on the empty paving.

"Miss Boleyn," said Colonel Bryce Epson-Smith, sweeping her a mocking bow. "How . . . fortuitous."

Kat's grip on the handle of her sunshade

228

tightened, then relaxed. Inclining her head, she gave the man a faint, bored smile. "Colonel."

"A gentle reminder about tomorrow night," he told her, his gaze traveling over her in a way that made her skin crawl. "After the play, of course. We wouldn't want to deprive London of one last glimpse of the divine Miss Kat Boleyn, in the event that you should elect to be . . . shall we say . . . stubborn?"

CHAPTER 37

It was midafternoon by the time Sebastian drove into the village of Avery in Kent. Having left Tom searching the docks of London for a man named Parker, Sebastian was forced to consign the chestnuts into the care of a lad at the livery stable and walk across the green to the rectory.

In the gentle sunshine, the redbrick walls of the rectory seemed more somber than ever, the heavy drapes closed tight at the windows. Sebastian plied the door's brass knocker, then listened to the summons echo into stillness in the depths of the house.

He was about to knock again when he heard quick footsteps in the hall. The door was yanked open by the housekeeper, Mrs. Ross, who blanched at the sight of him and put up a hand to straighten her crooked cap.

"My lord," she said with a gasp, "I do beg your pardon for leaving you standing here. I thought the housemaid, Bess, would get the door, but I suspect she's not back yet from the apothecary's. We've been at sixes and sevens here, ever since the Reverend took his turn for the worse."

"Reverend Thornton is ill?" said Sebastian, unraveling this.

Mrs. Ross nodded her head vigorously. "He had a bad turn, just after you left. And look at me, leaving you standing on the doorstep." She opened the door wider and stepped back. "Please, do come in, my lord."

"May I see him?" Sebastian asked, stepping into the shadowy hall.

"If you wish, my lord. But I don't think he'll recognize you. He doesn't even seem to know Dr. Newman, and they've been friends these twenty years or more."

She led the way up the stairs to a darkened bedroom lit only by a solitary lamp turned down low. The figure in the vast tester bed seemed shrunken, the wispy gray hair on his scalp damp with sweat, his eyes open but staring blankly.

"Reverend Thornton?" said Sebastian.

No answering gleam of recognition lit the man's half-open eyes. As Sebastian watched, a pool of spittle spilled over the edge of the clergyman's mouth to dribble down his chin. He made no movement to wipe it away.

"It's terrible to see him like this," said Mrs. Ross. "Such a brilliant man he was, so good and God-fearing." The front-door knocker sounded again and she jerked away with a quick apology.

Left alone, Sebastian stepped closer to the bed's edge. The rector continued to stare dumbly into space.

"What happened on that ship?" said Sebastian softly. "Hmm, my friend? It was something terrible, was it not? Did you try to stop it, I wonder, good, God-fearing man that you are? Or were you a willing participant?"

He became aware of voices on the stairs: Mrs. Ross's high-pitched, anxious notes answered by Aaron Newman's soothing words. A moment later, the physician entered the room alone.

"Any glimmer of recognition?" he asked Sebastian.

Sebastian shook his head. "How long has he been like this?"

"Since shortly after you left." The doctor came to stand beside his patient. Drawing a handkerchief from his own pocket, he gently wiped the spittle from his old friend's chin. "Mrs. Ross found him collapsed on his study floor."

"Has he said anything?"

"No. Nothing." The doctor glanced up. "I'm sorry if you were hoping to ask him any more questions."

Sebastian let his gaze drift around the room. It was an old-fashioned chamber, with solid oak furniture and a couple of gently worn, tapestry-covered chairs drawn up to the empty fireplace. Beside one of the chairs sat a woman's sewing basket and embroidery frame, as if their owner had only just put them down. "Has he ever spoken to you of what happened aboard the *Harmony?*" Sebastian asked, bringing his gaze back to the physician's face.

"You mean on his voyage home from India?" The doctor drew a straight-backed chair closer to the bed and sat. "Very little. Why?"

"I think the events on the ship are linked in some way to the deaths of Nicholas Thornton and the others. Sir Humphrey Carmichael and Lord Stanton were also passengers on that voyage."

"Good God." Then the inevitable conclusion must have occurred to him, because the doctor's eyes opened wide. "Surely you're not suggesting that —" He broke off, unable to put the thought into words.

"We have no way of knowing," said Sebastian. "But what was done to the victims' bodies does seem to suggest that the killer, at least, has reason to believe that the survivors of the *Harmony* resorted to cannibalism to stay alive."

The doctor's gaze fell to the shrunken, vacantly staring man in the bed. "No. I can't believe it. I can't believe he'd do such a thing. You didn't know him. How could a man who dedicated his life to God, who could quote Cicero and Seneca at length, who was working on a new translation of the *Confessions of St. Augustine* — how could that man do something that violates one of the most basic tenets of our civilization?"

"Some men will do anything to stay alive."

"Not this one," said the doctor, one fist closing tightly around his old friend's slack hand. "I don't believe it."

"Did he ever happen to mention the names of any of his shipmates, besides Carmichael and Stanton?"

Newman pursed his lips. "I believe there was another man and his wife. I seem to recall Mary Thornton mentioning them once or twice. A couple from somewhere up north." He paused, thoughtful. "There was a spinster of a certain age and a younger gentleman who was with the East India Company. There may have been others, but

I'm sorry, I couldn't put a name to any of them."

"It's a start," said Sebastian, turning toward the door.

The doctor stayed where he was, his gaze on the silent man in the bed. "If it's true," said Newman after a moment, "if the Reverend did do what you're suggesting . . . he would see it as his fault, what happened to Nicholas. How could any father live with that kind of guilt?"

"Obviously he could not," said Sebastian, and left the doctor there at the bedside of his dying friend.

CHAPTER 38

"Take extra-special care of them," Sebastian said when he turned the tired chestnuts over to Tom several hours later. "The lad at the livery stable down in Avery was a ham-fisted idiot. Don't let me go near that place without you again."

Tom grinned and took the reins. "I'll baby 'em, fer sure."

"Any luck with Parker?"

"Aye. 'Is name's Matt. Matt Parker. 'E works at the East India Company docks. Spends 'is evenings at a local called the 'Are and 'Ound, on the Ratcliffe Highway."

Sebastian regarded his tiger with awe. "How ever did you find that out?"

Tom's grin widened. "You don't want to know."

"Perhaps you're right." Sebastian turned toward the garden gate, but paused to say, "Now, if you could just find me a valet . . ."

Tom laughed. "I'm workin' on it, gov'nor.

I'm workin' on it."

The Hare and Hound was a nondescript, ramshackle pub reached through a narrow passage between an apothecary and a chandler's.

Sebastian pushed his way through a noisy crowd to the bar. He'd taken care to dress for the occasion in a shabby-genteel coat, hat, and breeches that formed part of his collection from Rosemary Lane. And still he was conscious of curious, vaguely hostile eyes upon him as he ordered a pint. Strangers were never welcome in such establishments.

Sipping his ale in thoughtful silence, Sebastian let his gaze drift around the dim room. The Hare and Hound appeared popular with men from the docks: sailors in blue flannel shirts and dockers in rough smocks. Sebastian was starting on his second tankard of ale when a group of dockers came in, big men with broad shoulders and beefy arms. Sebastian listened to their good-natured banter and soon picked out a sandy-haired giant with a badly scarred cheek the other men addressed as "Parker."

Sebastian returned his attention to his ale. The dockers played a game of darts, which Parker won. Sebastian ordered another pint, then looked around to find Matt Parker beside him.

"You watchin' me fer some reason?" Parker demanded, his light brown eyes narrowed with hostility.

"Actually, yes." Sebastian signaled for another pint. "I'd like to talk to you about your brother."

"Jack?" Parker's eyebrows drew together in a suspicious frown.

"Yes."

"And who the devil might you be?"

"My name is Devlin," said Sebastian, making no attempt to disguise the crisp, upper-crust tones of his speech.

Parker made a rude noise. "You sound like a bloody nob. What would a nob want with the likes of gallows bait like Jack?"

Sebastian considered offering the man money, then decided against it. There was a proud edge to the docker's bearing that told Sebastian the gesture would not be well received. "I understand your brother went to his death insisting the men who testified at his trial lied," said Sebastian.

"So? That was over four years ago now. No one ever paid it no heed before."

The bar maid plunked a frothing tankard of ale on the planks beside them. Sebastian pushed the tankard toward Parker. "That was before."

The docker left the ale untouched. "It's because of these murders, ain't it? First Carmichael, then Stanton. Now Bellamy."

"You're forgetting Nicholas Thornton."

"Thornton?" A flicker of confusion showed in the other man's eyes.

"Last Easter, down in Kent."

"I didn't hear about him. Don't remember no Thornton at the trial, either." Parker's tongue flicked out to moisten his lips. Absently reaching for the tankard, he brought the ale to his mouth and drank deeply.

"You're Bow Street, ain't you?" he said, setting the tankard down with a snap. There was dawning comprehension and fear in his eyes now — the fear of a man whose words have come back to haunt him. "You're here because o' them things I said at the hanging — about revenge and all. It was just talk. You hear? Wild talk. Jack was my little brother. He didn't do nothin' wrong. The mutiny weren't his idea. He didn't even take part in it. The other sailors, they give him a choice — come with them, or stay and die. Who wouldn't go? Is that any reason to hang a man?" Parker paused, his face slack with grief. "He was just seventeen years old, you know. Seventeen."

"No. I didn't know." Sebastian leaned forward. "Your brother maintained until the end that the men who testified at the trial lied. What about?"

Matt Parker drained his tankard, but shook his head when Sebastian moved to order another. "That David Jarvis — him whose father is cousin to the King. They said the lad was hurt in the mutiny. Said one of the crew members stabbed him in the side with a cutlass." Parker shook his head. "It weren't so. That young nob was just fine when the crew left the ship."

Parker dropped his voice and leaned in close. "Something happened on that ship when they was adrift. You think on what's been done to these murdered young gentlemen's bodies, and you'll know what I'm talkin' about."

Straightening, he was silent for a moment, his head turned as if he stared at something in the distance. Then his jaw hardened and he brought his gaze back to Sebastian's face. "You're right about one thing: I did swear to see all them titled buggers pay for what they done to Jack. But I'm a God-fearing man, and somehow I couldn't bring myself to do it. I figure the good Lord'll take care of them in His own way." A quiver of distaste passed over the docker's scarred

240

features. "Whoever's doing this — whoever is butchering those men's children — I'd say he's got a father's anger in him and a father's hurt."

Parker put his wrists together and held them out like a man surrendering to the law. "You can arrest me right now and take me in, but the killin' won't stop. Whoever's doin' this, he's damned himself to hell, and he knows it. He won't stop until he's killed them all."

"How many others were there?"

"I don't know," said Parker, his face unexpectedly pale. "Only Stanton, Carmichael, and Bellamy testified at the trial. But there were others, passengers and officers both. And God help their children."

"So now you know," said Kat softly, as they lay talking in each other's arms later that night. "You wondered what kind of secret could be so terrible that men would willingly put their own children at risk rather than reveal it. If what Matt Parker says is true, the survivors of the *Harmony* didn't just commit cannibalism. They also caused the death of Jarvis's only son."

Sebastian entwined his hand with hers and brought it to his lips. They'd made love slowly and sweetly, and still the feeling he'd had for days persisted — that gnawing certainty that something was terribly wrong. He just didn't know what. And he knew the fear of all lovers that he could lose her. Again.

"What are you going to do?" she asked, and it took him a moment to realize she was talking about the investigation.

He shifted his weight. "I think I'm going to pay another call on Captain Edward Bellamy."

"Do you honestly think he'll tell you what happened?"

"No. But he sure as hell can't have forgotten the name of his own cabin boy — if what Yates told you is right."

"You think the killer is the boy's father?"

Sebastian ran a hand down her naked side in a gentle caress. "Either him or Jarvis."

Kat was silent for a moment. Then she said in an odd, tight voice, "I can imagine Jarvis ordering those young men killed and mutilated."

Sebastian lifted his head to look at her. Even in the soft light of the flickering candles, she seemed pale and drawn. Yet he could find nothing to say or do to successfully encourage her to confide in him. "Yes. Except it doesn't fit somehow. How could Jarvis have found out what happened on that ship? And why not move against the men directly? God knows he's powerful enough."

"Jarvis has spies all over the country," Kat countered, sitting up. "How could the simple father of some dead cabin boy have found out what happened on that ship?"

Sebastian sighed and drew her back down to him. "I don't know. Perhaps when we find out who he was, we'll have the answer."

CHAPTER 39

Friday, 20 September 1811

The next day, Sebastian was reading the *Morning Post* while consuming a light breakfast in his morning room when he suddenly let out a crude oath.

"Is something wrong with the eggs, my lord?" asked his majordomo, starting forward.

"What?" Sebastian looked up, puzzled. "Oh. No, the eggs are fine, Morey. Thank you."

Shoving the plate aside, Sebastian turned his attention to the news article on page three: RETIRED GREENWICH SEA CAPTAIN FOUND DEAD IN RIVER.

The church bells were tolling a death knell when Sebastian drove into the outskirts of Greenwich.

Leaving the chestnuts in Tom's care, Sebastian let himself in the garden gate at the end of the long walk. He glanced up at the spreading limbs of the old oak, but the child Francesca was not there today.

With an oddly troubled heart, he mounted the steps to the house. He half expected the Captain's young widow to decline to see him. But he sent up the name he'd given her before, Mr. Simon Taylor, and after a few moments, the little housemaid Gilly returned to tell him Mrs. Bellamy would receive him.

She half sat, half lay upon a sofa drawn up so she could look out over the gleaming expanse of the river sliding past the house. At Sebastian's appearance, she tucked the black-edged handkerchief she'd been clutching up her sleeve. The ravages left by her tears were obvious.

"My apologies for intruding upon you at such a time," said Sebastian, bowing over her hand. "Please accept my condolences for your newest loss."

She did not seem to notice the subtle differences in his appearance and attire. She simply nodded, swallowing as if unable to speak for a moment, then gestured to a nearby chair. "Plees have a seat, Mr. Taylor. What may I do for you?"

Sebastian hesitated. According to the article in the *Post,* Bellamy was believed to have fallen into the water and drowned after suffering some sort of seizure while walking along the river. To Sebastian, it seemed improbable. But how do you ask a woman if her husband committed suicide?

He said instead, "What can you tell me about your husband's last voyage, on the *Harmony?*"

The question did not seem to surprise her. She brought up one fist to press her knuckles against her lips, and Sebastian found himself wondering how much of the truth the Captain had confided to his wife. "It preyed upon him always, that voyage," she said in a strained voice. "Not simply the loss of the ship, but the mutiny of the crew and those long, horrible days without food. He never got over it."

"It ruined his career," said Sebastian.

"Yes. But I often thought there was more to it than that. Such terrible dreams he would have. He'd wake up screaming, as if he'd looked into the very jaws of hell, calling that poor boy's name."

"What boy?" Sebastian asked sharply.

"Gideon, the cabin boy." She hesitated, then shook her head. "If I ever knew his last name, I've forgotten it. He died, you see, before they were rescued."

"What about the other young man who

died? David Jarvis. Did your husband ever mention him?"

"Sometimes. But not nearly so often. I believe Gideon reminded my husband of Adrian at that age. I often thought my husband blamed himself for the boy's death."

"Why is that?"

She looked confused. "Because he failed to keep the boy out of harm's way, I suppose."

She pleated the skirt of her mourning gown with shaking fingers. "He'd been particularly obsessed about the cabin boy's death these past few months." She hesitated, then added softly, "He began drinking far more heavily than before."

"Was he drinking heavily last night?"

She nodded, her lips pressed tightly together. Sebastian watched her swing her head away to stare out over the river. He supposed it was possible the old Captain had staggered into the river and been too drunk to haul himself out. But Sebastian doubted it.

"What will you do now?" he asked her. "Return to Brazil?"

She shook her head. "My father disowned me when I married Bellamy and followed him here to England. Besides, this is the only home Francesca has ever known."

"How is she taking it?"

The widow sighed. "Badly. First Adrian, now her father. It's too much."

Rising, Sebastian slipped one of his cards from his pocket and laid it on the table. "If there is anything I can do, please don't hesitate to contact me." Of course, the name on the card — his own name and title — did not match the name he had given her. But now was not the time to explain it to her.

"I'll see myself out," he said, and left her still staring silently out the window.

At the gate, he glanced back at the house's crepe-draped facade. He saw a flash at one of the third-story nursery windows — a child's pale face pressed for an instant against the panes. Then it was gone.

CHAPTER 40

Sebastian was in his library, glancing through the credentials of another round of applicants for the position of valet, when Morey knocked discreetly at the door.

"A young lady to see you, my lord."

Sebastian looked up in surprise. "A young lady?"

"Yes, my lord."

For a lady of quality to visit the home of an unmarried man was considered a serious breach of etiquette. Sebastian pushed to his feet. "Show her in immediately."

A tall young woman wearing a heavy veil swept into the room. She waited until the majordomo had bowed himself out, then thrust back her veil to reveal the no-nonsense features of Miss Hero Jarvis.

"Good God," said Sebastian before he could stop himself.

A breath of amusement flickered across her face. "Just so," she said crisply, jerking off her fine kid gloves. "Believe me, Lord Devlin, I am as appalled to be here as you are to have me. However, when I considered the alternatives, it soon became apparent that this was by far the simplest course. No one who knows either of us will give a moment's serious credence to any rumors that may arise should my visit here become known, which it will not. My maid awaits me in the entrance hall."

Sebastian blinked, then stretched out one hand to indicate the nearest sofa. "Please, have a seat."

"Thank you, but I have no intention of tarrying longer than necessary." Untying the strings of her reticule, she drew forth several sheets of paper, folded and worn as if with repeated readings.

"What is that?" he asked warily.

She held the folded pages out to him. "A letter written by my brother, David, and mailed from Cape Town. The *Harmony* docked there for minor repairs on the voyage home from India, and David entrusted the letter to an officer on a frigate that sailed before them. Look at it," she said impatiently, when he hesitated.

Taking the letter from her hand, he flipped it open. *Dearest Hero,* he read, then paused to glance up at her. "Why are you giving this to me?"

To his surprise, she tweaked the letter from his grasp. "I'm not. I simply thought it best that you actually see it so that you would have no doubt as to its existence. What I am giving you is this." She drew another paper from her reticule. This time, he took it promptly.

He found himself staring at a list of names written in a different scrawl he took to be Miss Jarvis's own. He threw her a quizzical look, then glanced quickly through the list. Some of the names — Lord Stanton, Sir Humphrey Carmichael, the Reverend and Mrs. Thornton — he recognized. Others he did not.

"My brother was a keen and enthusiastic observer of his fellow men," she was saying. "His letter contained delightful vignettes on each and every one of his fellow passengers and the *Harmony*'s officers. That is a listing of their names."

Sebastian brought his gaze back to her aquiline face. "How did you know I wanted this?"

"I am my father's daughter," she said enigmatically.

Grunting, he ran through the list again. It was divided into two sections labeled *Passengers* and *Officers*. Along with the names of the passengers he already knew were four he did not: Elizabeth Ware, Mr. and Mrs. Dunlop, and Felix Atkinson.

Elizabeth Ware must have been the spinster of uncertain age, he realized. Mr. and Mrs. Dunlop would be the couple with estates in the North, while Mr. Felix Atkinson, surely, was the gentleman from the East India Company.

Beneath the heading *Officers* were three names: Joseph Canning, Elliot Fairfax, and Francis Hillard. At the very bottom was written *Gideon, cabin boy.* Sebastian swore softly under his breath.

"What is it?" asked Miss Jarvis.

"The cabin boy's last name. You don't know it?"

"No. David referred to him only as 'Gideon.' " Her brows drew together in a light frown. "He's important. Why?"

Sebastian looked into her haughty, disdainful face, and somehow overcame the urge to answer her question. Folding the list, he tucked it into his pocket, then stood regarding her quizzically. "I still don't understand why you brought the list directly to me rather than simply giving it to your father."

To his surprise, she looked vaguely discomfited. Twitching the skirt of her dusky blue walking dress with one hand, she said airily, "It so happens that my father is unaware of the letter's existence. It would serve no purpose for him to learn of it now. I trust you will not mention it to him."

Sebastian leaned back against his desk and folded his arms at his chest, his gaze on Miss Jarvis's face. As he watched, an unexpected tide of color touched her cheeks. And he found himself wondering what else David Jarvis had written in that letter to his sister that she was unwilling to allow either Sebastian or her own father to read its contents.

As if aware of his train of thought, she said, "My brother was a very sensitive young man. He knew our father found him . . . disappointing. I don't believe I need to say more."

Her words awakened uncomfortable memories from Sebastian's own youth, memories of Hendon's palpable disappointment in his heir during the long, painful years following the deaths of Cecil and Richard. "No," said Sebastian, pushing away from the desk. "You've no need to say more. And I won't mention the letter to his lordship. Now don't you think it's time you collected your maid and ran away?"

Lowering her veil, she turned to go, then

hesitated to say, "I know my father believes me to be in danger."

"You disagree?" said Sebastian, surprised.

"If my reading of this situation is correct, yes."

"Then why are you here?"

"I looked into some of the names on that list. Mr. Felix Atkinson has two children, a son named Anthony and a younger daughter. Mr. and Mrs. Dunlop have three children. They're why I am here. And why I hope you will do all within your power to catch this madman, whoever he is. Before he strikes again."

CHAPTER 41

Sir Humphrey Carmichael was seated at his elegant desk at the Bank, his head bent over some ledgers, when Sebastian walked in and slapped a sheet of paper on the blotter before him.

"What the hell is this?" Carmichael demanded, looking up.

Sebastian went to stand with his back to the window overlooking the street. "It's a list of the passengers and officers of the *Harmony*. You do see the pattern, I presume?"

A muscle jumped along Carmichael's jaw, but he said nothing.

Sebastian leaned against the edge of the windowsill and crossed his arms at his chest. "You didn't tell me you and Lord Stanton were once shipmates."

Carmichael settled back in his chair, his lower lip curling in disdain. "What do you think? That I discuss the details of my private life with anyone who should happen to express an interest in them?"

"I think that for once in your life, you've found yourself in a situation you can't control."

"I don't know what you're talking about."

"Don't you? Did you hear that Captain Bellamy is dead?"

"I had heard."

"The tale is he fell in the river. I suppose it's even possible, given the way he's been drinking lately. But I suspect suicide is the more likely explanation. It must be a difficult thing to live with, knowing your actions in the past have led directly to the death of your only son."

"Get out," said Carmichael, his voice shaking with raw anger. "Get out of my office."

Sebastian stayed where he was, his gaze on the other man's livid face. "What really happened on that ship?"

"It's no mystery. The story was in all the papers."

"Your version of the story."

"There is no other."

"Really? That's not what Jack Parker's brother says. You do remember Jack Parker, don't you? Your testimony helped to hang him. Except it seems that according to Jack

Parker, Lord Jarvis's son, David, wasn't hurt in the mutiny after all. David Jarvis was alive and well when the crew left the ship."

Carmichael shoved to his feet. "They left us to *starve*. How can you believe anything one of those blackguards said?"

"Men with a rope around their necks don't usually lie."

Carmichael calmly resumed his seat and pulled the ledger toward him. "I'm a busy man, my lord. Kindly close the door on your way out."

Sebastian pushed away from the windowsill. But he paused at the door to look back and say, "By the way, you wouldn't happen to remember the name of the *Harmony*'s cabin boy, would you?"

Carmichael's head came up, all color slowly draining from his face. He sucked in a deep breath, but all he said was, "No. No, I wouldn't."

Sebastian was leaving the Bank, headed up Threadneedle Street, when he heard his father's deep baritone call peremptorily, "Devlin."

Sebastian looked around as the Earl's ponderous town carriage drew up, its crested door swinging open. "Step up," said Hendon. "I'd like a word with you." As if sensing Sebastian's hesitation, Hendon growled, "This isn't about your bloody aunt Henrietta and her matrimonial machinations. Now step up, will you?"

Sebastian laughed and leapt up beside his father.

"Why didn't you tell me someone tried to kill you on the Thames the other day?" Hendon demanded without preamble.

"How did you hear about that?"

Hendon pressed his lips together in a tight frown. "It's because of what you were asking about the other day. These murders. Isn't it?"

"Yes."

Hendon's chest swelled. "Damn it, Devlin. What kind of pastime is this for a man of your birth and station? Mixing with the lowest dregs of society? Nosing around for information like some common village constable?"

Sebastian kept his own voice steady. "We've been through all this before, sir."

Hendon worked his lower jaw back and forth in thought. "You're bored — is that it?"

"Not exactly —"

"Because if it is, there's no denying the Foreign Office could use a man with your talents. I don't need to elaborate. I know what you did in the Army." He paused. When Sebastian said nothing, he added gruffly, "We are still at war, remember?"

"I remember."

"Napoleon has a new spymaster in London, replacing Pierrepont. Did you know that?"

"I had assumed he would."

Hendon sat forward. "Yes, but whereas we knew of Pierrepont and could keep an eye on those he contacted, this man's identity continues to elude us."

Sebastian stared out the window at a ragged boy sweeping manure from the crossing. His next step, Sebastian had decided, would be to pay a visit to Lord Stanton —

"Devlin. Did you hear what I said? Even if Jarvis is able to persuade this actress to betray Napoleon's man, your contribution to —"

"What?" Sebastian brought his gaze back to his father's face. "What actress?"

"I don't know her name. I gather she was passing information to Pierrepont before he fled the country last winter. Jarvis has given her until tonight to give up the man's name or suffer the consequences."

Sebastian's hand tightened around the swaying carriage strap beside him. He was only dimly aware of his father's voice continuing. A succession of images from last February flickered through Sebastian's memory: Kat holding out a red leather book she'd somehow known to retrieve from its hiding place . . . Kat′ dressed in black, her face pale after Rachel York's funeral . . .

Kat as she'd been these last few days, nervous and afraid.

"*Devlin.* Are you listening to me?"

Sebastian sat forward abruptly. "Tell your coachman to draw up."

"What? What are you doing?" Hendon demanded as Sebastian thrust open the carriage door. *"Devlin."*

CHAPTER 42

Charles, Lord Jarvis leaned forward to study the row of hieroglyphs emblazoned against the brilliantly painted red and green tones of the sarcophagus. "Late seventh or sixth century B.C. wouldn't you say?"

He turned to the curator at his elbow, a painfully thin man whose shrunken skin and bony features reminded Jarvis of the Egyptian mummies the scholar had dedicated his life to studying. "I'd say so, yes," agreed the curator, clearing his throat.

The sarcophagus was part of a shipment of Egyptian artifacts only recently arrived at the British Museum, and Lord Jarvis was amongst the first in London to see them. His passion for Egyptology was one of the few distractions from statecraft Jarvis allowed himself.

He turned to the enigmatic statue of a cat displayed on a nearby plinth, its eyes, ears, and collar picked out in gold. "Ah. Lovely.

261

Just lovely."

The sound of footsteps echoing through the empty corridors brought the curator's head around, his features twisted by a look of annoyance mingled with nervousness. When Jarvis requested a private showing, he did not like to be disturbed. "Sir. The museum does not open to the public again until Octo—"

"Leave us," said Viscount Devlin, pausing in the doorway to the chamber, his fierce yellow gaze focusing on the curator.

The curator opened and closed his mouth several times, then scuttled away.

Jarvis uttered a bored sigh. "I trust you have a good reason for this interruption, Lord Devlin."

He was already turning back to the sarcophagus when the Viscount moved, so rapidly as to be but a blur at the periphery of Jarvis's vision.

Jarvis was a large man, tall and bulky with years of comfortable living. Yet by reaching across to grab a handful of Jarvis's waistcoat, Devlin managed to bring him spinning back around. Jarvis saw the flash of a blade, felt cold steel at his throat.

"Very well," he said dryly. "You have my full attention. Now what is this about?"

"I know you've threatened Kat Boleyn,"

said Devlin, his lips peeling back from his teeth as he spit out each word. "And I know why. But if you want the name of Napoleon's new spymaster in London, you're going to have to find another way to get it."

"If you think —" Jarvis began.

Devlin cut him off with a quick jerk of the knife that caused the edge of the blade to nick Jarvis's flesh. "No. The matter is not open for discussion. I'm here to tell you the new situation. All you do is listen."

Jarvis felt rage boil up within him, hot and impotent. He held it in check.

"By this time next week, Kat Boleyn will be my wife. You make a move to harm her or threaten her again in any way and I'll kill you. It's as simple as that. You know I'm a man of my word, and you know I'll do it. I trust I make myself clear."

Jarvis returned the man's hard stare.

"Of course," Devlin continued, "you could try to have me killed. But I don't think you're that stupid. The consequences for you if your lackey were to fail would be fatal."

With one smooth motion, Devlin withdrew the knife from Jarvis's throat and stepped back. It was with difficulty that Jarvis resisted the urge to bring his hands up to his throat.

The Viscount was already crossing the room. Jarvis stopped him before he reached the door. "You would do that? You would marry that traitorous whore?"

The Viscount's hand moved. Jarvis felt a passing breath of air, followed by an ugly *thwunk* as the blade sank into the wood of the sarcophagus behind him.

"Call her that again," said Devlin, "and the next knife bites flesh."

Sebastian found her in the shadows near the stage door. The air was heavy with the scent of dust and greasepaint. She had the hood of her cloak drawn up as if she were cold. Her pale face and haunted eyes were those of a woman with no hope, no future.

He walked up to her and put his hands on her shoulders. What she must have seen in his eyes caused the little color she had left in her face to drain away.

"I know why you've been afraid," he said. "It's over now. Jarvis won't bother you again."

He felt her tremble beneath his hands. "God save us. Please tell me you didn't kill him."

"Not yet. But I think I've convinced him of the folly of threatening my wife."

"Your *wife?*"

"I've found a bishop who's agreed to marry us by special license on Monday evening at seven. I pushed for sooner, but he insists he has other engagements."

"You can't marry me."

"You've been saying that for months, and I've respected it. But no longer. This is why you refused me before, isn't it? Because of your arrangement with the French."

She drew in a breath that shuddered her chest. "Oh, God. Partially. But only partially, Devlin. You know what I am, what I have been. An actress. A whore —"

He pressed his fingers to her lips. "Don't. Don't say it."

She stared up at him. "Why not? It's the truth. Would you have me live a lie?"

"No. I would have you live a life defined not by what you've been, but by what you are."

"My past is a part of what I am."

"A part. But only a part."

He slid his hands down her shoulders to capture her hands in his. "Marry me, Kat. It's the only way I can truly keep you safe. As Kat Boleyn, actress, you will always be vulnerable. As the future Countess of Hendon, no one would dare move against you."

"Your father —"

"Will adjust in time. Or not."

Her hands twisted beneath his. "How can I knowingly cause an estrangement between you?"

He gave a wry smile. "In case you hadn't noticed, there's already an estrangement between us."

"Society —"

"Society be damned. You think I care what Society might think of me?"

"No. I know you do not. But I care."

"Why?"

"This marriage would ruin you."

"Losing you would ruin me. I'm not taking no for an answer, Kat," he added quietly when she only stared at him with wide, bruised-looking eyes. "I listened to you before and almost lost you. I can't risk losing you again."

"You think this marriage will protect me from Jarvis?"

"Yes. Nothing I could do or say would signal to him more clearly my intention to keep you safe."

She was silent for so long he knew a quiet blooming of fear. Then she swallowed hard, her chin jerking up. "It's true, you know. I did pass information to the French. For years."

"Do you still?"

"No. Not since February."

"Then I don't care."

Her mouth parted silently, her forehead knitting with confusion. He knew she couldn't understand him, would never be able to understand how his experiences in the war had affected him in this way.

He ran one thumb across the back of her hand. "You did it for Ireland, didn't you?"

"Yes."

"Then how could you think I would hold your love of your country against you?" He brought her hands to his lips. "I'm frightened by the fact you put yourself at risk. And I'm hurt because you didn't trust me enough to tell me the truth, even before the threat from Jarvis. But my love for you is undiminished, Kat. It always will be."

A tear escaped from the edge of one eye to roll silently down her cheek. "I don't deserve this kind of love," she whispered. "This kind of devotion."

He gave her a tender, crooked smile. "I intend to spend a lifetime convincing you that you do. The notice of our approaching nuptials will be in the morning papers."

A shadow crossed her face. "Then there's something else you must do tonight."

"What is that?"

"Tell your father."

CHAPTER 43

There was a heavy mist that night that brought with it the crisp scent of outlying, newly plowed fields and the distant briny hint of the North Sea. Finding his father gone from his Grosvenor Square home, Sebastian walked the boisterous length of St. James's, a purposeful and solitary figure. The street rang with the clip-clop of horses' hooves, the laughter of gentlemen lurching along the footpath in evening dress or calling to one another from passing curricles. He visited first one gentlemen's club, then the next, until he came upon the Earl of Hendon in the reading room of White's, a book open on one knee, a glass of brandy on the table at his elbow.

Sebastian paused in the doorway. His father sat with his head bowed, his attention all for the volume before him. Hendon had no patience for the likes of Plato or Plautus, Euripides or Virgil. But he had great respect for the works of the Roman statesmen, from Cicero and Pliny the Elder to Julius Caesar himself, and he often spent his evenings thus, reading. In the gentle pool of golden light cast by the oil lamp beside him, he looked much like the father of Sebastian's childhood, in the years before his brothers' deaths and his mother's disappearance.

Remembering those days now, Sebastian felt a pain building in his chest and sought to ease it with a sigh. The relationship between the Earl of Hendon and his last surviving son had never been a comfortable one. But through it all — through the anger and hurt and confusion — Sebastian's love for his father had endured.

And so it was with a heavy weight of sorrow and no small measure of apprehension that Sebastian crossed the carpet to his father's side. "Come walk with me. There's something we must discuss."

Glancing up, Hendon met his son's eyes for one long moment, then slipped a marker in his book and stood. "I'll get my cloak and walking stick."

Side by side, they walked lamp-lit pavements gleaming with damp, a heavy silence between them. At last Sebastian said, "I wanted to tell you in person that I've sent a notice to the *Morning Post*."

Hendon's gaze swiveled toward him, and Sebastian knew by the narrowing of his father's eyes and the sudden slackness of his jaw that Hendon understood what Sebastian was about to say.

The Earl's voice was an explosion of sound that startled a dappled gray between the shafts of a passing hackney. "Good God. Don't tell me you've actually done it."

"Not yet. Monday evening at seven, by special license. I don't expect your blessing. But I would wish for your acceptance."

"My acceptance?" Hendon's lips twisted into a snarl. "Never."

Sebastian set his jaw. "Nevertheless, it will happen whether you accept it or not. There's nothing you can do to stop it."

"I swear to God, I'll disinherit you. All you'll get from me is what is not within my power to withhold from you. The title and the entailed estates."

"I expected as much."

"Did you, by God?"

Sebastian studied his father's dark, contorted face. "And would you respect me, I wonder, if I allowed such a consideration to dissuade me?"

Hendon's fist tightened around his walking stick. Then, to Sebastian's surprise, the Earl's jowly features softened for one brief instant. It was as if the fury momentarily ebbed, allowing a glimpse of the hurt and disappointment that fed it.

"Sebastian," said his father, disconcerting him, for it was rare that Hendon called him by his given name rather than his title. "For God's sake, think this through."

"You think I have not? This is what I have wanted for years. As well you know."

Hendon's features hardened. "I'll never regret what I did seven years ago."

Sebastian met his father's fierce gaze. "You did what you thought was right. I understand that now."

"Do you?"

"Yes. But that doesn't mean it *was* right. You were wrong about Kat — as she showed when she rejected the money you offered her."

"Was I wrong about her? Then why the devil has she agreed to this? Doesn't she understand what this marriage will do to you? For God's sake, Devlin! Consider the consequences. You'll be an outcast from everything familiar to you. Turned away from your clubs. Shunned by your friends. And for what? The love of a woman? Do you think your love so strong that it can survive the realization that you've allowed it to destroy your life?"

"Yes," said Sebastian tightly.

Hendon made an angry swiping gesture through the air with one gloved hand. "You think yourself the first man to love a woman who was forbidden him? I know what you're going through, Devlin. You think you'll never get over it. But you will. You will."

Sebastian stared at his father. "You? What woman did you love?"

"Never mind that," said Hendon gruffly, as if he regretted having said so much. "It was long ago."

They were on Grosvenor Street now. Sebastian paused at the base of the steps leading up to Hendon House. "Obviously not so long ago that you have forgotten it."

Hendon gripped the railing beside him. "If you insist on going through with this, I swear to God, I'll never darken your doorway again."

Sebastian drew a deep breath that did nothing to ease the ache in his chest. "At seven o'clock Monday night, I will make Kat Boleyn my wife. If it causes an estrangement between us, I am sorry for that. Good night, Father."

CHAPTER 44

"Oh, Sebastian. I am so sorry," said Kat later that night, when he told her of his interview with his father.

She lay in his arms, her glorious auburn hair spilling over his naked shoulder and down her back. He tangled his fingers in her hair, smoothing it away from her face. "It could have been worse."

"Do you think he'll change his mind?"

"No."

She put her hands on his shoulders, rising so that he looked up into her face. And what he saw there, for just an instant, brought a yawning uneasiness to the pit of his stomach.

Then her head dipped, her lips parting as she kissed him. "Make love to me," she whispered.

He swept his hands down her back, pulling her tight against him. "Every day for the rest of my life."

Sometime later, he awoke to the sounds of the night, the rumbling of a night soil cart on Harwich Street, the distant cry of the watchman. He lay for a few moments wondering what had awakened him, letting his gaze drift over the curving cheek and gently parted lips of the sleeping woman beside him. Smiling, he was just drifting off to sleep again when an oddly muffled *crack* from the back of the house made him open his eyes.

The servants had long since retired to their attic bedrooms. There should have been no one downstairs. He sat up, his breath coming hard and quick as he listened to the distant creak of floorboards, the thump of someone bumping into unseen furniture in the dark.

Sebastian slid from the bed, his bare feet noiseless as he crept toward the door. Pausing at the fireplace, he selected a heavy poker from the rack of tools. Behind him, Kat stirred, then stilled.

Slowly, he opened the door to the hall. The house lay in darkness, the heavy drapes at the windows blocking the faint glow of the waning moon and the streetlamps outside. He could hear footsteps now, on the stairs from the ground to the first floor, the scuff of boots, the rubbing of cloth. Two men, Sebastian decided, maybe three.

He hadn't expected Jarvis to move so quickly, so directly, against them. The poker gripped in both hands like a cricket bat, Sebastian crept to the top of the stairs, then paused. He'd have preferred to fight the intruders on the first floor, farther away from Kat, but he didn't have enough time to make it safely down the stairs and take up a position. And so he waited and let them come to him. It wasn't until he felt a draft of cool air move across his skin that he realized he was utterly naked.

The intruders reached the first-floor hall and turned toward the steps to the second floor, coming into his line of vision. They moved carefully, like men groping blindly in the darkness. But Sebastian had the night vision of a cat. He saw two men, one of medium height and build and wearing a slouch hat, the other taller, bulkier. Both carried stout cudgels. It seemed a crude form of attack for a man of Jarvis's ilk. But then, Jarvis would want to make the attack look random, the work of housebreakers surprised in the act.

They were on the second set of stairs now, the smaller man in the lead, the other some two or three steps behind him. Sebastian tightened his grip on the poker and waited. He waited until the first man reached the top stair. Lunging out of the shadows, Sebastian swung the poker with full force against the side of the intruder's head.

The impact made a sickening popping sound, iron smashing through flesh and bone. The man himself uttered only a small sigh, his cudgel clattering to the floor as the force of the blow spun him around and sent him toppling backward to thump down one stair after the other.

His companion flattened himself against the wall, his eyes wide. For one brief instant, Sebastian looked into the man's white face. Then the man screamed and dropped his club. Whirling, he bolted back down the stairs.

Sebastian chased after him, leaping over the bloody, lifeless sprawl of the first housebreaker near the base of the stairs. The second intruder hit the landing on the fly, then shot down the stairs to the ground floor. From overhead came the sound of Kat's voice. "Devlin? Where are you? What is it?"

Sebastian kept running. The intruder careened through the dining room, knocking over chairs, crashing into the sideboard.

Sebastian reached the dining room doorway just in time to see the man dive through the broken window to the terrace.

"Devlin?"

"Call for the watch," Sebastian shouted up the stairs. He leapt over an upended chair in his path, then skidded to a halt beside the open window, wary of blundering into an ambush. But he could see the intruder already crossing the garden, running for the back gate. Still carrying the poker, Sebastian stepped gingerly through the broken window and dropped to the terrace.

"Watch!" he cried, raising his voice. "Watch, I say!" Pelting across the terrace to the garden, he saw the intruder jerk open the gate and dart through it.

Sebastian chased him up the mews, the cobbles smooth and slick beneath his bare feet, the night air cold against his naked skin. The glow of a hastily lit lantern showed from the rooms over the stables. A second light flickered to life across the way.

"Watch!" Sebastian cried again as the man ducked through the arch and swerved left.

Still gripping the poker, Sebastian erupted through the arch, then hesitated. The street before him stretched quiet and empty in the misty lamplight. Pursing his lips, he blew out his breath and said, "Son of a bitch."

The shrill of a whistle brought his head around. The bulky figure of the neighborhood's night watchman blundered around the corner from Harwich Street, his whistle gripped between his teeth, his lantern swinging wildly. "What's this? What's this? What's this?" he cried, breathing heavily. "I say, young man. Your clothes! If a lady were to chance to see you —" He broke off, his eyes opening wide with recognition. "Goodness. *My lord.* 'Tis you."

"Two men broke into Miss Boleyn's house. I chased one of them here. Did you see where he went?"

The watchman lifted his gaze to the rooftops and kept it there. "I heard running footsteps, my lord. But I never saw anyone."

"Check up and down the street. He may have ducked down someone's area steps, or be hiding in the shadows of a doorway."

The watchman kept his gaze carefully averted. "Yes, my lord."

Sebastian started to turn away, but hesitated long enough to say, "By the way, there's a dead body at Miss Boleyn's house. You'll need to send someone to deal with it."

"Yes, my lord."

Sebastian swung back toward Kat's house.

As he crossed the garden, he could see the house ablaze with lights, hear a crescendo of female voices coming from inside. Climbing through the window again, he rummaged through the sideboard until he found a tablecloth to drape around his hips.

He found Kat, Elspeth, and the cook clustered in the first-floor hall. The man Sebastian had hit with the poker lay near the base of the stairs from the second floor. Blood splattered the walls of the stairwell and the banister, and soaked into the carpet. Sebastian took one look at what was left of the man's head and wished he'd thought to bring another tablecloth.

Kat came to stand beside him, her hands wrapping around his arm as she stared down at the man at her feet. Her face was white, but he suspected it was more from anger than fear. "It's Jarvis, isn't it? He sent these men."

Sebastian forced himself to take another look at the face of the man he'd killed. He studied the even features, the fan of smile lines at the edges of the widely staring eyes, and knew a flicker of surprise. "No. It's the man who threatened me outside my aunt's house last Monday." Hunkering down, he searched quickly through the man's pockets, but found nothing of interest. "This had nothing to do with Jarvis. Lord Stanton, perhaps, or Sir Humphrey Carmichael, or perhaps someone else who doesn't like the questions I've been asking. But not Jarvis."

"How many were there?"

"Two. The other one got away." He turned to head upstairs. "I need to get some clothes on. The watch should be here soon to deal with this fellow."

She followed him, carefully lifting the hem of her dressing gown as she stepped over the bloody corpse on her stairs. "You're certain it's the same man you saw before?"

"Yes." He pulled his shirt over his head and reached for his breeches. "I'll be back as soon as I can."

"Where are you going?"

"To have a little talk with Lord Stanton."

The sun was still a mere promise on the horizon when Sebastian popped the lock on the library window of Lord Stanton's Park Street town house and dropped inside.

He moved easily through the darkened house, hugging the wall on his way up the stairs to keep the steps from creaking. Lady Stanton had been advised by her doctors to retire to the country in an attempt to ease her prostration of grief. Only one of the bedrooms on the second floor — an opulent chamber overlooking the rear garden — was occupied.

Lord Stanton slept on his back in a gilded tester bed with red velvet hangings. Beneath the figured red coverlet, his heavy chest rose and fell rhythmically, his lips parting with each exhalation. Snagging a lyre-backed chair, Sebastian brought it, reversed, close to the bed's edge and straddled the seat. He pressed the muzzle of his small flintlock pistol into the hollow beneath the man's jawbone and waited.

The rhythmic breathing stopped on a strangled gasp. Stanton's eyes flew open, then fixed, wide, on the pistol.

Sebastian showed his teeth in a smile. "I trust you can see well enough to know what this is?"

Stanton nodded, his tongue flicking out to moisten his lips.

"Someone tried to kill me tonight. Not just me, but my future wife, as well. That was a serious error."

Stanton's voice was admirably strong and controlled. "If they told you I hired them, they lied."

Sebastian frowned. "Odd. I don't recall mentioning that there was more than one of them. But as it happens, there were two. One is now a bloody mess on Miss Boleyn's staircase. The other, regrettably, escaped."

Something flashed in the Baron's eyes, then was gone.

"This is the second time in the past few days that someone has tried to kill me. I must say, it's getting rather fatiguing."

"You're obviously making yourself unpopular."

"So it would seem. I keep thinking about our encounter in Whitehall the other day. You struck me at the time as a man with a secret, a terrible secret he was willing to do almost anything to keep from becoming known."

Stanton stared back at him, his lips pressed tight, his narrowed eyes radiating hatred and contained fury.

Sebastian leaned forward and dropped his voice to a whisper. "I don't know it all yet, but I'm getting close. At this point, I'm thinking it doesn't matter whether it was you or Sir Humphrey Carmichael or someone I haven't even met yet who sent those men into Miss Boleyn's house. But if any of you threatens her again in any way, you're dead. It's as simple as that."

"You're mad."

"I doubt you're the first to think so." Sebastian withdrew the gun and stood.

"I could call the watch on you," said

Stanton, his fists tightening on the covers at his chest.

Sebastian smiled and backed toward the door. "You could. But that would direct attention precisely where you don't want it, now, wouldn't it?"

CHAPTER 45

Saturday, 21 September 1811

Sebastian's sister lived in an elegant town house on St. James's Square. The house technically belonged to her son, the young Lord Wilcox, for Amanda was recently widowed. But Lady Wilcox ruled both her son, Bayard, and her seventeen-year-old daughter, Stephanie, with brutal purpose and an iron will.

Sebastian found her in the morning room arranging white and yellow lilies in a large vase. She was a tall woman, and thin, with their mother's pale blond hair still only barely touched by gray although she was twelve years Sebastian's senior. She looked up without smiling at his entrance.

"I trust you are here to tell me the notice in this morning's papers was an error."

"You saw it, did you?"

She set down the last lily with enough force that the rings on her hand clattered against the marble tabletop. "Dear God. It's true."

"Yes."

Her jaw hardened with cold fury. "You do realize that Stephanie's come out is less than six months away?"

Sebastian controlled the impulse to laugh. "Console yourself with the thought that most of the talk will have died down by then."

She studied him with one brow thoughtfully arched. "How did Hendon take it?"

"Predictably. He has promised never to darken my doorway again. I presume you intend to do the same?"

"As long as *that woman* is your wife? I should think so."

Sebastian nodded. "I'll bid you good day, then." And he walked out of her house and out of her life.

Sir Henry Lovejoy was at his desk, glancing over the coming day's schedule, when Viscount Devlin arrived at his office.

Henry sat back. "Good morning, my lord. And congratulations." He permitted himself a small smile. "I saw the announcement of your upcoming nuptials in the paper this morning."

The young Viscount was looking oddly

strained, but Lovejoy supposed that was to be expected in one about to embark upon such a life-altering event.

"Some men broke into Miss Boleyn's house last night and tried to kill us."

"Merciful heavens. Do you know who they were?"

Devlin shook his head. "Hirelings. You received the list of passengers and ship's officers I sent yesterday?"

"Yes, yes." Henry opened a drawer and pulled out a report. "Please, my lord, take a seat. I have my constable's notes right here. Of the ship's officers, the second mate" — Henry consulted his constable's notes — "Mr. Fairfax, died four years ago from a fall."

"A fall?"

"Yes. From a third-floor window in Naples. There was some speculation Mr. Fairfax may have deliberately thrown himself from the window, but as the gentleman was in his cups at the time, it was impossible to say."

Henry consulted the notes again. "The third mate, a Mr. Francis Hillard, was lost overboard while at sea off the Canary Islands two years ago, while the first mate — Mr. Canning — drank himself to death six months ago. A most unlucky lot, from the sounds of things."

Devlin grunted. "And the passengers?"

"The spinster, Miss Elizabeth Ware, died two years ago of hysteria."

"Hysteria?"

Henry nodded. "The constable spoke to her sister. Seems the poor woman went mad not long after her return to London. Stark, raving mad. As for Mr. and Mrs. Dunlop, they were living in Golden Square up until several weeks ago, but they appear to have packed and fled the city somewhat precipitously. That leaves only Mr. Felix Atkinson of the East India Company. He lives with his wife and two children in a house in Portland Place."

"Have you spoken to him?"

Henry slid the paper with the address across the desk to the Viscount. "I am no longer a part of the investigation, remember?"

The Viscount smiled and rose to leave.

"There is one other thing," said Henry.

Devlin paused. "Yes?"

"Captain Quail. I've had another of my constables checking into his whereabouts on the nights of each of the murders."

"And?"

"It seems the Captain was neither at home nor with the Horse Guards on any of the nights in question." Henry peeled his glasses off his nose and rubbed the bridge. "I also looked into the Captain's activities in the Army. I understand why you suspected him."

"But there's no connection between Quail and the *Harmony.* At least, not that I know of."

"No." Henry replaced his glasses and reached for his schedule again. "There does not appear to be, does there?"

Sebastian was halfway across the entrance hall of his Brook Street house, heading toward the stairs, when his majordomo cleared his throat apologetically.

"I trust you have not forgotten, my lord, that you have an interview with a gentleman's gentleman scheduled for this morning?"

Sebastian paused with one foot on the bottom step, his hand on the newel post. "What? Good God."

"I've taken the liberty of putting the gentleman in the library."

Suppressing an oath, Sebastian turned toward the library. The prospective valet proved to be a tall, cadaverously thin man with a bony face and prominent, thick lips.

"My apologies for keeping you waiting,"

said Sebastian, reaching for the valet's credentials. Sebastian was heartily sick of this entire hiring process. Unless this candidate engaged in pagan sacrifices or wiped his nose on his sleeve, Sebastian was determined to hire him. "I understand you were most recently employed by Lord Bingham."

The gentleman's gentleman inclined his head. "That is correct."

"And why, precisely, did you leave Lord Bingham's service?"

"I'm afraid Lord Bingham shot himself last Tuesday."

Sebastian looked up. He vaguely recalled hearing something about Lord Bingham earlier in the week, but had been too preoccupied to pay it much heed. "Right. Well, tell me —"

The sounds of an altercation in the hall reached them through the library's closed door, Tom's ringing cockney tones blending with Morey's hissed "*Not now. He's with —*"

The door burst open and Tom catapulted into the room. "Wait till you 'ear this, gov'nor. I been lookin' into that cove, Quail, and you know 'ow 'e told you 'e didn't know Barclay Carmichael? Well, it seems Carmichael won five hundred quid off 'im at faro right afore Carmichael was found butchered in the park last summer."

The valet's already pale skin bleached white. "Merciful heavens. It's true, what they say."

Sebastian swung to look at the man. "What? What do they say?"

The valet pushed to his feet and backed toward the door, his hat gripped tightly in both hands. "That you involve yourself in . . . in *murder.*"

Sebastian rose from behind his desk and took a step forward. "Yes, but never mind that. You're hired. You can start work today. My majordomo will show you —"

But the gentleman's gentleman had already bolted through the door.

"You didn't want 'im anyway," said Tom with a sniff. " 'E looked like a queer cove to me."

"All I get is queer coves. Obviously because word has gone out amongst the gentlemen's gentlemen of the city that I am a queer cove."

Tom sniffed again. "I checked 'afore I come here. Quail's at 'is 'ouse. In Kensington, just off Nottinghill Gate. Want I should get the curricle?"

CHAPTER 46

Captain Peter Quail occupied a pretty little brick row house on Campden Hill Road, with a shiny black painted front door and a small garden filled with a profusion of late-blooming roses. As Sebastian reined in his chestnuts beside the gate, a delicate-looking young woman with a basket looped over one arm and a pair of secateurs in her hand looked up from deadheading a large shrub near the fence.

Sebastian handed the reins to Tom. "Walk them."

The woman appeared to be in her mid-twenties, with a finely featured face and soft blond curls that tumbled from beneath a straw bonnet tied at her chin with a cherry red ribbon. She wore a lightweight, cherry red spencer over a simple sprigged muslin morning gown, and watched Sebastian's approach with the wary eyes of a woman whose fragile world has already been rocked too many times by the unpredictable activities of her erratic husband.

"Mrs. Quail?" Sebastian asked, politely removing his hat as he opened the low front gate.

"Yes."

He gave her a reassuring smile. "I'm Lord Devlin. I served in the same regiment as your husband in Portugal. Perhaps you've heard him speak of me."

The wariness in her pale blue eyes receded, and she smiled. "I have heard Peter mention you, yes. How do you do, my lord? What brings you here?"

Sebastian let his gaze drift over the house's curtained windows. "Is the Captain at home?"

Mrs. Quail closed her secateurs and laid them in the basket of roses. "Why, yes. If you'd like to —"

The front door jerked open to slam against the inside wall with a bang. Captain Quail clattered out onto the small porch and down the steps to advance on them with a quick, long-legged stride. He was only half dressed, the tails of his shirt untucked, the neck half open to reveal a triangle of bare chest.

"What have you told him?" he demanded, his handsome jaw clenched, his eyes hard on his wife's face.

She took a step back. "Nothing. Lord Devlin just —"

"Get inside," he ordered, his good arm swinging through the air to point back at the house.

Her face drained pale, then flushed scarlet. She threw Sebastian a quick, mortified glance, then looked away. "Excuse me, my lord."

Sebastian watched her hurry toward the house, her head bent, and felt his hands curl into fists at his side.

"What are you doing at my house?"

Sebastian brought his gaze back to Quail's handsome face, with its rugged chin and clear blue eyes and aquiline nose. "You lied to me. You told me you didn't know Barclay Carmichael, when in fact he won five hundred pounds off you shortly before he was killed."

The Captain's jaw tightened. "Get off my property. Now."

With deliberate slowness, Sebastian settled his hat back on his head and turned toward the gate. "You might warn your wife to expect the constables soon."

"Constables?" Quail stood in the center of his yard, his empty shirtsleeve flapping in the cool breeze. "Why? I had nothing to do with that man's death, I tell you. He was killed by the West End Butcher."

Sebastian paused with one hand on the gate. "You didn't by any chance have a younger brother, did you? A brother who served as a cabin boy on a merchant ship?"

Quail's eyes narrowed. "No. What are you talking about?"

"The *Harmony*."

"Never heard of it."

Sebastian studied the man's closed, hard face, and found only confusion and anger. He turned away.

"You don't think it's him, do you?" said Tom, scrambling back up onto his perch as Sebastian took the reins.

Sebastian gave his horses the office to start. "Unfortunately, no. Which means that however much I'd like to kill him, I can't."

Kat was peering through the bowed window of a perfumery on Bond Street when she heard a man's cheery voice say, "Top o' the morning to you, my lady."

She swung to find Aiden O'Connell smiling at her with lazy green eyes. "*Now* you come?" she said.

His smile widened to bring a beguiling dimple to one cheek. "I had to leave town unexpectedly for a few days." He captured her hand and brought it to his lips in a parody of gallantry. "Forgive me?"

She took her hand back. "No."

He laughed. "Why did you want to see me?"

He fell into step beside her as she turned to walk up the street, her sunshade held at a crisp angle. "Actually, I was going to suggest you might want to leave the country."

"Really?" He kept the smile in place, but his gaze sharpened. "Why?"

"Someone was about to betray you to Lord Jarvis."

The dimple faded. "Who?"

Kat twirled her parasol. "Jarvis gave me a choice: your identity or my life."

"And so you betrayed me."

"As it happens, no. Lord Jarvis's threat to me became known, and it was suggested his own health might suffer as a consequence."

"Ah. I think I understand. I saw the notice of your approaching nuptials in this morning's paper. Congratulations."

"Thank you. But your congratulations are premature." She swung to face him. "I want your help leaving the country."

He opened his eyes wide. "Really? And your marriage to Lord Devlin?"

"Would ruin him."

The Irishman was silent for a moment. Then he said, "You love him that much?

295

That you would go away to save him from himself?"

"Yes." Turning, she continued up the street. "It's to your advantage to help me leave. You know that. Without Devlin's protection I would remain vulnerable to Jarvis."

"Why do you need my help? Ships leave England from any number of ports every day."

"Because Jarvis's men may still be watching the ports. I can't take that chance — and neither can you. I don't have much time," she added impatiently when he said nothing. "The wedding is scheduled for Monday night."

O'Connell continued studying her in silence for a moment, then let out his breath in a strange sound that could have meant anything. "I'll see what I can do."

CHAPTER 47

The children were playing in the square across from the house. The boy looked about twelve, towheaded, with ruddy cheeks, and limbs just beginning to lengthen beyond boyhood. The girl was some four or five years younger and still very much a child, with a ragged, beloved doll she kept tucked under one arm as she ran, laughing, after her brother.

Sebastian stood and watched them for a time, then turned to mount the steps to Felix Atkinson's house in Portland Place.

He found Atkinson still at home and finishing his coffee in the morning room. He looked surprised and vaguely annoyed to have Sebastian's card brought up to him.

"Please have a seat, Lord Devlin," he said curtly. "Although I must warn you, I haven't much time. What may I do for you?"

Sebastian took one of the chairs near the cold hearth and said in a pleasant voice, "I understand you were a passenger on the *Harmony*'s return voyage from India some five years ago."

Atkinson set aside his cup with a shaky hand. "Yes, that's right." He was a prim-looking man of medium height and build, in his late thirties now, perhaps a little older. He wore his light brown hair oiled and swept to one side in a futile attempt to disguise a receding hairline, and he had a habit of putting up one hand to touch it, as if to reassure himself it was still in place.

"You've noticed, I assume," said Sebastian, "that someone seems to be killing the sons of your fellow passengers?"

Atkinson's hand crept up to touch his hair, then slipped away. "Well. You don't mince words, do you, my lord? To answer your question: Yes, I have noticed. Perhaps you noticed on your way into the house that I have at least two Bow Street Runners watching my children at all times." He pushed to his feet. "I appreciate your concern for my family's welfare even if I fail to understand what affair any of this might be of yours. However, I am a busy man, Lord Devlin, so I really must ask you to excuse —"

"Sit down," said Sebastian, his voice no longer pleasant.

Atkinson sank back to the edge of his chair.

"It must have been a living hell on that ship after the crew left, taking with them most of the food and water." Sebastian leaned forward. "I imagine you thought you'd never see your family again."

Atkinson cleared his throat and looked away. "It was difficult, yes. But we were all Englishmen and -women, thank God."

"I would have expected the water to run out before the food."

"So we feared. The crew left us but one barrel of water, you know. But one of the gentlemen aboard — Sir Humphrey, to be precise — rigged up a kind of distillery using a teakettle and a gun barrel. It didn't produce much, but it was enough to keep us alive. That was when the lack of food became the major issue. Most of the ship's stores had been lost in the storm, and the crew took what was left."

"Tell me about the cabin boy," said Sebastian, his gaze on the other man's face.

A tic began to pull at the edge of Atkinson's mouth. "The cabin boy?"

"What was his name again? Gideon?"

"I think so. Yes."

"Do you by any chance remember his family name?"

The twitch became more rapid, distorting the lower part of the man's face. "I don't know that I ever heard it. Why?"

"He was injured, was he not? In the storm."

"Yes."

Sebastian leaned forward. "I wonder, how long after the crew left did he die?"

Atkinson leapt from his seat and began to pace the room. "I don't know. I can't recall. It was a very difficult time."

Sebastian watched the man striding back and forth. "I suppose you've heard the rumors?"

Atkinson stood very still, his entire face now twitching with distress. "Rumors? What rumors?"

"It was inevitable, I suppose, given the way the bodies of the victims have been butchered. I mean, a shipload of starving passengers and a dying boy . . ." Sebastian shrugged. "You can imagine the conclusions people are drawing."

"They're lies." Atkinson's voice rose to a shrill pitch. "All lies. It never happened." He brought up a handkerchief to press against his lips. "Do you hear me? It never happened."

Sebastian stretched to his feet. "Unfortunately, someone out there obviously believes it did happen. And unless you help us catch him, that boy of yours playing in the square will continue to be at risk."

"How can I help you catch this killer when I don't know who he is? You think if I knew, I wouldn't tell you?"

Sebastian let his gaze drift toward the window overlooking the square. In the sudden silence, the laughter of the children came to them, light and sweet. "If there's one thing the last few days have taught me," said Sebastian, "it's that some men will do anything, sacrifice anything and anyone, to save their own lives."

He turned toward the door. "Good day, Mr. Atkinson. Do give my best to your family."

CHAPTER 48

Aiden O'Connell trolled the pleasure haunts of the haut monde, looking for a tall man with long black hair and the wink of pirate's gold in one ear.

He found Russell Yates at Gentleman Jackson's in Bond Street. For a moment, Aiden simply stood on the sidelines, watching the ex-privateer spar with the Champion himself.

Yates was an enigma, a born gentleman with a comfortable fortune who amused himself by running rum and the odd French agent beneath the noses of His Majesty's Navy. Some did it for money, and some did it out of a fierce conviction; Yates did it for fun.

Aiden waited to approach him until the other man had left the ring, a towel draped around his neck. "I need to talk to you," said Aiden quietly.

Yates scrubbed the towel across his sweaty

face, his eyes alert and gleaming with interest. "What is it?"

Aiden leaned in close to drop his voice. "A mutual acquaintance of ours needs to go away."

Kat was organizing papers at her desk when Russell Yates sent up his card. For the sake of Sebastian's investigation, she checked her first impulse, which was to have the shipowner told she was not at home.

"This is unexpected, Mr. Yates," she said, rising to greet him when Elspeth showed him up. "Please, have a seat. Have you recalled something of relevance concerning the *Harmony?*"

Yates stretched out in one of the chairs beside the fireplace, a large, powerfully built man who exuded virility and a rakish air of danger. "Actually, I'm here because of an interesting conversation I had with Aiden O'Connell this morning. He tells me you've decided to travel abroad. Permanently."

Kat raised one eyebrow. "Now why would he tell you a thing like that?"

"Mr. O'Connell and I have made these sorts of arrangements before."

"I see." Kat came to sink into the chair opposite him. "And can you arrange it? Before tomorrow night?"

"I assume you wish to go to France rather than to the Americas? The Americas are so dreadfully, well, *colonial.* Still. Something about the mind-set, I suppose."

"France would be fine," Kat said in a tight voice. She knew it should matter to her, where she went, but somehow it did not. She found the thought of life without Devlin — anywhere — too unbearable to contemplate for long enough to come up with a coherent plan beyond removing herself from the temptation of saying yes to everything he was urging.

"I have a sloop leaving Dover with tomorrow's tide. It can have you in Calais in four hours."

Kat felt an ache pull across her chest. It was one thing to reach the decision to leave, but something else entirely to actually make the arrangements. "Good," she said briskly, pushing up from the chair and reaching for the bell to summon Elspeth. "Now you'll have to excuse me. I have much to prepare —"

"O'Connell also told me something of why you're leaving," said Yates.

She swung slowly to face him again.

"I saw Lord Devlin's announcement in this morning's *Post.* There aren't many actresses who would abandon everything they know — home, career, friends — to save the man they love from ruining himself. You're a remarkable woman."

"I wouldn't say so."

"No. I don't suppose you would." He rested his elbows on the delicate arms of the chair, his fingers templed before him. "Right now, you believe you have only three alternatives. You can take your chances with Lord Jarvis — never a good idea. You can ruin Viscount Devlin by marrying him. Or you can flee the country. But there is a fourth option."

She gave a short, humorless laugh. "There is?"

"We could help each other."

She cocked her head. "How could I help you?"

"You've heard the whispers about me, no doubt?" He smiled when she hesitated. "Don't be shy. The rumors have been circulating for years. The tales of my exploits on the briny seas diminished them for a time, but only for a time. Lately the gossip has become both more vicious and more troublesome. People are watching me. I fear the moral climate of our age is becoming more oppressive. Have you noticed?"

"The inclination of which you speak has never been condoned. Not in our culture."

"How true. One can gamble away a fortune, drink oneself to death, openly set up half a dozen mistresses, or regularly debauch young virgins fresh from the countryside, and no one in Society will give it a second thought. But direct your love toward a member of the wrong sex, and the punishment is not mere social ostracism, but death. A death as ugly and unpleasant as that which Jarvis promises you."

Kat studied the man's dark, square-jawed face. "You have enemies who would wish to see you destroyed?"

"One. One very powerful enemy. He dares not move against me directly, but it is not so difficult to manipulate rumor and public opinion."

Kat came to sink back into the chair opposite him. "It's Jarvis, isn't it?"

"As a matter of fact, yes."

"I don't understand. Why would Jarvis dare not move against you directly?"

"Because it just so happens that Lord Jarvis is hiding a dangerous secret. A secret that, if it were to become known, would destroy his influence at the palace and very likely lead to his own death."

"You have proof of this?"

"If I did not, I would be dead. Jarvis knows my death will lead to the publication of what he most desires be kept undisclosed. Hence his caution."

"I would think such a threat from you would be sufficient to motivate his lordship to suppress any rumors about you, not foment them."

"You might think so. But there's a flaw in that logic. If I were to move to bring down Lord Jarvis, he would retaliate by having me killed. We would effectively destroy each other."

"So what does any of this have to do with me?"

"It occurs to me that the easiest and quickest way to lay the rumors to rest would be for me to take a wife. A famous wife known for her beauty, sensuality, and charisma."

Kat laughed. "You can't be serious."

"I am utterly serious. It would be a mutually beneficial arrangement: I would protect you from Jarvis, while you would provide me with what I suppose one could call a disguise. With Kat Boleyn as my wife, anyone questioning my virility or sexuality would be laughed out of the room."

"Why me? Why not choose a bride from the selection available at Almack's?"

He smiled. "This isn't the kind of arrangement I'd care to explain to some innocent debutante just out of the schoolroom. You need have no worry I would press to consummate the marriage. I offer you companionship and witty conversation at the supper table, but our amorous adventures, obviously, would be directed elsewhere. All I ask is that you pursue them with discretion — as shall I."

Kat pushed up from her chair to pace the room. She should have dismissed the suggestion out of hand. Instead, she found herself saying, "Devlin would never forgive me were I to embark on such a marriage."

"You think he would forgive you for running away to France?"

When Kat said nothing, he added, "I can have a marriage contract drawn up preserving your control over whatever wealth you bring to the marriage as well as your subsequent earnings."

"No. This is impossible."

"Don't dismiss the idea too hastily. Give it some thought."

She brought up one hand to rub absently at her temples. "This proof you claim to possess against Jarvis. How do I know it exists?"

He smiled. "I expected you to be suspicious." Slipping his hand into his coat, he drew forth a case of soft brown leather tied with a thong. "So I brought it."

The documents in the case were thorough, damning, and irrefutably authentic. "Good God," whispered Kat when she had finished reading through them.

"Exactly." Yates tucked the documents away and rose to his feet to cast a significant glance around the elegantly proportioned room with its peach silk hangings and theatrical memorabilia. "You don't need to give all this up."

"What you're suggesting is outrageous."

He shrugged. "Think about it."

Kat stayed where she was, her hands gripped tightly together in front of her.

At the door he paused to look back, his pirate's earring winking in the sunlight streaming in through the front windows. "Oh. I almost forgot. The name of the *Harmony*'s cabin boy you were asking about? It was Forbes. Gideon Forbes."

After Yates left, Kat paid a boy a shilling to carry a brief note to Brook Street, giving Sebastian the dead cabin boy's name. Then she thought about sending Elspeth up to the attic to pull down her trunks.

Instead she stood at the front window, looking out at Harwich Street and the familiar crowded rooftops, chimneys, and soot-stained spires of the city she had called home for more than ten years.

CHAPTER 49

Later that afternoon, Sebastian drew up the curricle on the gravel sweep before a small Elizabethan sandstone manor. Lying to the north of London, near St. Albans, the childhood home of Gideon Forbes proved to be a pleasant, well-kept estate with fat-bellied cows and well-tended fields. As he swung down from the curricle, Sebastian could hear the sound of children's laughter mingling with the barking of a dog in the distance.

"It's funny," said Tom, squinting up at the manor's forest of chimneys. "But when you think about what musta happened to that lad, somehow you don't expect 'im to 'ave grown up someplace that looks so *ordinary.*"

"I know what you mean," said Sebastian. Acting on Kat's message, he had found it easy enough to trace Gideon Forbes here, to this idyllic corner of the Hertfordshire countryside. Gideon's father was a country squire named Brandon Forbes; the boy's mother was some four years dead. But whatever Sebastian had been anticipating, it wasn't *this*, this utterly English landscape of unpretentious gentility and bucolic peace.

A shout brought Sebastian's head around. A sturdily built man in serviceable buckskin breeches was walking toward the house from across a park of oak trees and sun-spangled grass that waved gently in the breeze. He looked to be in his midforties, his dark hair newly touched by gray, the lines on his long face just beginning to settle and deepen with age. A liver-colored hound loped at his heels. "May I help you?" he called.

Sebastian went to meet him. "Mr. Forbes? I'm Viscount Devlin. I'd like to talk to you about your son Gideon."

The man blinked several times, his eyes narrow and a bit wary. "All right," he said at last. "Come walk with me."

They followed a footpath that curled away toward a distant string of cottages, the hound racing ahead of them. "It's because of these terrible murders, isn't it?" he said after a moment. "That's why you're here. You think there's some connection to the wreck of the *Harmony.*"

Sebastian studied the man's sun-darkened

face. "Did you attend the trial of the mutineers?"

"No." Forbes stared off across the fields, to where two little girls played with a much younger boy still in leading strings. "I'm afraid Gideon's mother was sickening by then. She'd never been well after the birth of our last daughter, you see, and I didn't want to leave her. But I followed it in the papers."

"Did you go to the hangings?"

Forbes shook his head, his lips twisting in a grimace. "Nah. What would be the point?"

"Revenge, perhaps?"

"It wouldn't bring the boy back, now, would it?"

Sebastian nodded toward the laughing children in the distance. "Are they yours?"

Forbes's features lightened into a proud smile. "That's right. Catherine there is eleven; Jane is seven, while Michael has just turned two. And I've two older boys by my first wife: Roland, who helps me here at the manor, and his younger brother, Daniel. Daniel's up at Cambridge."

As Sebastian watched, the boy on the leading strings took a tumble and started to cry. His half sisters rushed to pick him up again. "You've remarried?"

"Aye." He sighed. "I've buried two wives,

God rest their souls. I pray to the good Lord I won't bury the third."

Sebastian brought his gaze back to the man's plain, long face. "Do you think these murders have something to do with the *Harmony?*"

"Looks that way, doesn't it? I mean, I didn't think much about it after Carmichael's and Stanton's sons were killed. But now, with Captain Bellamy's son, and what the papers are saying was done to young Thornton last Easter . . ." He hesitated. "Well, it makes you think, doesn't it?"

"Did you ever talk to Captain Bellamy about what happened to your son?"

"Aye. Bellamy came to see me when it was all over. Brought me this." He pulled a worn Spanish piece of eight from his pocket and held it out. "It was Gideon's. He'd had it from the time he was a little one. Carried it with him everywhere."

"Did he tell you how the boy died?"

"Spar fell on him during the storm. He didn't die right away, though. Gideon was a plucky one, no doubt about it. Maybe if they'd been rescued sooner, he'd have made it. But without food or water . . ." The man's voice trailed away. He hesitated, then blew out his breath in a long sigh. "I never should have let him go to sea. Not that young. But from the time he was a little tyke, it was all he could talk about. The sea and tall ships and all the foreign lands he wanted to visit. In the end, he wore us down. One of his mother's cousins knew Captain Bellamy and arranged to have him take the lad on as cabin boy. Gideon was aiming to be a sea captain, you know. He'd have made it, too. If he'd lived."

Sebastian studied the man's pleasant, weathered face. "The young men who've been killed have all been found with various objects stuffed in their mouths — a papier-mâché star, a mandrake root, a page torn from a ship's log, and the hoof of a goat. Do you have any idea what it could mean?"

As Sebastian watched, Forbes's face became tight with an effort to control his emotions. "I didn't read anything about that."

"It does mean something, doesn't it? What is it?"

Forbes swung away to stare out over the park, toward the laughing children. "Gideon had a poem he liked. You know the one? Something about mermaids singing?"

" 'Go and Catch a Falling Star,' " said Sebastian softly. "By John Donne?"

Forbes's throat worked as he swallowed. "That's it. 'Go and Catch a Falling Star.' " He brought his gaze back to Sebastian's face. "Bellamy told me they buried Gideon's body at sea. But that's not what you think happened to him, is it? Is it?" he said again, when Sebastian remained silent.

Sebastian met the other man's intense gray eyes. "No. No, I don't."

CHAPTER 50

Kat was drinking tea on the terrace at the rear of her house, overlooking the tree-shaded garden, when her maid came hurrying across the pavement.

"I asked her to wait in the drawing room while I announced her," said Elspeth, wringing her work-worn hands against her apron. "Truly I did, but she said —"

Kat cut her off. "Who, Elspeth?"

A woman's voice reached her, low and stern. "Good morning, Niece."

Kat stared across the sun-dappled terrace at the thin matron who stood in the open doorway. It had been more than ten years since Kat had stolen away from this woman's home — a frightened, desperate child willing to face the uncertainties of life on the streets rather than continue to endure this woman's grim whippings by day and the degrading violations that came in the terrifying darkness of the night.

Her name was Emma Stone, and she was a close associate of "Holy Hannah" More and William Wilberforce and the growing group of moral reformers known as the Evangelicals. Emma Stone had made the Evangelical's Society for the Suppression of Vice and Immorality her own special project, perhaps as a public form of atonement for the shame of having a sister as scandalously immoral as Kat's mother.

They had come to London together, Emma and Arabella Noland, two Irish sisters, pretty but poorly dowered. The elder, Emma, had married a barrister named Maurice Stone. Arabella, the younger and prettier, had chosen a different path, becoming the mistress of first one wealthy nobleman, then the next.

"You are not welcome in my house, Aunt," said Kat, keeping her voice level with effort.

"Believe me, it is only my sense of duty to my dead mother and the laws of our dear Lord that have brought me here."

Kat gave her aunt a cold, tight smile. "Your devotion to your Lord's laws seems very selective." She cast a deliberate eye over her aunt's unrelieved mourning gown of black bombazine. "Is he dead then?"

"Mr. Stone has been gone from me these past three years."

"And still you wear deep mourning for him? How" — Kat paused, searching for the right word — "hypocritical of you."

Two bright spots of color appeared on the other woman's cheeks. "I did not believe the lies you told ten years ago. I'm not about to believe them now."

"No. Of course not." Kat crossed her arms before her. "I assume you're here for some reason. Please state what it is and go away."

The color in Emma Stone's cheeks deepened. "I should have expected such a reception. There aren't many women in my position who would have taken you in when I did — the illegitimate offspring of a harlot and the man who had her in his keeping. And how did you repay me? By fleeing my protection without a word of warning or thanks."

"I'm the oddest creature," said Kat in a tight voice. "I decided if I was going to be forced to slake a man's lust, then I might as well get paid for it."

A tremble of raw fury shook Emma Stone's thin frame. Kat expected her to launch into an impassioned defense of her dead husband, or simply go away. Instead, she clenched her jaw so tightly she was practically spitting out her words. "I am here because of the notice of your approaching nuptials in the *Morning Post.*"

"Really, Aunt? You shock me. I had no idea you interested yourself in the affairs of Society."

"I do not. Which is why I remained unaware of your relationship with Lord Devlin until the betrothal was brought to my attention by my dear friend Mrs. Barnes. You recall Mrs. Barnes?"

Kat remained motionless. Eunice Barnes was both her aunt's near neighbor and a fellow soldier in the Society for the Suppression of Vice.

"She is the only one of my acquaintances who realized that the brazen hussy calling herself Kat Boleyn and flaunting herself on the boards at Covent Garden was none other than the niece I had once sheltered."

"And she kept such delicious gossip to herself? I am impressed."

Mrs. Stone acknowledged the barb with a twitching of her upper lip. "Had I been aware of the nature of the relationship you had developed with Viscount Devlin, I would of course have overcome my repugnance and approached you sooner."

"Your repugnance. Yes, I suppose it must be quite a soul-trying exercise for a saintly woman such as yourself to venture into this den of sin and debauchery. You'd best say what you came to say and run away quickly before you become contaminated."

Mrs. Stone jerked open the strings of her reticule to draw forth two small miniatures painted on oval porcelain plaques and framed in gold filigree. "Your mother stayed with me for a short time before she fled London. Did you know?"

Kat kept her surprise to herself, although in truth she had not known. Had Emma Stone's despicable husband made his vile advances on Kat's mother, too? Kat wondered. Had he found a grown woman — even one heavy with child — better able to defend herself than a thirteen-year-old girl?

"The ungrateful wretch fled my house as you did, leaving only a curt note of thanks and these two miniatures, which she begged me to accept as payment."

"And you didn't sell them?" However much Emma Stone might prate on about the Kingdom of Heaven, Kat knew the woman still maintained a healthy interest in the material comforts of this world.

Mrs. Stone's head reared back in exaggerated affront. "Do you think I would take payment for sheltering my own sister in her time of need? The Good Book says, 'Jesus Our Lord hath given unto us all things that pertain unto life and godliness, through the knowledge of Him that hath called us to glory and virtue, and to godliness brotherly kindness, and to brotherly kindness charity.' "

Kat kept her gaze on her aunt's lined face. The passage of time had not been kind to Emma Stone, crimping the skin around her mouth and etching her habitually disapproving expression deep. "I assume there is a point to all this, Aunt?"

Emma Stone held out the first miniature. "This one is of your mother. I assume you recognize her?"

Kat cradled the porcelain oval in her hands, the painting so exquisitely rendered that it caught her breath. It was a face Kat hadn't seen in more than ten years, the wide green eyes slanted up slightly at the ends like a cat's, the cheekbones high and flaring, the nose almost childlike above full, sensuous lips. Kat could trace some of those features in her own face, mingling with traits she'd come to think of as purely her own, although she knew they must come from the unknown lord who'd been her father.

She skimmed her fingertips across the smooth surface, as if by touching the painted likeness she might somehow touch the laughing, breathing mother who'd once loved her. A welling of emotion closed her throat. It was a moment before she could look up and say, "And the other miniature?"

Emma Stone pressed her lips together in grim censure. "The other miniature is the reason I have come. It is of the last man who had my sister in his keeping. Your father."

With a hand that was not quite steady, Kat reached to take the small painting held out to her. Somehow, even before her hand closed over the miniature, she knew what she would see.

He was younger, of course, at least twenty-four years younger. The deftly rendered hair was still dark, the features solid but still firm. She had his chin, Kat realized; she supposed it was understandable that she had never noticed it before. But she should have recognized the eyes, she thought. How could she never have realized that the vivid blue eyes that stared back at her from her own reflection were those of Alistair St. Cyr, the Earl of Hendon?

CHAPTER 51

"Once I give this information to Bow Street," said Sir Henry Lovejoy, "I have little doubt but what they'll move to arrest Mr. Forbes." Henry focused his gaze on Lord Devlin. "Do you think he's guilty?"

They sat in the modest drawing room of Henry's Russell Square house, the remnants of tea spread on the table before them. Shifting in his chair, the Viscount stretched out his legs and crossed them at the ankles. "Forbes seems the most likely suspect, obviously. But is he guilty? I honestly don't think so. The pieces of the puzzle are all fitting neatly together, but the picture they make seems somehow off-kilter. I can't explain why."

"He's the only man with a motive that I can see."

"There's no doubt it's a powerful motive," Devlin agreed, "knowing your son was killed and eaten by a shipload of starving men and women."

"Did they kill the boy, do you think? He might simply have died. He was injured, after all. Without adequate food or water . . ."

"He could have died of his injuries. But there have been other instances in which starving Englishmen and -women have been reduced to feeding upon their dead companions — or have drawn lots. The fact that this company kept quiet about what they did suggests the boy was simply killed out of hand." He blew out a long breath. "I doubt we'll ever know the truth."

"No, you're probably right." Henry sighed. "I'll take this information to Sir James at Bow Street tonight."

Devlin fixed him with an uncomfortably fierce yellow stare. "I suppose you must, but —" He broke off.

Henry raised one eyebrow. "You think there's something you've missed?"

"I don't know. I wish I understood better the part Jarvis's son played in all this."

"There is no evidence that Matt Parker's brother spoke the truth. Who would take the word of a hanged sailor against the testimony of the likes of Sir Humphrey Carmichael or Lord Stanton?"

The Viscount set his teacup aside and

stood up. "In this instance? I would."

Sebastian returned to his house on Brook Street to be intercepted in the hall by his majordomo.

"There is a woman here to see you, my lord. A *foreign* woman and a child. They insisted upon waiting, so I have put them in the drawing room."

"A Mrs. Bellamy?" said Sebastian sharply.

"That is the name she gave. Yes, my lord."

Sebastian turned toward the stairs. "Send up some tea and cakes, Morey, and tell them I won't be but a moment."

He found Mrs. Bellamy seated in one of the cane-backed chairs beside the front bow window. At the sight of him, her mouth parted in surprise and she dropped the black-edged handkerchief she had been clutching. The child, Francesca, perched on the edge of a sofa near the empty hearth, a scorched leather-bound volume clutched against her thin chest, her eyes huge in a wan, pale face.

"Mrs. Bellamy, Francesca. My apologies for keeping you waiting. You should not have troubled yourself to make the journey up to London to see me. I would have been more than happy to wait upon you in Greenwich, had you but sent word."

The Captain's widow cast her daughter a quick, enigmatic glance. "Oh, my lord! I did not wish to trouble you at all. I thought Mr. Taylor must have left your card with me by mistake, and I came only in the hopes you might be able to direct me to him. It was Francesca who insisted we stay."

Sebastian went to pour the tea that stood, neglected, upon the table. "Please accept my apologies for the deception I practiced upon you in Greenwich. I feared if I approached Captain Bellamy under my own name, he might refuse to see me."

Her brow wrinkled in confusion. "And why would that be, my lord?"

"I suspect the Captain was warned not to speak to me." He held out a cup. "Please, have some tea."

She took the cup automatically, but did not drink it.

He turned toward Francesca. "And you, Miss Bellamy? Would you care for some tea and cakes?"

"No, thank you," she said with painful seriousness, and held out the leather-bound book. "We've brought you this."

"What is it?" asked Sebastian, not moving to take it from her.

It was Mrs. Bellamy who answered. "The ship's log. From the *Harmony*. The evening

327

he — he fell in the river, Captain Bellamy spent hours sitting at the table after supper, reading the log and drinking rum. Before he went out, he threw it on the hearth and lit a fire. But the fire didn't catch properly and Francesca pulled it out."

Sebastian watched the child run one hand over the log's charred binding. "Have you read it?" he asked, glancing at the widow.

She flushed and shook her head. Too late, Sebastian remembered what Tom had told him in Greenwich, that the Captain's young Brazilian wife was illiterate. "No," she said. "But Francesca has."

Sebastian's gaze met the child's, and he saw there the horrified confirmation of everything he'd suspected and more. "You read what happened after the mutiny?" he asked softly.

"I read it all."

Dear God, thought Sebastian. Aloud, he said, "And still you brought it to me?"

She nodded, the muscles in her jaw held tight. "It's why Adrian died, isn't it? It's why they all died. Because of what Papa and their parents did on that ship."

Impossible to lie to the child. All he could say was, "I suspect so."

"Do you know who is doing it?"

"Not yet."

She laid the log on the tea table and pushed it toward him. "Perhaps this will help."

CHAPTER 52

Hendon spent most of Saturday afternoon at Carlton House, dealing with a fretful Prince. He was leaving the palace and heading up the Mall when Kat Boleyn drew up her phaeton and pair beside him with a neat flourish.

"I'd like a word with you, my lord," she said. "Drive with me a ways?"

Hendon looked at the woman before him. She wore a hunter green driving gown embellished with brass epaulets and set off by a cocky green chip hat with a curling ostrich feather. Hendon didn't hold with females driving phaetons. He dropped his gaze to the restive horseflesh between the traces and was tempted to plead some excuse. But the fact that she had deliberately sought him out raised a glimmer of hope in his breast. Perhaps he might find some way to scotch Devlin's marriage scheme after all.

He stepped up to the curb and said quizzically, "You wish me to ride with you in that rig?"

She let out a peal of musical laughter. "I promise not to overturn you, my lord. George," she said to the groom seated beside her, "wait for me here."

"Yes, miss."

Hendon climbed up to settle in the space vacated by the groom. She gathered her reins, but before she gave the horses the office to start, she handed Hendon a small painted porcelain oval — a miniature of a dark-haired woman with flashing green eyes and a smile that had once stolen Hendon's heart.

"Do you recognize this?" Kat Boleyn asked.

Hendon's fist closed around the filigree-framed porcelain so hard the metal bit into his flesh. "No."

She cast him a swift glance. "You lie, my lord. The truth is writ plain on your face. Her name was Arabella Noland, and she was your mistress, was she not?"

"What if she was? You think that showing me her portrait now will somehow soften my attitude toward your plans to marry my son? Well, let me tell you something, girl: you're fair and far out!"

She said nothing, her attention all for the task of guiding her horses through the heavy Saturday-afternoon traffic.

"Where did you get this?" he asked at last.

"It was given to me by Arabella's sister, Emma Stone."

"That hateful woman," said Hendon. "Why should she do such a thing?"

"Mrs. Stone also gave me this portrait of you." She held out another miniature, and after a moment, Hendon took it from her.

"They are a matched set. Did you give them to Arabella? I wonder. Were they part of your farewell gift to her when you discovered she was with child?"

"No," he said gruffly, unable to grasp her point. "They were a birthday gift. Why?"

She cast him a look he couldn't begin to comprehend. "But you knew she had a child by you."

Hendon worked his jaw back and forth. He saw no point in denying it. "Have you told Devlin of this?"

"No." She feathered the turning onto Whitehall. "*Did* you know of the child?"

"I knew. It's why she left me."

"She left you?"

Hendon grunted. "I assumed you must know the whole story. It was my intention to take the child away after it was born. Give it to a good family, to be raised in the country."

"You would have taken her child away?"

The edge in her voice caught him by surprise. He shrugged. "It's the usual practice. Arabella was distraught at the suggestion, but I thought she'd come around. Instead, she left without even telling me she was going."

Wordlessly, Kat Boleyn eased her pair around a brewer's wagon obstructing the road. Hendon let his gaze rove over her high cheekbones, the impish line of her nose, the sensuous curve of her lips. He'd always thought she had something of the look of Arabella. And then, from somewhere unbidden came a powerful sense of disquiet.

"Why did Emma Stone give you these miniatures?" he asked again.

"Emma Stone is my aunt."

Hendon opened his mouth to deny it, to deny everything she was suggesting. Then he shut it again. If any other young woman had come to him with such a claim, he would never have accepted her statements at face value. But this woman of all others had no reason to claim him as her father and every reason not to.

"My God," he whispered. "I always thought you resembled her, but I never imagined . . ." His voice trailed off. He stared across the tops of the elms in the park, their leaves suddenly so brutally green against the blue of the sky that he had to blink several times.

"What are you going to do?" he asked at last.

"Tell Devlin. What else can I do?"

He studied the beautiful, hauntingly familiar face beside him. He had always thought of her as his adversary, the woman he had to fight to prevent her from ruining Devlin's life. He found that he still thought of her that way. He had to think of her that way. He could allow himself nothing else. Not now. "You could simply go away," he suggested.

"No," she said fiercely. "I won't hurt him like that again. Not a second time."

"Then let me be the one to tell him."

He thought at first she meant to refuse him. She drew in a quick breath, then another. And it was only then that he realized she was fighting back tears.

"Very well," she said, drawing up before the palace. "But you had best tell him right away, because the next time I see him, I will tell him if you have not."

CHAPTER 53

Outside, the sun shone brightly on the last of what had been a fine September day. Sebastian could hear the sound of children laughing and calling to one another as he walked into his library and laid the *Harmony*'s long-lost log on his desktop. For the briefest instant, he found himself hesitating. Then he opened the charred leather binding and stepped back into a dark and terrible episode.

The voyage's first weeks out of India had been uneventful, and he skimmed them quickly. Some captains kept extensive, chatty logs. Not Bellamy. Bellamy's entries were terse, impatient — the hurried scribblings of a man who kept his log to satisfy his ship's owners rather than himself. He made only brief lists of his passengers, officers, and crew. Sebastian ran through the names, but there were no surprises. There had been twenty-one crew members. There, near the bottom of the list, Sebastian found the name *Jack Parker,* but he recognized none of the others.

He flipped through the days, the long layover in Cape Town, the fine sailing as they headed up the west coast of Africa. And then, on the fifth of March, Bellamy had written:

2:00 a.m. Strong gales with a heavy sea. Clewed up sails and hove to.

6:00 a.m. Strong gales continue from the WSW. Carried away the main topmast and mizzen masthead.

3:00 p.m. Shipped a heavy sea, carried away the jolly boat and two crewmen.

There was only one scrawled entry for the next day, 6 March.

10:00 a.m. Gale continues. No idea of our position at sea. Reckoning impossible in storm.

Two days later, Bellamy wrote:

8 March, 7:00 p.m. Shipped a heavy sea, washed away the long-boat, tiller. Un-shipped the rudder. Cabin boy, Gideon,

suffered a broken arm. Plucky lad.

As bad as things had been, on the ninth of March they got worse.

11:00 a.m. Pumps barely able to keep water from gaining. Crew restive. Cargo thrown overboard, but ship still lying heavy in the water and listing badly to starboard.

2:00 p.m. Ship suddenly righted though full of water. A dreadful sea making a fair breach over her from stem to stern. We are surely lost.

5:00 p.m. Gale dropped to strong breeze. Employed getting what provisions possible by knocking out bow port. Saved twenty pounds of bread and ten pounds of cheese, some rum and flour, now stored in maintop.

10 March. 6:00 a.m. Isaac Potter slipped into hold and drowned before we could get him out. Committed his body to the deep.

10:00 a.m. Crew restive. It is obvious that if we don't spot a ship soon, the *Harmony* must be abandoned. Yet with no jolly boat or long boat, all cannot be saved.

11 March. 2:00 p.m. Crew mutinied and abandoned ship, taking most of remaining provisions and water. Officers and passengers left aboard. God save our souls.

13 March. 5:00 p.m. Stern stove in. I know not how we stay afloat. Made tent of spare canvas on forecastle. Able to salvage a bit of rice and more flour from below. Rationing half a gill of water each per day, but even at this rate it will not last long.

14 March. 7:00 a.m. Small shark caught by means of running bowline. Sir Humphrey rigged up a teakettle with a long pipe and a stretch of canvas to fashion a kind of distillation. But it affords only one wineglass of water a day each, barely enough to maintain life. Gideon feverish.

16 March. 10:00 a.m. Sir Humphrey has improved upon his distillation process. We can now manage nearly two wineglasses each per day. Barnacles gathered from side of vessel and eaten raw, but they will not last.

23 March. Suffering much from hunger. Gideon hanging on, though I know not how. No nourishment now for seven days.

24 March. 2:00 p.m. Saw a ship to windward. Made signal of distress, but stranger hauled his wind away from us.

25 March. 7:00 a.m. I like not the mutterings amongst the passengers. They have been awaiting the death of the cabin boy, Gideon, intending to feast upon his dead body. But he has not died, and now there is talk of killing him.

5:00 p.m. A dark day for us all. Over the objections of myself and Mr. David Jarvis, the passengers and ship's officers voted to hasten Gideon's death. Mr. Jarvis sought to protect the lad, but the others rushed him and in the altercation a cutlass was thrust through young Jarvis's side. I thought for a moment Gideon would be saved, for they would make their meal of Mr. Jarvis instead. But, though injured, the young man defended himself stoutly, and they returned to Gideon.

Reverend Thornton delivered the last rites while Lord Stanton held Gideon down and Sir Humphrey Carmichael slit his throat. The poor lad's blood was caught in a basin and shared amongst the passengers. Then the body was cut up into quarters and washed in the sea. They drew lots for the choicest parts. The Reverend and Mrs. Thornton drew the poor lad's internal organs; Sir Humphrey an arm; Lord Stanton and Mr. Atkinson shared a leg, and so on. Even those such as Mr. Fairfax and Mrs. Dunlop, who had argued against the killing of the lad, did not fail to join in once the evil deed was done.

Only Mr. David Jarvis, wounded though he was, refused to partake of the feast. "Why should I condemn my soul to hell," he told them, "so that I might live for one or two days more? I know well who you will fall upon once you've picked clean the bones of this poor lad."

I myself found I could not quiet my stomach sufficient to eat the poor lad's flesh. But when they passed the cup of his blood, God help me, I drank.

Pushing up from his desk, Sebastian went to pour himself a glass of brandy. But the brandy tasted bitter on his tongue and he set it aside.

Through the window overlooking the street he gazed down on a lady's barouche driven at a smart clip up the street. A child chasing a hoop along the footpath glanced up to shout something, and the golden sunlight fell gracefully on his honey-colored hair and ruddy cheeks.

It was easy to condemn the passengers and officers of the *Harmony,* Sebastian realized, easy to sit in security and comfort and reassure oneself of one's own superior moral fiber and courage. But no man can truly know how he will act until faced with such a choice: to hold to his convictions and embrace death, or to kill and live?

Reaching again for his brandy, Sebastian drank it down. Then he went back to his desk and read.

26 March, 8:00 a.m. English frigate hove in sight. Hoisted the ensign downward and the stranger hauled his wind toward us. Remains of cabin boy thrown overboard. Mr. Jarvis holding on to life, but he lost consciousness as the *Sovereign* hove to, and I doubt he will live to see another dawn.

There was one last line, entered in a shaky scrawl, then nothing.

10:00 a.m. Committed his body to the deep.

CHAPTER 54

Sebastian closed the log, then sat for a time staring down at the charred leather. It was one thing to suspect that the passengers and officers of the *Harmony* had resorted to cannibalism and murder, but something else entirely to read the terse record of their long, horrible ordeal.

The *Harmony*'s log explained much about the recent killings that had before seemed incomprehensible. He now understood that the strangely varying mutilation to which each of the victims had been subjected corresponded exactly to the lots drawn by their parents after Gideon's murder. Adrian Bellamy had been spared the others' butchery not because his killer had been interrupted, as they'd supposed, but because his father, Captain Bellamy, had not himself partaken of the dead cabin boy's flesh.

Yet the deliberate ordering of the killings struck Sebastian as less logical. It made sense that Barclay Carmichael had died before Dominic Stanton, since Sir Humphrey Carmichael had personally slit Gideon's throat while Lord Stanton had held the boy down. But Reverend Thornton had simply given the boy last rites. Why had his child been the first to die? And why had Captain Bellamy's son been slated as second on the list? Whatever his reasoning, the killer had considered his ranking of the victims so important that he had reserved the mandrake root for Adrian Bellamy even when the naval lieutenant's absence had forced the killer to move on to the next victim on his list.

But what struck Sebastian as the most vexing question of all was, *How* had the killer known in such excruciating detail the events that had transpired aboard that ship? The only logical explanation that presented itself was that the killer had been there on the ship himself.

Was that possible? What if one of the crew members had been left behind when the others mutinied and abandoned ship? Bellamy's log entries had been brief and sporadic; would he have bothered to name one or two crewmen who'd been abandoned by their shipmates? Sebastian was just flipping back to Bellamy's listing of the *Harmony's* original twenty-one crew members when the sound of the knocker followed by his father's voice in the hall brought his head up.

"I thought you'd sworn never to darken my doorway again," said Sebastian when the Earl appeared at the entrance to the library.

Hendon jerked off his gloves and tossed them along with his hat and walking stick onto a nearby table. "Something has come up."

He went to stand before the empty hearth, his hands clasped behind his back, his weight rocking from his heels to the balls of his feet. "I've never claimed to be a saint. You know that," he said gruffly.

Sebastian leaned back in his chair, his gaze on the Earl's heavily jowled face. He had no doubt as to why his father was here. A man who had once offered a young actress twenty thousand pounds to leave his son alone was not likely to sit idle and let their marriage take place now without doing everything in his power to stop it — and then some. Sebastian gave his father a cold smile. "I know you're no saint."

"I've kept mistresses over the years. After your mother left, and before."

"I've made Kat my mistress. Now I intend

to take her as my wife."

"For God's sake, Sebastian! Just hear me out, please. This isn't easy. One of the women I had in my keeping was a young Irishwoman by the name of Arabella. Arabella Noland. Her father was a clergyman from a small market town to the northwest of Waterford, a place called Carrick-on-Suir. Ever hear of it?"

"No."

"It was the birthplace of Anne Boleyn."

Sebastian knew a deep sense of uneasiness, although he had no idea where his father could possibly be going with all this. "And?"

"She came to London with her sister, Emma. Emma married a barrister by the name of Stone. She's made something of a name for herself over the years as a moralistic writer, much in the vein of Hannah More. Perhaps you've heard of her."

"I've heard of her."

"Yes. Well, the younger sister, Arabella, was by far the prettier and the more lively. There was no dowry to speak of, and the family was from the meanest gentry — and Irish to boot. Arabella —"

"Became your mistress? Is that what you're saying? When was this?"

"Twenty-some-odd years ago. You were

still in leading strings."

Sebastian pushed up from his chair. "If you think by means of this tale to dissuade me from my marriage to Kat —"

"Let me finish. We were together for more than three years. Then she learned she was with child."

Sebastian watched as his father swung away to brace his outstretched arms against the marble mantelpiece. It was a moment before he could go on. "You know how such things are often handled. A servant delivers the infant to the parish along with a small sum of money, or the child is farmed out to a nursemaid in some mean hovel. They never survive. Perhaps that's the whole point. I don't know. But it's not what I was suggesting. I found a good home for the child — a family of respectable yeoman farmers whom I had every intention of supervising carefully."

"But she didn't want to give up the child, I take it?"

Dark color stained the Earl's cheeks. "No. She begged me to abandon the scheme. I tried to make her understand that anything else was impossible. I even thought I'd succeeded. But then, several months before the child was to be born, she disappeared. I searched for her, but to no avail. Sometime later I received a note from Ireland. It said simply, 'You have a daughter. She is well. Do not attempt to find us.' "

Hendon pushed away from the mantel and swung to face Sebastian. "This morning, Emma Stone paid a visit to Kat Boleyn. It seems the woman is Kat's aunt. She brought her these." Reaching into his pocket, he drew forth two miniatures that he laid on the desk beside Sebastian. "They're portraits of her parents."

The woman in the first painting was a stranger, although it was easy enough to trace the likeness to Kat in the beguiling juxtaposition of that childish nose and the full, sensuous lips. The second portrait was of the Earl of Hendon as he had been twenty-five years ago. Sebastian stared down at the twin porcelain ovals framed in filigree and felt an explosive welling of denial and fury and fear. *"No."*

He slammed away from the desk. *"Mother of God.* Is there nothing to which you will not stoop in your effort to prevent this marriage?"

"No," said Hendon in rare honesty. "But even I could not have invented this."

"I don't believe any of it. Do you hear me? *I don't believe it."*

Hendon's jaw worked back and forth.

"Talk to Miss Boleyn. Talk to Mrs. Emma Stone —"

"Have no fear that I shall!"

"They'll tell you the same tale."

Sebastian swept his arm across the desktop, sending the miniatures flying. "Goddamn you. Goddamn you all to hell."

Hendon's eyes — those vivid blue St. Cyr eyes that were so inescapably like Kat's — twitched with pain. "You can't blame me for the fact that you fell in love with that woman."

"Then who the hell do I blame?" raged Sebastian.

"God."

"I don't believe in God," said Sebastian, and he slammed out of the house.

CHAPTER 55

Sebastian went first to Harwich Street.

"Where is she?" he said when the maid Elspeth opened the door.

Elspeth stared at him with wide, frightened eyes. "Miss Boleyn isn't here."

Sebastian pushed past her. "Kat?" he called, and heard his voice echo through the empty house.

He ran up the stairs to the drawing room, then took the stairs to the second floor two at a time. "Kat!"

A minute later, he was back downstairs. "Where is she, damn it?" he demanded, coming upon Elspeth in the entrance hall.

The maid looked up from the oil lamp she'd been trimming. "I don't know. She went out."

"You know something you're not telling. What is it?"

"I don't know anything! Something strange is going on, but I don't know what it is. I swear I don't."

"Did she say when she'd be back?"

"Tomorrow. She said she probably wouldn't be back until tomorrow."

"Probably?"

"All I know is what she said."

Sebastian slammed his open palm against the paneled wall and left.

He went next to Emma Stone's small house in Camden.

The woman was famous for writing wildly popular "improving" tracts with titles such as "Christian Piety" and "Moral Sketches for the Next Generation." Had Hendon named anyone else, Sebastian could have dismissed his wild claims without hesitation. But Sebastian found it impossible to imagine Mrs. Emma Stone lending herself to one of the Earl's schemes.

Pausing on the footpath, Sebastian stared up at the proper brick facade before him. He knew only the faintest outlines of Kat's earlier history, but what he knew fit uncomfortably well with Hendon's tale. She'd told him once that her father was an English lord, but her mother had left London before Kat was born to take refuge in her native Ireland. Sebastian knew what the soldiers had done to Kat's mother and stepfather. He knew too that after their deaths Kat had been taken in by her mother's sister. Sebastian had formed a hazy image of a self-righteous, ostentatiously religious woman who'd punished her niece's accusations of her husband's misconduct with the whip.

Sebastian studied the silent rows of neatly curtained windows. Had it been from this house that Kat had fled as a child into a life on the streets? She had never named her aunt as Mrs. Emma Stone. But then, there was much that Kat had never told him.

He became aware of the sensation of being watched. As he climbed the short flight of steps to the front door, he saw the lace curtain at one of the upstairs windows shift slightly, then settle back into place.

He half expected his knock to go unanswered. Instead, the door was opened almost immediately by a thin slip of a maid with jade green eyes and a scattering of freckles across her nose who looked at him with undisguised curiosity and asked breathlessly, "Are you Lord Devlin?"

"Yes," said Sebastian in surprise.

The girl stepped back and opened the door wide. "Mrs. Stone said to bring you straight up."

Sometimes our worst dreams don't come when we're asleep.

The nightmares that came to Sebastian in the bowels of the night were familiar things, disjointed memories of slashing sabers and exploding ordnance punctuated by the screams of dying men and maimed horses. He'd learned to live with those dreams, with those memories. But he wasn't sure how he was going to learn to live with this.

He wandered the darkened streets of London, down narrow lanes of shuttered shops and quiet houses. A mist had settled over the city, painting the pavement with a wet sheen that reflected the light from the streetlamps and an occasional passing carriage. He kept trying to comprehend the incomprehensible, how a love once so beautiful and life-sustaining could have suddenly been transformed into something unclean and vile. Of all the taboos with which Englishmen and -women fortified themselves against the horrors of savagery and bestiality, only two were so unforgivably loathsome as to be spoken of in frightened whispers: the prohibition against the eating of human flesh, and the sexual union of those bound by the closest of family ties. Father and daughter. Sister and brother.

He knew he should recoil in horror. A part of him did recoil in horror. But a part of him still ached for the future that had been snatched from him, for the woman he would have made his wife.

He wanted to get on his horse and gallop out beyond the last straggling hamlets. He wanted to ride through woods lashed by a wild wind, with none but the cold and distant stars for companions. He wanted to ride until he reached the crashing waves of the sea and felt the salty spray rise up to meet him as he spurred ever on, to oblivion.

A burst of laughter from an open door brought his head around. He paused for a moment, shuddering, recognizing the danger of being alone and far too sober.

Wiping a hand across his face, he turned his steps toward Pickering Place, unaware of the slight figure watching him anxiously from the shadows.

Paul Gibson pushed past the billiard tables toward the more select rooms filled with scattered faro and whist tables that lay beyond. The air he breathed smelled strongly of brandy and tobacco and the unmistakable sweet tang of hashish.

He was in one of the most expensive — and decadent — of the gaming hells off Pickering Place, and he had to keep reminding himself to clench his jaw shut for fear of staring around like some gape-mouthed lout just up from the country. Gibson had been in his share of hells and brothels before — and opium dens, too, for that matter. But he'd never been in a place quite like this one. The walls were hung with watered silk, the mirrors large and framed in ornate gilt wood, the cloths on the supper tables of starched linen. From somewhere in the distance came the lilting strains of a string quartet, the music forming an odd counterpoint to the high-pitched laughter of women and the ceaseless rattle of the dice box.

Gibson lifted a glass from one of the waiters who circled the rooms bearing trays of claret and brandy. A woman wearing a scarlet gown with a shockingly low décolletage cast him a speculative glance, then brushed past him. Gibson thought the diamonds in her ears looked real, but then, what did a poor Irish doctor know? He fortified himself with a sip of brandy and pushed on.

Scanning the gaming tables and the crowd around the whirling roulette wheel, he followed the gently curving staircase up to the next floor. The lights here were dimmer, but not dim enough to hide the bare flesh and unmistakable postures of the men and women who cavorted in groups of two, three, or more on low sofas and scattered cushions. Gibson felt his cheeks heat with embarrassment, and looked pointedly away.

He found Viscount Devlin sprawled on the velvet cushion of an embrasure overlooking the darkened street below, one fist wrapped around the neck of a bottle of good French brandy. As Gibson watched, a half-naked woman stroked one hand over his chest and down his stomach, but Devlin shook his head and brought his hand down on hers to stop its slow descent. The woman mewed softly in disappointment, then moved away. The Viscount raised the brandy to his lips and drank deep. Gibson had been afraid he might find his friend in one of those knots of groping, naked flesh. But Devlin seemed more interested in drinking himself to death than in drowning his pain in sex.

"There you are, me lad," said Gibson heartily, for the benefit of anyone who might be listening. "Sorry I took so long. You haven't forgotten you promised to meet my sister tonight, have you?"

Devlin swung his head to stare directly at him. The feral yellow eyes were glittering and dangerous. "Your sister?"

"Ah. See, you have forgotten. I've a hackney waiting outside. I know the Beau has dictated that no gentleman should condescend to ride in a hackney, but my carriage is being repaired, so I'm afraid there's not much we can do about it."

"You don't own a carriage," said Sebastian. "Nor do you have a sister."

"Now that's where you're out, my friend. I do indeed have a sister. But seeing as how she's taken the veil in a nunnery near Killarney, I don't think you'd want to meet her. Especially not in your present condition."

Devlin laughed and pushed to his feet. His cravat was rumpled and his hair more disheveled than normal, but his gait was steady enough as they walked down the stairs. It was only when they reached the narrow lane outside the gaming hell's discreet door that the Viscount paused to lean against the rough brick wall and squeeze his eyes shut.

"Bloody hell," he said after a moment.

Gibson studied his friend's pale face and tightly clenched jaw. "I haven't seen you this foxed since that night in San Domingo."

"I haven't been this foxed since that night in San Domingo. In fact, I'm not sure I've ever been this foxed." Devlin opened his eyes and stared at him. "What the devil are you doing here?"

"Tom was worried about you."

The dangerous glitter was back in the Viscount's eyes. "The devil you say."

"That's right." Gibson clapped his hand on his friend's shoulder, then laughed softly when Devlin winced. "And tomorrow, when you sober up, you can thank him."

The doctor waited until they were in the hackney headed toward Tower Hill before saying, "I don't suppose you've heard the news."

Devlin had been gazing silently out the window, but at that he swung his head to stare at Gibson. "What news?"

"They've arrested the Butcher of the West End. A country gentleman from Hertford-shire."

Devlin was suddenly, almost frighteningly sober. "Brandon Forbes?"

"That's it."

"But he didn't do it."

Gibson raised one eyebrow. "Can you prove it?"

"No."

"Then he'll hang for it, for sure. Either that, or some mob will pull him out of his cell and tear him to pieces. People are afraid. They want someone's blood, and quick."

"Stop the carriage," said Devlin.

Gibson sprang to signal the driver. "Why?

What is it?"

Devlin shoved open the door. "I think I'm going to be sick."

CHAPTER 56

Sunday, 22 September 1811

Charles, Lord Jarvis spent as little time as possible in his house in Berkeley Square. But he always attended Sunday-morning services at St. James's chapel with his harridan of a mother, his half-mad wife, and his determinedly unwed daughter, Hero. After church, it was his practice to pass several hours in his library dealing with affairs of state before sitting down to Sunday dinner with his family. He was very conscious of the need for the better classes to set a proper example for the lower orders, and church attendance and devotion to family were an important part of that example. It was a duty he had sought to impress upon his daughter, although with indifferent success.

On this particular Sunday, he returned from chapel to find the reports of several of his agents awaiting his attention on his desk.

Devlin's interference with his plans to use the actress Kat Boleyn to ferret out the identity of Napoleon's new spymaster had forced Jarvis to fall back on more traditional means, but so far his agents had proved unsuccessful. He was glancing through their reports when he was interrupted by a cautious knock.

"Yes, what is it?" he said without looking up.

"A Mr. Russell Yates to see you, my lord."

Jarvis's head came up. "What the bloody hell does he want?"

"Shall I tell him you are not at home, my lord?"

Jarvis tightened his jaw. "No. Send him in."

Russell Yates came in, bringing with him the scent of well-bred horses and a cool morning rain. From his manly chest and powerful shoulders to the glint of pirate's gold in his left ear, he exuded an aggressive form of masculinity not often seen amongst the members of the *ton*. And it was all for show.

Jarvis had dedicated his life to reading people and manipulating them. He was good at it, and he rarely made mistakes. Yet once Jarvis had underestimated this man. It would not happen again.

Very deliberately, Jarvis leaned back in his chair, but did not rise. "Have a seat, Mr. Yates."

Yates adjusted the tails of his dark blue morning coat and settled in a leather chair beside the empty hearth. "Please accept my apologies for interrupting you on the Sabbath day, my lord."

Jarvis merely inclined his head. It was flowery flummery and they both knew it.

"I am here, first of all," continued Yates, "to share with you the news of my good fortune. The lovely Miss Kat Boleyn has consented to become my wife."

Jarvis drew a gold snuffbox from his pocket and flipped it open. "Indeed? It was my understanding that Miss Boleyn had consented to become the Viscountess Devlin."

"Things changed."

"So it seems." Jarvis lifted a pinch of snuff to one nostril. "You understand, I assume, that Miss Boleyn has some . . . shall we say, unfortunate associations in her past?"

"Actually, that is my primary purpose for coming to see you today. While it's true Miss Boleyn has in the past engaged in certain activities that are better forgotten, the same could be said of many of us." Yates's smile widened to show his teeth.

"Even you, my lord, have been involved in episodes that would be best left unknown."

Jarvis closed his snuffbox with a snap. He was not one to bluster or rage, for he had learned long ago to control his emotions. He did at times give vent to anger, but only when it served his purpose. It would not serve his purpose now.

He tucked his snuffbox away and said calmly, "The understanding we reached on these matters still stands. I assume you are here merely to reassure me that as long as Miss Boleyn's secrets are safe, others are safe?"

"That's a fair representation of the situation, yes."

"Good. Then we understand each other."

Yates rose to his feet. Jarvis waited until he was at the door to add, "It does seem a waste."

Yates turned. "How's that, my lord?"

"Such a beautiful woman, married to a man uninterested in women."

If he'd been hoping for a rise, Jarvis was disappointed. Yates merely smiled and said, "Good day, my lord."

Some twenty minutes later, Jarvis was still sitting at his desk when his daughter, Hero, appeared at the door.

"The most vexatious thing, Papa. Grandmama has thrown her chamber pot at the upstairs parlor maid, and now both the maid and Cook have quit."

"The cook?" Jarvis looked around, his attention caught. "Why the cook?"

"Cook is Emily's aunt."

"Emily? Who the deuce is Emily?"

"The upstairs parlor maid."

"Good God," roared Jarvis. "And what would you have me do about it? The petty affairs of this household are not in my province."

"I don't expect you to do anything about it," said Hero. "I have simply come to warn you that dinner will be delayed."

"Dinner? But . . . who is cooking it?"

"I am," said his daughter with unruffled equanimity, and closed the door behind her.

Jarvis stared at the closed panel for a moment, then rose to pour himself a brandy. It had been a trying week.

The day might have been overcast, but the light streaming in through Paul Gibson's kitchen windows was still bright enough to hurt Sebastian's eyes. He squeezed them shut and ran a hand across his beard-roughened chin. "Remind me why I stayed here, rather than going home? I need a shave. And a bath. And clean clothes."

Paul Gibson answered him from across the room. "You needed to talk."

Sebastian opened one eye. "I did? How much did I say?"

"Enough." Gibson came to stand on the far side of the battered kitchen table. "I'm sorry, Sebastian."

Sebastian looked away.

"Here." Gibson plunked a tankard of ale on the boards before him. "This will help your head. You'd best drink it before you hear this morning's news."

Sebastian brought his gaze back to his friend's face. "Why? What's happened?"

"It's Felix Atkinson's twelve-year-old son, Anthony. He's missing."

CHAPTER 57

Sebastian found Felix Atkinson in the drawing room of his prosperous West End home. The East India Company man stood with his back to the room, his gaze fixed on the scene outside the window overlooking Portland Place. In a damask-covered chair off to one side, a pale-haired woman in her early thirties wept quietly into a handkerchief. As far as Sebastian could see, her husband was making no attempt to comfort her.

"I'd like a word with you," Sebastian told Atkinson. "Alone."

Atkinson swung to face him, all bluster and trembling affront. "Really, my lord. Now is hardly the time —"

Sebastian cut him off. "I don't think you want Mrs. Atkinson to hear what I have to say."

A rush of color darkened the other man's cheeks. He cast a quick glance at his wife, then looked away. "We can speak in the morning room."

They had barely crossed into the morning room before Sebastian's hands closed over Atkinson's shoulders and spun him around to slam his spine up against the nearest wall.

"You bloody, self-obsessed, lying son of a bitch," said Sebastian, spitting out each word through gritted teeth.

Atkinson gasped and made as if to pull away. "How dare you? How dare you lay hands upon me in my own h—"

Sebastian pressed his forearm against the man's throat, pinning him to the wall. "I know what happened on that ship. I know about Gideon Forbes, and I know what really happened to David Jarvis."

Atkinson went utterly still. "You can't."

"I read the log."

"The log? But the log was lost. Bellamy said the log was lost."

"He lied." Sebastian shoved his forearm up under the man's chin harder. "You all lied. What did you do? Get together after Thornton's and Carmichael's sons were killed and swear one another to secrecy?"

"What choice did we have?"

"You could have told the truth."

Atkinson's tongue darted out to moisten his lips. "How could we? No one would have

366

understood about the boy. You have no idea what it was like on that ship. The fear. The endless days and nights of hunger. That kind of hunger, it's like a yawning pit of fire in your belly, consuming you. You'll do anything when you're hungry like that."

"You might. Yet people starve to death on the streets of London all the time. They don't kill and eat each other."

Atkinson sucked in a breath that shook his entire frame. "The boy was dying. All we did was hasten the hour of his death. David Jarvis should never have tried to stop us."

"Is that what you tell yourself? What about the *Sovereign?*"

"We didn't know the frigate was out there! We thought we would die without seeing another ship. How could we have known?"

"That's why men shouldn't take it upon themselves to play God." Sebastian shifted his grip. "I'm going to ask you a question, and I want you to think very hard before answering. After the crew mutinied and abandoned ship, were any of the men left aboard?"

"Crewmen, you mean? No. Only Bellamy, the three ship's officers, and the boy. Why? Who do you think is doing this? You have some idea, don't you? Who is it?" His voice rose. "What aren't you telling me?"

Sebastian simply shook his head. "It hasn't struck you as peculiar that this killer knows exactly which lots you each drew after the boy's murder?"

The tic began to play at the edge of Atkinson's mouth. "Peculiar? It's terrifying! It's as if he were there on the ship with us. But that's impossible, isn't it? Isn't it?"

Sebastian gave the man a nasty smile. "You tell me."

"I told you before. I don't know who's doing this. *I don't know.*"

"It's too late to save yourself. When Jarvis hears you murdered his son, you're going to wish you did die on that ship."

"It wasn't me! I didn't have a cutlass! It was one of the others."

"You think that will make a difference to Jarvis?"

Atkinson's entire face convulsed. "No. I know it won't. We all know it won't. Why else do you think we've kept silent?"

"Why? Because you value your own lives more than you value the lives of your sons." Sebastian let the man go and stepped back. "When was your boy taken?"

Atkinson adjusted his cravat and gave the lapels of his coat a twitch. "This morning, early. He was gone from his bed when the

368

household awakened."

"He was taken from the house? I thought you had Bow Street Runners watching him."

"Two of them. Someone broke the lock on the back door."

"And where were your Runners while all this was happening?"

"One was watching the front of the house from across the street."

"And the other?"

"Was found insensible in the garden."

Sebastian suppressed an oath. If the killer followed his established pattern, the boy's butchered body would be discovered in some prominent spot early tomorrow morning. It was still possible that the boy was alive someplace. But their chances of finding him before he was killed diminished with each passing minute.

"Let me see the boy's room," said Sebastian.

Atkinson stared at him. "What?"

"You heard me. I want to see the room from which the boy was taken. Quickly."

Anthony Atkinson had occupied a chamber on the third floor, just off the schoolroom. It was a typical boy's bedroom, its shelves crammed with books and birds' nests and all manner of wondrous and special things.

Standing on the braided hearthrug, Sebastian thought about the towheaded lad he'd glimpsed in the Square, his cheeks flushed, his eyes bright with merriment. The boy might have been younger than the other victims, Sebastian realized, but he was a sturdy, healthy lad; he would not have been easy to subdue. Especially without waking either his family or the servants.

A small girl's voice came from the doorway to the schoolroom. "Are you looking for Anthony? He's not here."

Sebastian turned to find young Miss Atkinson watching him with wide, solemn eyes. He went to hunker down before her.

"Did you hear Anthony leave this morning?"

She shook her head. "No. I didn't hear anything."

"Have you noticed anyone watching you the last few days? A man, perhaps? Or maybe a woman?"

Again, she shook her head.

Frustrated, Sebastian shoved to his feet. It was when he was turning to leave that he saw it: a glint of blue-and-white porcelain peeking out from beneath the counterpane. He knew what it was even before he stooped to pick it up.

It was a Chinese vial. An opium vial.

CHAPTER 58

Sebastian was paying off his hackney outside Newgate Prison when he heard a man's high-pitched voice calling his name.

"Lord Devlin."

Sebastian turned to find Sir Henry Lovejoy coming out of the prison's formidable gates.

"I stopped by your house this morning, my lord, but was told you were not in. I assume you've heard the news about young Anthony Atkinson? Dreadful business this. Just dreadful."

Sebastian stepped out of the path of a passing ironmonger's wagon. "Who was it pushed for the arrest of Brandon Forbes?"

"Sir James Read and Sir William both. Lord Jarvis has brought considerable pressure to bear on Bow Street to solve this case, and the magistrates are always anxious to curry favor with the Palace."

Sebastian squinted up at the prison's dark,

oppressive facade. "And now that Anthony Atkinson is missing? Will Mr. Forbes be released?"

Sir Henry sighed. "I fear not. Sir James in particular contends that the disappearance of the young Atkinson boy in no way absolves Mr. Forbes of the earlier murders."

"That's preposterous."

"That's the law. Thanks to your admirable detective work, it appears that Mr. Forbes possesses a powerful motive to have committed the murders, and I fear the gentleman has no verifiable alibi for the nights in question."

Sebastian swore long and hard. "So what exactly is being done to find Anthony Atkinson?"

"As I understand it, Bow Street has some twenty men combing the countryside around Forbes's estate."

"Bloody hell. The boy's not there."

"So it would seem."

Sebastian found Brandon Forbes seated at a writing desk in one corner of a surprisingly large room overlooking the street. The rattle of the jailer's keys brought the gentleman's head around. At the sight of Sebastian, he grunted.

"It's you I've to thank for my being here,

I take it."

Sebastian ducked his head through the doorway and waited while the jailer locked the door behind him. Newgate could be relatively comfortable for those with a few extra pounds to buy themselves a private cell, some furniture and bedding, and food. But the dank air still reeked of excrement and despair, and the threat of the hangman's noose was like an unseen presence in the room.

"Indirectly," Sebastian admitted.

Forbes laid aside his pen. The bluff, good-humored country squire who'd walked the fields of his Hertfordshire estate was gone. The man before Sebastian now was pale and anxious. "You think I did it?" he asked. "You think I butchered all those young men?"

"No."

Forbes grunted. "Why not? Everyone else does. My arrest ties it all up in a neat package."

"Except for this morning's disappearance of young Anthony Atkinson."

"Yes, well, I could have an accomplice, couldn't I? That's what they're saying. Someone who nabbed young Atkinson to confound the authorities and make it appear that I'm innocent."

"I don't think so."

Forbes pushed up from his desk and went to stand at the window overlooking the front of the prison. "That's where they hang them, you know. Those who have been condemned to death. Right there in front of the prison. You ever see a hanging?"

"Yes."

"I saw one once. In St. Albans when I was a boy. My father took me to see it over my mother's objections. Some lad who'd pinched a bolt of cloth from a shop. I was ten at the time, and I don't think the boy was much older. They botched his hanging something terrible. Took him fifteen or twenty minutes to die. In the end, the hangman wrapped his own arms around the poor lad's legs and pulled in an attempt to break the boy's neck, but even that didn't work. He suffocated slowly. Very slowly."

"I won't let you hang for this," said Sebastian.

A wry smile touched the man's lips. "Pardon me if I'm not comforted."

Sebastian searched the other man's plain, weather-darkened face. "Is there anything else you can tell me about your son — anything at all — that might help?"

"No."

"No one you know who might have felt

compelled to avenge the boy's death?"

The man's face paled, and Sebastian knew he was worrying about the suspicion that would now also fall on his surviving sons, the boy studying at Cambridge and his older brother. "No!"

"I didn't mean your older sons," said Sebastian.

Forbes went to sit on the edge of the bed, his hands clasped between his knees, his head bowed. After a moment, he said, "It is possible that someone . . ." He hesitated, then swallowed hard. "You see, Gideon wasn't actually my own child. Oh, I raised him as my son, and God knows I loved him like a son. But he was not the issue of my loins."

"What?"

Forbes kept his gaze on the stone paving beneath his feet, a tide of color staining his cheeks. "It's not the sort of thing a man speaks of ordinarily. But . . . My second wife — Gideon's mother — she was already some three months gone with child when I married her."

Sebastian leaned forward. "The father — who was he?"

"I don't know. She never told me and I never asked. Her parents never knew she was with child. I gather they had objected

375

to the match because of the man's religion."

"Where was your wife raised? In Hertford-shire?"

"No. She was from a village called Hollingbourne, in Kent."

Sebastian thrust up from his seat. "Is that near Avery?"

Forbes's head came up, his mouth slack with surprise. "How did you know?"

CHAPTER 59

Sebastian could hear thunder rumbling in the distance by the time he reached Brook Street. He set his groom, Giles, scrambling to saddle the Arab, then sent for Tom.

Sebastian was in his library, loading a small pistol, when Tom scooted into the room. "I want you to find Sir Henry," said Sebastian, slipping the flintlock into his pocket as he briefly ran through the conversation with Forbes. "Tell him what I've discovered and where I've gone." He squinted up at the leaden sky and paused to throw a cloak over his shoulders. It was going to be a wet ride.

"I could come with you," Tom said. He had to trot to keep up as Sebastian crossed the gardens toward the stables, jerking on his leather riding gloves as he went. "You could send Giles with the message and —"

"No. This man is a killer. I want you well away from him. You deliver the message to

Sir Henry, and then you await me here. That's an order." Sebastian gathered the black's reins, but paused to give the boy a hard look. "Do you understand me?"

Tom's shoulders slumped. "Aye, gov'nor."

Sebastian settled into his saddle and felt the mare tremble beneath him, as if she could sense his urgency and was eager to be off. But he held her in check long enough to lean down and say to Tom, "Disobey me in this, and I swear to God, I'll take it out of your hide." Then he tightened his knees to send the Arab thundering down the mews.

The rain began in earnest just after Sebastian clattered across the bridge into Blackfriars Road. This was a mean part of London, the streets narrow and unpaved and filled with clutches of ragged, hollow-eyed children and crippled beggars who forced Sebastian to hold the Arab in until he was well past Greenwich Road. By the time he reached Blackheath, the rain had become a steady, wind-driven torrent that stung his cheeks and ran down the back of his neck and rapidly turned the pike into a dangerous quagmire.

How many hours had passed since Anthony Atkinson's abduction? he wondered, pushing on. Four? Five? A part of him acknowledged that the boy might already be dead. But he clung to the hope that Anthony might yet live. It couldn't be easy for a man dedicated to saving lives to steel himself to the brutal murder of a child.

It struck Sebastian as ironic, how a single, easily overlooked piece of information could provide a solution if one simply shifted his perspective and considered it from a different angle. He'd wondered how the killer had learned the details of the *Harmony's* ordeal, yet he'd given little thought to Reverend Thornton's wife, who must have faced her coming death last Christmas weighed down by the onerous guilt upon her soul. From where could she have sought absolution for the sins of murder and cannibalism? Not from the rector her husband, whose guilt was as great as her own. And so she must have chosen to unburden herself to her dear family friend and physician, Dr. Aaron Newman, never imagining that the man to whom she'd confided her terrible secret was actually the dead boy's natural father.

Yet even armed with the truth of what had happened to Gideon Forbes and David Jarvis, Newman must have known himself to be at *point non plus.* It had been impossible for him to move against the *Harmony's* survivors in a court of law; even if the ship's passengers hadn't included some of the most powerful men in the Kingdom, Newman had no proof of what had occurred on that ship beyond a dying woman's testimony given without other witnesses. And so he had decided to wreak his own terrible form of revenge, killing not his son's murderers, but their sons.

Thou shalt give life for life, eye for eye, tooth for tooth, hand for hand, foot for foot, burning for burning. And if an ox have gored a son or have gored a daughter, according to this judgment shall it be done onto him . . . How much suffering and death had been wrought upon the world, Sebastian wondered, by a literal interpretation of that ancient biblical passage? Wrapping the folds of his cloak around him, he kneed the mare on ever faster through the pounding rain.

He noticed the two horsemen at the first toll. They rode up, hats pulled low, collars turned against the wind and rain just as Sebastian was passing through the gate. One of them, a tall man with a broken nose, reached down to hand their toll to the gatekeeper. He glanced up, his gaze catching Sebastian's eye just as Sebastian set his spurs to the mare's flanks.

After that, he was aware of them behind

him, two rough-coated men riding as hard as he. Any men out on such a day would be riding hard. But when Sebastian deliberately slowed his pace at a small hamlet, the men dropped back.

Bloody hell. He suppressed the urge to whirl and confront them. He didn't have *time* for this.

He drove the mare on faster. He could feel her dainty hooves slipping in the soupy churned mud of the road. Rain slid in cold rivulets down his cheeks, ran into his eyes. He was shaking his head, trying to clear them, when the mare stumbled.

She pitched forward with a frightened squeal. He just managed to kick his feet free of the stirrups before she went down and rolled. His back slammed against the ground hard enough to drive the wind from his body, leaving him gasping in agony.

He was aware of the sounds of the mare scrambling to her feet, but he couldn't move. Rain beat against his face, ran into his open mouth as he fought to draw the breath back into his aching chest. Floundering in the mud, he managed to prop himself up on one elbow. He opened his eyes just in time to see the muddy sole of a man's boot driving toward his face. Then all was black.

CHAPTER 60

He awoke to pain and the mists of confusion. The confusion lifted slowly. He remembered the mare stumbling, the sound of boots in the mud, an explosion of pain in his face. He could taste blood in his mouth, feel more blood mingling with mud and rain. Then he realized the pain in his jaw came not only from that kick, but also from the gag that pried his lips apart, making it difficult to swallow.

Cautiously, he opened his eyes. He lay on his back, his hands twisted awkwardly beneath him and tied at the wrist. His ankles were tied, too, and suspended oddly in the air. Squinting against the rain, he saw that someone had taken one end of the rope that bound his ankles and looped it over an oak branch that stretched above him. He remembered the way Barclay Carmichael had been found butchered and hanging upside down from a mulberry tree in St.

James's Park, and knew a rush of raw fear.

His hat and cloak were both gone, along with the reassuring weight of the pistol he'd slipped into his coat pocket. He'd obviously been dragged away from the road, for he was now in a clearing of what looked like a thick stand of oaks. The smell of wet grass, dirt, and leaves was strong. He could hear the rain still pounding on the leaves overhead, but the canopy sheltered him from the worst of the downpour.

Shifting his head slowly so as not to attract attention, he scanned the small clearing. He could see only one man; a small, thin man with overlong blond hair who leaned against the trunk of a tree some twenty-five feet away. Beyond him, Sebastian could see his own black Arab and one other horse, a big bay.

There had been two men following him, Sebastian remembered. The second man must have ridden away, either for reinforcements or to notify whoever had hired them. The man leaning against the tree had the air of someone waiting.

Sebastian studied his guard more closely. He stood with one knee bent, the sole of his boot propped against the trunk behind him, his hat pulled low on his forehead against the rain. He looked young, very young, his clothes rough. Rougher than those of the killer who had attacked Sebastian on the hoy, more like those of the men who had broken into Kat's house Friday night.

A sudden wave of nausea roiled Sebastian's stomach, so that he had to squeeze his eyes shut for a moment. But he knew he needed to make his move now, before anyone else returned. His breath coming shallow and quick, Sebastian opened his eyes and squinted up at his feet.

They might have found his pistol, but it had evidently never occurred to the men who had bound and gagged and tethered him by his ankles to a tree that a nobleman might be carrying a knife in his boot; he could still feel the subtle pressure of that small, deadly blade against his calf. The hard part would be getting the knife out without attracting his guard's attention.

Moving slowly, Sebastian straightened his legs as much as possible and locked his knees while shifting his weight subtly to the right. The sheath was well oiled, and he was hoping gravity alone might be enough to loosen the knife.

It wasn't.

He threw a quick glance at the man leaning against the tree. He hadn't moved. Gritting his teeth, Sebastian gave a series of short, sharp kicks upward with his right heel. The knife slipped out of its sheath to land with a soft thump in the wet leaf litter beside his hip.

By lifting his hips in the air, Sebastian was able to shift his bound arms over far enough to close his fingers around the handle of the knife. He reversed the blade, angling it carefully toward the rope that bound his wrists. The point nicked the pad of his palm and he swore silently to himself. Then he felt the blade bite into the rope.

It wasn't easy, holding his hips in the air, balancing his weight on his shoulders while sawing blindly. Rain pattered on his face, ran into his eyes. Twice the knife slipped, slicing into his wrists. He could feel the blood slippery on his hands, on the knife.

He became aware of a vibration in the wet earth beneath him: horses' hooves coming fast from somewhere off to the left where the road must lie. He willed them to keep going. They slowed.

The man beside the tree hunched his shoulders against the rain, his head still bowed as if he were oblivious to the sounds of approach. Sebastian felt the last of the rope give way beneath his blade just as a man's shout cut through the dripping woods. The hireling beside the tree lifted his head and glanced back at Sebastian. Sebastian lay perfectly still, his hands twisted out of sight beneath him, the knife clutched in one blood-slicked fist.

Lord Stanton rode into the clearing, mounted on a fine gray and flanked by two coarsely dressed men. "Is he alive?" Stanton demanded.

The blond-headed hireling pushed away from the tree and went to hold the Baron's horse. "Last I looked."

Stanton grunted and swung down from the saddle. Sebastian looked beyond him to the other two men. One — the tall, thin-framed man with a broken nose — he recognized from the tollgate. The man helping the blond youth with the horses was the survivor from Friday night's assault on Harwich Street.

His boots crunching a litter of twigs and wet leaves, Stanton halted in the center of the clearing, his gaze on Sebastian's face. "So. You're still alive."

Sebastian blinked, his mouth held rigid by the gag.

The Baron swiped one forearm across his wet face. "You have no one but yourself to blame for this situation. Indeed, I went out of my way to discourage your involvement. I feared all along it would come to this."

Sebastian stared up into the Baron's pale, fleshy face and marveled at the man's capacity for self-deception. If Sebastian had been less agile or his hearing less acute, it would have come to this in the dead of the night on Harwich Street, or before, on the hoy on the Thames.

"Have you succeeded, then?" Stanton asked. "Do you know who killed my son?"

His eyes wide, his grip on the knife handle behind his back tightening, Sebastian nodded.

Stanton motioned to the tall, thin-framed man with the broken nose. "Take the gag out of his mouth so he can talk."

Sebastian waited, tense and ready, while the man came to crouch down beside him.

"Lift yer 'ead so's I can get at the knot," he ordered.

Sebastian obligingly raised his head. He waited until the man was fully occupied picking at the knot; then Sebastian moved.

Tilting his hips up so that his shoulders took all his weight, Sebastian grabbed a fistful of the man's coat with one hand, holding him steady while he drove the knife deep into the man's chest.

The man convulsed, pale eyes widening with shock. But Sebastian was already jerking the dagger out of the man's chest. Holding the hireling's body like a shield, Sebastian jackknifed up and hacked desperately at the rope binding his ankles.

"What is he doing?" he heard Stanton bellow. "Don't just stand there, you fools. Stop him."

The young yellow-haired man reached Sebastian just as the knife freed his ankles. "Oye! What the —"

Sebastian twisted so that his falling feet came down against the side of the man's head with a solid *thwunk.* The man staggered to his knees.

Sebastian hit the sodden ground in a roll and came up onto his feet at a run. With Stanton and the third hireling between Sebastian and the horses, he had no choice but to plunge downhill, away from them. He felt a stinging slice across his upper arm the instant before he heard the boom of a pistol reverberate through the forest.

Bloody hell. The smooth leather soles of his riding boots slipping and skidding in the wet leaf mold, Sebastian zigzagged through gnarled old oak trees, one hand clamped against his bleeding arm.

"You, Horn," he heard Stanton shout, "stay with the horses in case he tries to circle back. Burke, come with me."

Wet branches slapped Sebastian in the

face. His coat caught on a hawthorn and he breathed another quick oath, ripping it free. Given enough time, he had no doubt he could outrun Stanton and his men, but time was the one thing Sebastian didn't have.

He scanned the trees ahead, swerving toward an ancient oak with stout branches arching low to the ground. Slipping his knife back into its sheath, he was reaching for the lowest branch when his gaze fell on the tumble of stones lying half hidden in the leaf litter at the tree's roots. He hesitated, then swooped to select a particularly lethal-looking chunk with jagged edges. He hefted it for a moment, testing its weight. Then he scrambled into the tree.

CHAPTER 61

Sebastian found his left arm unexpectedly weak, so he made more noise than he would have liked climbing into the ancient oak. Crouching on the lowest branch, he rested his back against the rough trunk, his breath coming hard and fast.

From some distance to his right came Stanton's voice. "Devlin? You might as well give yourself up and stop this foolishness. You don't have a chance. There are still three of us."

Sebastian could see them now, Stanton and his man Burke. They were keeping close together, and they were going the wrong way, cutting along the side of the hill. For a moment Sebastian considered simply staying where he was. Except he knew that if they gave up and left, they would take his horse with them.

Casting a critical eye over the oak's nearest boughs, he found a small, half-dead branch and leaned his weight against it until it broke off in his hand with a *crack* that echoed through the forest.

Stanton drew up, his gaze darting first one way, then the other. "It's him." He held the flintlock close, one finger curled around the trigger. Sebastian doubted Stanton had taken the time to reload, but it was a double-barreled pistol, which meant he still had one shot left. "Where did that come from?"

Sebastian knew a grim kind of amusement. The Baron's combination of arrogance and incompetence might have been comical, except there was nothing funny about a man who could kill and eat a young boy, or whose attempt to cover up his ugly past had already caused the death of his own child.

Balancing carefully on his limb, Sebastian opened his hand and let the branch fall. It hit the rocks below with a clatter.

"There." The man named Burke swung around. "He's over there."

Like hounds following the scent of a fox, the two men swept across the hillside, their gazes hard on the undergrowth of hawthorn and holly. They never thought to look up.

"I don't see him." Burke paused almost directly beneath Sebastian, his gaze searching the rainy hillside. "Where is he?"

"My shot clipped him." Stanton crouched down to touch the leaf litter beneath the tree with one splayed hand. "Look. There's blood. He must be —"

Slipping the handle of his knife between his clenched teeth, Sebastian gripped the rock with both hands and dropped straight down on the henchman, his full weight smashing the rock onto the man's head.

The man collapsed beneath him, then lay utterly still.

Stanton backed away, the pistol clutched in a two-handed grip, his mouth going slack with shock. "My God. You smashed his head in."

Wordlessly, Sebastian slipped the knife from his teeth and held it loosely in his right hand.

Stanton extended the pistol, his elbows locked. But he was shaking so badly the gun barrel waved wildly. "Stay back. I'll shoot. You know I will."

Sebastian's lips pulled into a tight smile. "You have only one shot left. What if you miss?"

The Baron's throat worked as he swallowed hard. The finger on the trigger twitched. Sebastian flipped the knife so that he held the blade between his thumb and forefinger, his gaze on the other man's eyes.

He thought for a moment Stanton meant to put the pistol up. Then a wild kind of determination flared in the man's eyes. Sebastian sent the knife whistling through the air just as Stanton squeezed the trigger.

The shot went wide, but Sebastian's blade caught the big man in the throat. Blood spurted from the wound, spilled from both corners of his open mouth in dark rivulets. His legs buckled beneath him, his eyes rolling back in his head.

Sebastian surged to his feet. He could feel the sleeve of his coat wet and heavy against his arm and realized suddenly it wasn't just wet from the rain. He was losing more blood than he'd first realized.

Staggering slightly, he walked to where Stanton lay. Blood still pulsed from the man's throat, but it was slowing. Reaching down, Sebastian loosed the Baron's grip on the pistol and thrust it into the waistband of his own breeches. The gun was empty now, and a thorough search of Stanton's coat failed to turn up the powder and shot required to reload. But there were times when even an empty pistol had its uses. He searched both men for his own small flintlock, as well, but did not find it. Gritting his teeth, Sebastian retrieved his knife. He might need it again.

Leaning against the tree trunk, he yanked off his cravat and used it to bind up his arm as best he could. He stayed for a moment, trying to calm his roiling stomach and clear his head. Then he headed up the hill toward his black mare and the young blond man Stanton had called Horn.

Horn stood beside the horses, his head jerking this way and that as he searched the surrounding wood with wide, anxious eyes. Hunkering low, Sebastian crept up behind him, his knife in one hand, Stanton's flintlock pistol in the other. The pistol was empty, of course, but Sebastian was betting on the hireling being too scared to realize that.

Treading softly in the wet, leafy humus, Sebastian pressed the barrel of the pistol behind Horn's ear. "Move and I'll blow your brains out."

The youth froze.

Sebastian clicked back the hammer for dramatic effect. "This is your lucky day, my friend. You get to live."

"Jesus Christ. Don't kill m—" The man's voice broke off in a whimper as Sebastian brought the pistol's handle down like a club on the back of his pale blond head.

Yanking off Horn's dark neckcloth, Sebastian used it to quickly bind the unconscious youth's hands, just in case. A quick search of Horn's pockets again failed to yield Sebastian's flintlock, and he realized it must have been lost on the road when the Arab fell.

Pushing to his feet, his head swimming sickeningly, Sebastian turned toward the horses. The horses snorted with fear, smelling blood. He reached for the Arab's reins and she tossed her head, her eyes wide. "Easy girl," he crooned. "Easy."

Hauling himself into the saddle, he started to turn toward the road. Then he hesitated, his gaze lingering on the clearing. Beyond the silent heap of the young blond man, Horn, Sebastian could see the bloodied body of the first man he'd killed; the bodies of the other two — Lord Stanton and his hireling Burke lay someplace out of sight farther down the hill. It occurred to Sebastian with a strange sense of detachment that he'd just killed three men. Yet, when he searched inside himself for some flicker of remorse, all he felt was a strange, detached kind of numbness. He knew the men he'd killed had been trying to kill him, but he wasn't sure that should matter.

Wiping his sleeve across his wet face, he

turned the Arab's head toward the road and spurred her forward, toward Avery.

CHAPTER 62

The mare was tiring by the time the river came into view, its storm-churned surface as agitated and gray as the sky above it.

Mud flying from his horse's hooves, Sebastian tore up the hill to the wide green where the ancient Norman bulk of St. Andrews brooded over a deserted, rain-drenched graveyard. He leapt down, his boots squelching in the mud, his gaze scanning the quiet scene. He'd been hoping to find Lovejoy and his constables already here, ahead of him.

A half-grown lad hurrying past on his way to the High Street cast Sebastian a queer look.

"You, lad," said Sebastian. "Has there been a magistrate here? From London?"

"No." The boy backed away, his eyes wide as he stared at Sebastian's blood-splattered silk waistcoat, his torn and bloodied coat.

Sebastian fumbled for his purse. "Here's a

shilling for you, if you'll walk the mare up and down the lane. And a promise of two more when I come back."

The boy looked hesitant, but relented at the sight of the coins in Sebastian's hand.

Sebastian splashed up the walk to the physician's white frame house. He plied the front knocker hard, then listened to the sound of it echo away to nothing. "Anyone there?" he shouted against the roar of the rain.

The house before him lay still and silent.

He took a step back, his gaze scanning the yard. Water gushed off the eaves. He could see a stable with room for two horses at the base of the garden and beside it an open-sided shelter where the physician doubtless kept his carriage. The space was empty.

The sprigs of hay found on the bodies of young Stanton and Carmichael suggested they'd been held and killed in a barn or a stable. Yet surely Newman hadn't brought his victims here to Avery, where the chances of accidental discovery loomed large. So if not here, then where?

"Hello?" Sebastian called again.

He was about to swing away when he heard the latch turn. The door opened a crack and the housekeeper peered out at him, her features pinched with suspicion and anxiety. He was acutely conscious of his beard-roughened chin, his disheveled clothes.

Then she must have recognized him, because her expression cleared. "Goodness, it's you, my lord. Whatever has happened to you? Do come in and sit down, quickly."

Sebastian stayed on the porch. "Where is Dr. Newman?"

"I'm afraid the doctor is not in, my lord." She spoke with a studied deliberation that made Sebastian want to grab and shake her, just to get her to speak faster. "Went off late last night, he did, in his gig. Told me not to expect him back before Monday."

"Have you any idea where he might have gone?"

The housekeeper frowned. "I'm afraid he didn't say." She hesitated, then added slowly, "I know he sometimes goes to Oak Hollow Farm for a few days, so I suppose it's possible he —"

"Oak Hollow Farm?" said Sebastian sharply.

"It's a property he inherited from his uncle. It did have tenants, but they emigrated to America last year, so it's empty now. He's been spending quite a bit of time there these last few months. Actually, I believe he was there just last —"

"How do I get there?"

The question seemed to surprise her, but after a moment, she stepped out onto the small portico to point into the driving rain. "You take that lane, just to the north of the church. Keep going past the village of Ditton until you see the ruins of an old medieval tower. The farm's there, just below the ridge."

"Thank you." Sebastian stepped back into the rain. "There'll be a magistrate and constables here soon from London. Give them the information you've just given me."

"A London magistrate?" The housekeeper clucked her tongue. "Whatever for?"

But Sebastian was already running toward his horse.

CHAPTER 63

Crumbling and open to the sky, the medieval watchtower stood on a rocky ridge overgrown with brambles and hawthorn.

Sebastian paused beside the broken entrance, now a gaping hole that showed only a tumble of weed-choked fallen stones within. The rain had slowed to a steady drizzle, the wind a lonesome thing that whistled through the old arrow slits and ruffled the Arab's wet mane. The air was filled with mist and the smell of wet leaves and grass and a faint hint of woodsmoke that drifted up from below. But the tower was long deserted, the ancient stone walls blackened by the fires of centuries of vagrants who'd found shelter there.

Sebastian nudged the mare forward, to the edge of the ridge. Oak Hollow Farm lay just beyond the tower, in a shallow depression below the cusp of the hill overlooking the distant downs. A single line of smoke drifted up from a chimney at the far end of the farmhouse.

The house was a low, rambling structure, built of coursed rough stone with mullioned windows and a thatched roof. Once, the farm must have been prosperous, but signs of recent neglect lay everywhere: in the cottage garden of roses and lavender and marigolds left to run rampant, in the broken hinge of the wood house door that creaked slowly in the wind. Beyond the house, the farm's cluster of stone outbuildings and wooden pens stood empty and silent beneath the gray sky.

Rather than come at the farm directly, from the open road, Sebastian cut through the copse of mingled chestnuts and oaks below the ridge. A few hundred yards uphill from the house, he dismounted, staggering slightly as an unexpected wave of light-headedness washed over him. Gritting his teeth, he looped his horse's reins around a low branch and continued on foot.

At the edge of the wood he paused, watching for any movement, any sign of life beyond that pale line of drifting smoke. Nothing. He knew he was making a dangerous assumption — that Newman was in the room with the smoking chimney — but he tried not to think about that as he darted across the open field and ducked around the side of the house. Pressing his back against the wall, he paused for a moment and waited for his head to clear. Then he edged around until he was close enough to peer through the room's heavy, leaded glass window.

He found himself looking at a kitchen, a big farm kitchen with a wide-mouthed, smoke-darkened stone hearth that stretched across most of the far wall with a clutch of dusty pots that dangled from a blackened beam. At the battered, scrubbed table in the center of the room sat Dr. Aaron Newman, his back to the window. As Sebastian watched, the doctor wrapped his fist around the neck of a brandy bottle and raised it to his lips to drink deeply. A well-kept fowling piece — an over-and-under flintlock shotgun with a brass butt cap and steel trigger guard — lay on the table just inches from his hand.

Anthony Atkinson was nowhere in sight.

Sebastian blew out a long, slow breath. The boy could be anywhere in the house or outbuildings, or he could be dead. But Sebastian had come to the conclusion there was a good chance the child still lived. Newman had planned each of his murders with a chilling degree of precision and ruthlessness. The man might be a physician rather than a surgeon, but he would still be familiar with the effects of time on a corpse. And anyone intending to drag a dead body into London in the dead of the night would want to avoid dealing with a cadaver in the full grip of rigor mortis.

With effort, Sebastian checked his first impulse, which was to burst into the kitchen and end it all right here, right now. Against that shotgun, he had only the knife in his boot. And while ordinarily that would have been enough, Sebastian knew he would be taking a terrible chance now. His left arm hung nearly useless at his side, and he was dangerously light-headed, whether from loss of blood or concussion, he had no way of knowing. Better to get the boy away by stealth, quickly and quietly. He could deal with Aaron Newman later.

Turning away from the window, Sebastian flattened his back against the house wall, the stones cold and sharp against his palms. His gaze swept the kitchen yard, with its wood house and smokehouse, and moved on to the buildings clustered around the farmyard, the henhouse and pigsty, wagon shed and stables, barn and calf pens. All appeared empty, the old manure heap in the center of the yard now blackened with age and rain. Neither the doctor's gig nor his horse was anywhere to be seen.

Sebastian brought his gaze back to the stable. Constructed of the same coarse, rough stone as the other farm buildings, it had a thatched hipped roof with a central gable for the hayloft, and a wide set of double doors that doubtless gave access to a carriage room. The carriage doors were closed, but Sebastian could see freshly churned mud in the yard before them.

Sucking in a deep breath tinged with woodsmoke and the smell of damp stone, he eased away from the window and worked his way back toward the corner of the house. Wary of being seen if Newman should chance to stand and glance out the window, Sebastian approached the farmyard by swinging out in a wide arc, his boots squelching in the mud as he neared the abandoned pigsty.

It was raining harder now, big drops that pattered on the thatched roofs and ran down the back of Sebastian's collar as he sprinted across the farm road to the carriage doors. The doors were old and warped, and slid apart with a harsh grating that was lost in the sound of trees bending in the wind and rain slapping into mud. Squeezing through the narrow opening, Sebastian quickly eased the doors shut behind him.

He found himself in a space some twenty feet deep and twelve feet wide. The air here was thick with the smell of dust and hay and fresh manure. A black gig, its padded leather seat still wet with that morning's rain, stood in the dim light. Halfway down the wall to his right, an arched opening framed with dressed stone gave access to a darkened corridor.

Skirting the gig, Sebastian ducked through the arch to find himself in a cobbled passage. Beyond a narrow flight of stairs leading up to the hayloft stretched a row of three horse stalls, with a harness room and feed bin ranged along the opposite side of the passage. A Dutch door at the far end of the passage doubtless led to a fenced side yard.

"Anthony?" Sebastian called, the clatter of his bootheels on the cobbled floor echoing in the stillness. A big bay tethered in the first stall lifted its head, its ears flicking forward as it whinnied loudly. From the copse up the hill came a distant answering nicker.

"Bloody hell," whispered Sebastian, slipping the knife from his boot. If Newman heard the horses and decided to investigate . . .

Sebastian moved quickly down the passage. The second stall stood empty in the dull light cast by its high cobwebbed window. Outside he could hear the rain pick up again, beating harder on the thatched roof overhead. His stomach clenching with the knowledge of what he might find, Sebastian moved on to the last stall.

The boy lay curled up against the thick planked walls of the third stall, his hands and feet bound, a gag prying his mouth open in an awkward rictus. His eyes were closed, his face pale and streaked with dirt and the tracks of dried tears. But Sebastian could see the shudder of his stained white nightshirt where it stretched across his chest.

"Anthony?" Sebastian hunkered down to touch the boy's shoulder. "I'm here to take you home. Everything's going to be all right."

The boy's eyes fluttered open, then closed again, his breath coming slow and shallow. Newman had obviously dosed the boy liberally with laudanum.

"Don't be afraid of the knife. I'm going to use it to cut you loose." His hand sweaty on the handle of the blade, Sebastian sliced through the ropes at the boy's hands and feet, then loosed the gag at his mouth.

"You need to wake up for me, Anthony."

He grasped the boy's shoulders to give him a little shake. "Can you stand?"

Anthony's eyelids opened again, his eyes glassy, his head rolling on his neck.

"Come on then." Slipping his hands beneath the boy's armpits, Sebastian hauled him upright, staggering slightly as he took the boy's weight. For one perilous moment, the barn's dusty light dimmed, and Sebastian's head swam.

"I don't think I can carry you, lad." Sebastian wrapped an arm around the boy's waist. "You've got to at least hold on and try to walk. Can you do that?"

Anthony's lips parted, his thin chest shuddering as he sucked in a deep breath and nodded.

"Good lad." Sebastian lurched toward the passage. He wasn't sure if he was holding the boy up, or if it was the other way around. The rain pounded on the roof, pattered against the high windows. He was concentrating so hard on putting one foot in front of the other that it wasn't until they'd reached the arched entrance to the carriage room that Sebastian heard the slap of boots in the mud outside and the rasp of the carriage doors opening.

CHAPTER 64

Sebastian shoved the boy behind him. "The door at the other end of the passage," he whispered. "Get yourself out of here, then run like hell for the wood." As long as Sebastian could keep Newman at the entrance to the carriage room, the shadowy recesses of the passage would be out of his line of vision.

Aaron Newman loomed in the open carriage doors, a lean figure silhouetted against the rain-filled yard. "Stay right there and put your hands where I can see them," said the doctor, the fowling piece gripped in both hands. "Do it, my lord. Or I swear to God, I'll shoot you."

Sebastian braced his hands against the stone doorframe beside him and said, "It's over, Dr. Newman."

The doctor's hands tightened on the shotgun's ornate stock. "I beg to differ with you, my lord, but I don't see it that way."

Sebastian was aware of the boy's frightened breathing behind him, the furtive patter of bare feet on the cobbled floor as Anthony crept toward the far end of the passage. Sebastian managed to keep his voice calm, although he could feel his pulse racing in his neck. "I didn't come alone. Sir Henry Lovejoy and some half a dozen of his constables are on their way here."

Newman raised one eyebrow. "You came ahead, did you? How foolhardy of you."

By now Anthony had reached the far end of the passage. "I know about your son," said Sebastian, scuffing one bootheel across the cobbles to cover the scrape made by the door's bolt being drawn back. "I know what they did to him on the *Harmony.* I understand your anger and your desire for justice. But why not kill the men responsible for what happened to him? Why murder their innocent children?"

Newman shook his head, a muscle jumping along his tightened jaw. "Death ends all suffering. I wanted them to pay for what they did to Gideon and for what they did to me. I wanted them to feel what I have felt, to suffer what I have suffered. They killed my son. I killed theirs."

"Edward Bellamy didn't kill your son."

"He didn't protect him, either. My son

was entrusted to his care. Bellamy was captain of that ship. If anyone had the power to stop what happened, it was him."

Sebastian felt the brush of cool air from the door easing open at his back, heard the slow creak of a hinge as Anthony Atkinson moved oh so carefully.

"Yet you killed the Reverend Thornton's son first. Why?"

"Thornton was a man of God. *A man of God.* He urged them to kill my son. *Urged* them! Mary Thornton told me about it when she was dying. About how the good Reverend reassured the others that God would forgive them. Well, he was wrong, wasn't he?"

"Did you kill her? Mary Thornton, I mean."

Newman shook his head. "God killed her."

Sebastian was watching the man's wild gray eyes. And so he knew the instant the doctor heard the bang of the Dutch door flying fully open, the distant slap of running feet hitting the muddy yard.

His lips peeled away from his teeth in a painful grimace. *"You bastard."* Sebastian jerked back just as Newman tightened his finger on the shotgun's trigger and fired.

The first barrel discharged in a deafening blast of fiery powder and shot that sent bits of stone coping and wooden splinters from the stairs flying. The air filled with thick smoke and the stench of cordite.

Sebastian took one step toward the open door at the end of the cobbled aisle, then knew it for a mistake. Newman still had another barrel. Silhouetted against the open doorway, Sebastian would be impossible to miss.

He dove instead into the first stall, his injured shoulder exploding in fire as he careened into the plank wall and slipped to his knees. The carriage horse whinnied in alarm, its head tossing, its hooves clattering on the straw-covered cobbles.

Sebastian rolled quickly to his feet, his head spinning as he drew back into the shadows. He could feel the drops of mingled sweat and rainwater dripping from his hair to roll down his cheeks, hear the doctor's boots in the cobbled passage. Slipping his knife from his boot, Sebastian reached out and unhooked the bay's tether. He held the length of leather clutched in his fist, the edges of the stiff hide digging into his palm as he waited for Newman to come into view.

He watched the doctor pass the stall, his gaze fixed on the open doorway at the end of the passage. The bay snorted and tossed its head, just as Sebastian let the tether drop.

The sound of the leather slapping against the stall's heelpost brought Newman's head around, his eyes wide. Sebastian pricked the bay's flanks and sent it charging out of the stall. Newman took a quick step back, his finger tightening on the trigger in a reflex action. The fowling piece exploded in a deafening concussion that filled the stables with flames and smoke. Shot ripped through the nearest heelpost, torn shards of wood and splinters flying through the air as Sebastian dove into him.

The force of the impact sent Newman crashing back against the harness room wall. Their feet tangled, Newman going down to smack his back hard against the cobbled floor. Sebastian slammed on top of him, the knife blade held tight against the doctor's throat.

In the sudden stillness, his ears still ringing from the shot, Sebastian could hear the sawing of his own breath and the roar of the rain through the open doors. And something else. The distant thunder of approaching horses ridden fast.

Newman's lips parted, his chest shuddering as he sought to draw air into his aching lungs. "Kill me," he said in a hoarse whisper. "Why don't you just kill me?"

Sebastian shook his head. He thought

413

about Francesca Bellamy, about Lady Carmichael, about Dominic Stanton's mother, now half mad with her grief. And he felt a rush of fury that submerged all shreds of pity or understanding. "No. You said it yourself. Death ends all suffering. And you deserve to suffer. For what you did to those innocent young men and for what their deaths have done to those who loved them."

They heard a shout from the yard and a boy's thin voice saying, "In the stables. They're in the stables."

Newman's eyes squeezed shut, his breathing still ragged. "I did it for Gideon. I was never able to do anything for him in life. The least I could do was avenge his death."

"No." Sebastian closed his fist on the doctor's coat and hauled him to his feet. "You did it for yourself."

CHAPTER 65

Sir Henry Lovejoy hunched his shoulders against the rain as he watched his constables bundle the Kentish doctor out of the stables.

"I thought this wasn't your case?" said Devlin, coming up beside him.

"It's not," said Henry, swinging his head to look at the Viscount. He stood hatless in the rain, his once fine coat, waistcoat, and breeches torn and smeared with mud and blood and bits of leaves and straw. "Good God. We need to get you to a surgeon."

"It'll keep." Devlin scrubbed a hand across his face, wiping the rain from his eyes. "How's the boy?"

"He's a good lad. He'll be all right. Thanks to the laudanum, I don't think he remembers much. But I've no doubt his testimony — combined with whatever evidence a search of the farm buildings yields — will be more than enough to see the good doctor hang."

Devlin's features remained impassive as he stared off across the mist-filled valley. "There are some bodies in the wood just past the second tollgate out of London. You might want to send a couple of your men to deal with them."

"Bodies?"

"Lord Stanton and several of his henchmen. They tried to kill me."

"And so you killed them?"

"I was in a hurry."

Henry sighed.

"Sir Henry."

Henry turned to see Constable Higgins coming toward them across the yard, his plump cheeks red with exertion, something small and white clutched in one fist. "Constable?"

"I thought you'd want to see this," said Higgins, holding out a small porcelain figurine. "We found it in a bag under the seat of Newman's gig."

"What is it?" said Henry.

The Viscount reached to take the delicate statue in his hands. "A mermaid. It's a mermaid."

Henry groped for his handkerchief. "Merciful heavens."

"What will happen to them?" Devlin asked, staring down at the figurine. "I mean

Atkinson and Carmichael and the absent Mr. and Mrs. Dunlop."

"Nothing, I suspect. I've never known the Crown to prosecute cases of cannibalism on the high seas."

"Actually, I was thinking about what they did to David Jarvis."

Henry shrugged. "We've no way of knowing who struck the fatal blow."

"The crew was hanged for his death."

"The crew was hanged for mutiny."

Devlin's lips flattened into a sardonic smile. "Of course."

Henry knew a profound inner sense of uneasiness. "You're planning something. What is it?"

A gleam of amusement touched the Viscount's haunted yellow eyes. "I don't think you want to know."

"I think I've patched you up more in the past nine months than I did during the war," said Paul Gibson, wrapping a length of bandage around Sebastian's upper arm. "Here. Put your finger on that."

They were in Sebastian's library, with Sebastian seated, shirtless, on the edge of his desk. He smiled and held the end of the bandage in place while the doctor rummaged in his bag for a pair of scissors.

"What is war, after all, but an organized, sanctioned form of mass murder?"

Gibson cut the length of gauze and tied it off, his attention seemingly all for his work. "I don't suppose you've heard the latest rumors?"

"What rumors?"

"About Russell Yates and Kat Boleyn. They've been married by special license."

"What?"

Gibson pushed out his breath in a sigh. "I was afraid you didn't know anything about it."

"No," said Sebastian. "I didn't." He fixed his gaze unseeingly on the bowl of bloody water beside them while his friend went to work on the knife cuts on Sebastian's wrists. Ever since he'd turned Aaron Newman over to Sir Henry down at Oak Hollow Farm, Sebastian had been trying to figure out how, with marriage out of the question, he was going to keep Kat safe from Jarvis. But it seemed Kat had found a way to protect herself.

Now, freed from the desperate rush to catch a killer and devise some way to shield Kat from Jarvis's malevolence, Sebastian suddenly found himself with nothing to distract him from the brutal reality of a future without Kat as his love, without Kat in his life. He felt a hideous emptiness yawn deep within his being, and for one blinding moment, the agony of it was so raw that it took his breath.

"Sebastian —" Gibson broke off as the sound of running feet and the bang of a distant door foretold the arrival of Tom.

"I've found one," said Tom, his breath coming fast and his cheeks flushed. "I found you a valet. 'E's been a gentleman's gentleman for more'n twenty years. 'E knows all about yer interest in murder and the rigs from Rosemary Lane you sometimes wear, and it don't bother 'im a bit. In fact, 'e'll be a right handy one to 'ave around next time we find ourselves with a murder to investigate, 'cause 'e knows near every rookery and cracksman and Black Legs in town."

Sebastian slid off the edge of the desk. "And how, precisely, does he come to have this information?"

" 'Is ma owns the Blue Anchor."

"She what?" The Blue Anchor was the most notorious flash house in town, frequented by the worst sort of Morocco Men, dashers and beau-traps.

Tom swallowed. "I know what yer thinking, but you got it wrong. Calhoun's ma was determined 'er son weren't going to grow up to be no receiver or fancy man, and 'e 'asn't." Tom hesitated. " 'Cept for one brief spell 'e did in Newgate, and that weren't 'is fault."

Gibson choked and turned away to hide his amusement.

"What did you say this paragon's name is?" asked Sebastian.

"Jules Calhoun. 'E says 'e can come round tomorrow evening for an interview, if'n yer interested." Tom cast a worried glance at Gibson, who was now openly laughing. "Are you interested?"

"After weeks of making due with the footman? Of course I'm interested." Sebastian pointed a warning finger at his tiger. "But if so much as a shoestring goes missing in this house, it'll be on your account."

Tom's face cleared. " 'E's a right one. You'll see."

Tom dashed off, while Gibson set about collecting his various implements and returning them to his bag. After a moment, he said, "Have you seen her yet?" There was no need to identify which *her* he referred to. Kat's name hovered between them still.

Sebastian crossed the room to splash brandy into two glasses. "No. Not yet."

Gibson looked up from his task. "You're going to have to find some way to put it all behind you, Sebastian. Kat. The war. The things you saw, the things you did." *This desperate, futile quest to find your mother.* Again the words hung in the air, unsaid but there.

Sebastian came to hand his friend his drink. "And have you put it all behind you then, Paul? The war? The loss of your leg?" *The hunger for the sweet relief to be found in an elixir of poppies?*

The skin beside Gibson's eyes crinkled in amusement as he raised his brandy in a silent toast. "No. But we doctors are always better at giving advice than taking it."

CHAPTER 66

Monday, 23 September 1811

Kat was in her dressing room, supervising the packing of her trunks, when she looked up to find Devlin standing in the doorway.

"I'd heard you were hurt," she said, her worried gaze tracing the cuts and purple bruises that discolored his face, the arm that hung stiff and awkward in a sling at his side.

"It's nothing." He turned his head to survey the litter of half-packed trunks and tumbled gowns strewn about the room. "It's true then, what they're saying? You have wed?"

She nodded, barely trusting herself to speak. "Yes."

He studied her face. "Why Yates?"

"He can protect me. He has evidence that would destroy Jarvis, were it to be made public."

"But, Kat, what kind of a marriage can this be, with a man who . . ." He left the rest of the sentence unsaid.

Her voice shook as she answered him. "The only kind I want." She cleared her throat, trying to ease the tight constriction that felt as if it might choke her. "I've let it be known that the *Post* scrambled the announcement of my coming marriage. There will doubtless be some talk, but it should die down."

He shrugged one shoulder, but said nothing. She knew it meant nothing to him, the public whispers and speculations.

The old urge to go to him was still there — the urge to take him in her arms and enfold him in the comfort of her embrace. The strength of that wanting — despite all she knew, despite the shame now attached to what they had been to each other — shocked and appalled her. She gripped her hands together against her skirt. "Have you spoken to Hendon?"

His face was oddly blank, as if carefully drained of all emotion. "I've nothing more to say to him."

"It's not his fault, what happened between us. God knows he tried to discourage it."

"He took your mother as his mistress."

"And you took me as yours."

"I would have made you my wife."

"Yes. Well . . . at least we were spared that."

He searched her face, his yellow eyes hard, questioning. "What about you? Do you forgive him?"

Kat let out a sigh that shuddered her breasts. "For my mother's sake, no. He would have taken her child away from her. Yet he wanted what was best for me, didn't he?"

"Or what was best for himself. Does he plan to acknowledge you?"

She felt a wry smile tug at one corner of her lips. "That's asking a bit much, isn't it? For the Earl of Hendon to acknowledge an actress as his daughter — an actress who everyone knows was mistress to his son?"

"Kat —" He reached as if to touch her, but she jerked away.

"No. You mustn't."

She watched his hand fall back to his side. She found she was no longer able to fathom his thoughts, the exact tenor of his emotions. She knew Devlin better than she'd ever known anyone in her life, but she knew him as a lover. How was she ever to learn to know him as a brother?

"I look at you," he said, his voice a torn whisper. "I look at you, and I see my father's eyes staring back at me. And still in my heart, I can't accept it. Surely if you were my sister, I would know it?"

They studied each other across the crackling distance that separated them. She said, "How could we ever have imagined such a thing?"

He shook his head. "I am trying. But I don't know how to make my love simply go away."

She saw the pain in his eyes and knew there was nothing she could say, nothing she could do to ease it. She wanted to say, *I love you. I will always love you.*

Instead, she said, "We must."

The Earl of Hendon found his firstborn child, Amanda, seated at her embroidery frame in the morning room.

"I've come to tell you I have another daughter," he said, standing in the center of the rug as she continued to set neat stitches in the chair cover she was making. "An illegitimate daughter."

Amanda let out a peal of laughter, her needle flashing in and out. "Good God. Are you getting soft in your old age? What precious little thing has managed to convince you she's your long-lost offspring?"

"Kat Boleyn."

All trace of amusement fled her face. She set the embroidery frame aside. "You can't be serious."

"But I am."

Amanda raised one eyebrow. "How clever of you. So that's why the marriage has been called off. However did you manage to convince her?"

Hendon worked his jaw back and forth. "What do you think? That I contrived this tale to drive a wedge between her and Devlin? I'm not that clever. She is my daughter. Of that, there is no doubt."

He watched a slow, unpleasant smile spread across Amanda's face. "So now they believe they've been committing incest all these years? And of course you said not a word to disabuse them of that notion."

Hendon tightened his jaw.

"He'll discover the truth, you know. Someday. And when he does, this will be just one more lie you've told him, one more lie he'll never forgive you for."

Hendon let his gaze rove over her haughty face, with its unsuccessful blending of his own blunt features with the fine-boned beauty of her mother. He wanted to deny it. Instead he turned and left her there with her embroidery hoop beside the cold hearth. He had almost reached the doorway when he heard her start to laugh.

He kept walking.

■ ■ ■ ■

Charles, Lord Jarvis stood beside the library windows overlooking the rear garden of his house in Berkeley Square. He was calm. Rage made men do stupid things, and Jarvis was never stupid. He had suffered a setback — several setbacks — and he had some scores to settle. But he was in no hurry, and he was already beginning to see a way the situation might be turned to his advantage.

His butler scratched discreetly at the door. "Lord Devlin to see you, my lord."

Jarvis kept his back to the room, his gaze on the garden below. "I'm not at home."

"Yes, my l—"

"I suspected you might deny me," said the Viscount in a bland voice. "So I've come anyway."

Jarvis's head snapped around, his eyes narrowing. The Viscount had his left arm in a sling and a patch of sticking plaster on his forehead. Jarvis grunted. "Who did the damage? Lord Stanton or this Kentish doctor I've been hearing about?"

"Both."

Jarvis reached for his snuffbox. "Say what

you have to say and then get out of my house."

Devlin smiled. He carried a leather book tucked under one arm, a large volume with a charred binding that he set on the corner of Jarvis's desk. "I've brought you this."

Jarvis frowned. "What is it?"

"The *Harmony*'s log. I think you'll find it makes interesting reading."

Jarvis stayed where he was.

Devlin turned toward the door, but paused with one hand on the knob to look back and say, "I'd like to have known your son. You have much to be proud of. Good day, my lord."

When Devlin had gone, Jarvis stared at the charred log on his desk. It was a moment before he crossed the room to pick it up.

He read the log seated in the embrasure beside the window. It was some time before he finished, closing the log with a quiet snap. The sun had sunk low behind the neighboring rooftops, lengthening the shadows in the library.

And still he sat there, until the last of the day faded from the sky, and the lamplighter on his rounds set a flickering flame to the oil lamps in the square.

ABOUT THE AUTHOR

C. S. Harris graduated Phi Beta Kappa, summa cum laude, with a degree in classics before earning a PhD in European history. A respected scholar of the French Revolution and nineteenth-century Europe, she is also the author of the nonfiction study *Women, Equality, and the French Revolution,* written under the name of Candice E. Proctor. After years of living in England and various far-flung regions of the old British Empire, she now makes her home in New Orleans with her husband, retired Army Intelligence officer Steve Harris, and two daughters. Visit the author at www.csharris-.net and csharris.blogspot.com.